' "There! See them. See the army of the true Tsar. See how they have come in their thousands to die for their Emperor."

From a hidden *balka* beyond the Tatars, came pouring like ants from a crack in the earth, a stream of dark humanity: the motley tattered multitude of Pugachev's infantry, the sunlight striking from the weapons of a peasant army. Scythe blades, sickles, axes and pitchforks waved above the yellow dust that rolled from under the trampling, shuffling feet, and with them came the rebels' few pathetic cannon, hauled by half-naked men . . .

Henryk held up his hand for silence. "Any man among you who wants to leave is free to go . . . If you stay then it will be to fight." '

DESTINY OF EAGLES

THE BANNERS OF LOVE
THE BANNERS OF WAR
THE BANNERS OF POWER
THE BANNERS OF COURAGE
THE BANNERS OF REVOLT

and published by Corgi Books

Sacha Carnegie

The Banners of Revolt

CORGI BOOKS
A DIVISION OF TRANSWORLD PUBLISHERS LTD

THE BANNERS OF REVOLT

A CORGI BOOK 0 552 11124 4

First published in Great Britain by Peter Davies Ltd., London

PRINTING HISTORY
Peter Davies edition published 1977
Corgi edition published 1979

This book is set in 10/11pt Baskerville.

Corgi Books are pusblished by Transworld Publishers Ltd.,
Century House, 61–63 Uxbridge Road,
Ealing, London, W5 5SA.
Made and printed in Great Britain by
Hunt Barnard Printing Ltd., Aylesbury, Bucks.

My grateful thanks to Don Pottinger
my collaborator in planning and research

For my wife, Diana, and son, Jocelyn

PROLOGUE

Early spring of 1772.

'The troubles of the last four years are over and God will surely smile on Poland again,' said the old country people. 'Now perhaps we can forget the fighting and the bloodshed and live our lives in peace.'

The peasants went out to the sowing without having to post look-outs among the wooded hills to warn of the approach of armed horsemen; the dust kicked up by the marching feet of Russian infantry; the approaching thunder of heavy guns. Slowly they began to resume their normal lives, thinking only of the present, trying not to look into the future, for Poland had never been free from war, or not for long. Surrounded by enemies she and her people were well-used to fire and sword. But now at last, it seemed, they could go to their beds secure in the knowledge that the night would not to be stained by the reflection of burning villages or torn by the screams of the dying.

They had almost forgotten why this particular war had taken place at all. Something to do with the damned Russians, as usual, and the King. Men came to the villages; men who could read and write and who had been to Warsaw and Krakow; these learned people said the King was on the Russian side because he had lived in St Petersburg where he had shared the bed of Catherine the Empress. She had sent him back, or so they were told, to be King of Poland.

Not that it mattered to the peasants who sat on the throne.

They never saw him; he did nothing for them. All they cared about was finding enough to live on after paying their dues of grain and livestock to their masters. They cared more about the weather than what went on at Court.

They did not understand why some of the nobles had gathered armies round them to resist the Russian invader and to fight against their own King. Poland, and especially the Polish Ukraine, had been well soaked in blood throughout the centuries. Must it always be like that? But you did not disobey your master, not unless you wanted the skin flayed from your back or hankered after an early death kicking at the end of a hempen rope. Though, to be honest, some masters were kind and just and treated you and your family not as pigs but as human beings.

Such a one was the master of Lipno, Count Henryk Barinski. That is, the people of Lipno always thought of him as their true master even though he was only the younger brother.

Count Adam was more aloof; he did not laugh with them. Oh, he was fair enough and did not use the knout except when it was really deserved; he gave back more than he took and listened patiently to their problems and complaints but yet—as old Todor, the venerable village elder, said in the safety of his own little wattle house, 'Count Adam's a cold fish, or to us he is. Give me his brother any day, he should be master of Lipno even though he spends most of his time riding about trying to find a Russian to kill.'

'Not only Russians,' put in one of Todor's old cronies. 'Frenchmen too, and Prussians.'

'Turks as well.'

'I don't wonder, with that dirty great scar across his face. A Turkish scimitar on the night they burnt Volochisk to the ground.'

'Oh-ah!' They sighed heavily, remembering that terrible night.

'D'you remember the flames? Reached half way to

Heaven. The night they took our Kasia away to their harems, the heathen swine.'

'She may be dressed in grand clothes that would buy us twenty cows for every dress,' said Todor's wife Natalya, turning, scarlet-faced, from the stove, 'but to Lipno she'll always be our Kasia.'

'It was a great day for all of us when she became Count Henryk's wife, though the butler, Stepan, said the old Count—'

'May God rest his soul, the bad-tempered old—'

'Now then, that's enough, Mishka. I'll have nothing said against their father. Not in this house. He was of the old school, that's all. He fought with Sobieski.'

'No, he didn't. That was his father.'

'All right, so it was his father.' Todor's wife stirred furiously at something seething in the iron pot. They buried their leathery bearded faces in the mugs of vodka.

'She's right,' mumbled a voice. 'He could not understand all the changes. And Henryk, his favourite son, always away fighting in some God-forsaken war. You remember, he even fought as a sailor for some years in the English Navy.'

'Against the Turks.'

'The Spaniards.'

They argued about this for some time until Natalya banged down the wooden platters on the table. 'It was the Frenchies,' she said. 'The Countess told me so herself.'

'And yet it was the Frenchies who helped us against the Russians. I can't make head nor tail of it all.'

'Us!' she exploded. 'So it's *us* now, is it? I didn't notice you marching out with your musket to hold back the Russian army.' Snorting and muttering she began to ladle out the thick cabbage soup.

'Count Henryk made sure there's a musket and a sabre hidden in every thatch, and pistols buried under the sunflowers.'

'God grant they are never needed.'

They all nodded at her heartfelt words. Todor crossed himself, glancing at the tiny sanctuary flame flickering before the ikon niche cut from the hard earthern wall.

An angry gust forced snow under the door.

'Never mind,' said a very old man with tiny eyes and bedraggled white beard. 'Never mind, friends. Have you noticed the rooks? It's going to be an early spring.'

'Every year he says that and it never is.'

'Ah, but this year I'll be proved right, mark my words.'

And he was.

* * *

But some of the Polish people did not rejoice and for them God was not smiling on Poland.

They were the Confederates; the Patriots who, for four hard and bitter years, had carried on the unequal struggle against an enemy backed and encouraged by their Sovereign, the despised 'King' Stanislas Poniatowski—Catherine's lap-dog, as some called him.

Compared with the might of Russia their little armies had been pathetic; brave but pathetic; owing to the petty jealousies and squabbles which have always split the unity of Poland, even with the enemy at the very gates, the little armies never joined as one large army under one leader.

There was Branicki, Grand General of Poland, already an old man, tired and ready for his library and warm fireplace. There was Radziwill, Prince of Poland and Commander of the Northern Front. There was Josef Pulawski and his son, Kasimir.

And there were Count Henryk Barinski, Jan Dombrowski and Sergeant Nym (late of the Royal Bodyguard—cavalry escort to His Royal Majesty King Stanislas Poniatowski) with some three hundred superbly trained light horsemen behind them. None of these rejoiced. To them God was on the wrong side. He had been on the wrong side since the fall of Wawel Castle, the ancient seat of the Polish Kings, perched on the heights above the City of Krakow, on 22 April 1772.

From that disastrous day the French refused more help and the Poles themselves drifted away back to their homes, vanishing in the night or openly riding off in groups, no longer willing to risk death or mutilation for a cause so obviously lost.

A few small bodies of men, including that under Henryk Barinski, carried on the hopeless struggle for a few weeks until, in May, it was all over: the Confederate Wars were finished and Poland lay open to the ravages of her enemies.

The few remaining leaders were scattered like grains of dust in the storm: Kasimir Pulawski crossed the Atlantic to America to die in battle at Savannah, killed by a British musket ball or bayonet in the War of Independence. Jan Dombrowski went back to his small estate in the Ukraine. Sergeant Nym returned to his wife, Maryshka, in the little village of Rabka in the foothills of the Carpathians, there to await future events.

And Henryk Barinski came home to his wife, Kasia, and their son, Jacek, arriving at Lipno just as dawn was breaking beyond the hills which lay between their estate and the limitless steppes stretching to the Dnieper and beyond, to the Don, the Volga and the vast wilderness of the Khirghiz Steppe.

He greeted her, half-dead from exhaustion, caked in mud, dust and the acrid stink of an unwashed body; his horse, Rasulka—pet name for his wife—stood shivering, white with lather, gasping with open mouth and swollen tongue.

He was thickly bearded, the scar half hidden, livid against the pallor of his face; his old wounds hurt him like the pincers of Hell; his eyes were red, his faded green hunting tunic stained and filthy but what did it matter? He was home.

Although the sight and feel of Kasia drove everything else

from his mind and after he had slept and they had woken to satisfy each other and sleep again, for many hours, he woke with his mind filled once more with the bitter taste of defeat and the sickening knowledge of what was to happen to their country.

The lion was crippled and about to be torn apart. Russia. Prussia. Austria. The three jackals had come together in an unholy alliance. Already twenty thousand Prussians had marched into the Silesian provinces; the Russians had claimed all the lands to the west bank of the Dnieper and soon, very soon, the Austrian legions would swarm into Galicia—including the rolling hills and steppe-land of Lipno.

Poland was to be dismembered. And no country in Europe would raise a finger, let alone a soldier, to save her.

Henryk Barinski had not come home to settle to a life of peace with the woman he loved above all in this miserable little world; he would not—could not—stay with her and help to bring up their son; not while, all around them, their country was sinking into even deeper slavery and degradation.

And, from what she heard from his disjointed mutterings as he slept, Kasia understood this only too well and her heart grew heavier than ever before.

PART ONE

Chapter One

COLONEL Skurin, commanding officer of the Smolensk Regiment, in the service of Her Imperial Majesty, Catherine the Second, Empress of all the Russias, reined in his horse as he came within sight of the green roofs of Lipno.

This was the third time he had ridden between the lime trees and the poplars, the third time in eight years. The first time as an enemy; then almost a friend. And now? He shook the rain-drops from his braided tricorne hat and drew his cloak more tightly round him.

The first time he had ridden into snow showers leading his men; the second in sunshine, alone; this time the rain dripped drearily from the trees, and his horse's hooves splashed in the puddles. And this time he was, once again, quite alone. His regiment did not march behind him, there was no thud of a drum, nor tramp of heavy feet.

The trees covering the surrounding hills were thickly hidden by misty rain and below in the valley the river rushed dark and swollen. Nothing moved on the wet road of the little village except the usual rootling pigs enjoying the rain on their hairy backs, and the self-important geese. He saw a face here and there, pressed to the minute windows, only to vanish if he glanced towards them.

As he approached the mansion of Lipno he found himself holding back his restless horse, so that they were progressing slower and slower. Perhaps he should not have come? What could he say? Would Henryk be here? Would Kasia be here? Count and Countess Barinski. But he thought of them as Henryk and Kasia.

Having all his life since the age of fourteen been a dedicated soldier who had fought in every major battle of the Seven Years War, he had never had much time for a social life, nor for women except for the occasional whore picked up during some campaign. Once, under the twin influences of battle and drink, he had raped a peasant girl in East Prussia but he preferred to forget the incident.

His keen blue eyes were less bleak, his mouth no longer set in such a tight downward crescent. He looked forward very much indeed to seeing Countess Barinska again. At the thought he touched his horse with his spurs.

* * *

Kasia Barinska dropped her embroidery into her lap and looked across at her husband. He sat by the window watching the rain streak the glass driven by a rising wind. It was going to be a wonderful spring, or so Todor had told her only yesterday; but now the clouds were low and dark grey and soon she would have to summon Stepan with the candles and a fresh supply of wood for the fire.

From upstairs she heard the happy laughter of their son as he drove old Katushka mad with his teasing. She smiled. 'It's always amazed me,' she said, 'how well the very young and the very old get on.'

Henryk did not answer; he was occupied trying to follow the course of the raindrops with his finger. The pang that drove through her heart was sharp as a stiletto. For days he had been like this. Buried deep in thoughts which, for the first time since they had met twenty-three years ago, he did not share with her; by his face, dark and gloomy thoughts. To do with Poland, with defeat—that she did know. But the future? That was what worried her to distraction, though she never said a word. He would speak; in his own time he would speak, with his head on her shoulder he would tell her what tormented him.

'I suppose it is us, our generation, who are the unwanted ones. We bring up the young and look after the old and perhaps neither of them really want us.'

Henryk shook his head as if to clear it of unwelcome occupants.

'I'm sorry, darling. I . . .' He paused, looking back at the window. 'It's only—oh, I can't explain. I . . .'

'I know, my love, I understand.'

This time he turned and faced her. 'Thank you for understanding. It means a very great deal. I'll tell you. Soon I'll tell you, I promise. And don't think I don't love you any less because . . .'

'I don't,' she said. Her smile was happy as she took up her embroidery.

'Pleased with yourself, aren't you?'

They laughed.

'I love you, Kasia.'

'Surprisingly enough, I love you too. Now, go on counting raindrops if that's what you enjoy.'

He watched her long fingers as they moved swiftly with the needle; the black waves of hair half hiding her face as she bent over her work; the rounded swell of her breasts under the dark blue brocade of her dress. Strange, he thought. When I was young I never imagined it would be possible to love a woman—the same woman—for the whole of my life. And yet it has happened. God may not have been kind to Poland but He has been kind to me. He moved towards her and, at that moment, there was a loud thumping on the door which could only mean Stepan, in a bad mood.

'Colonel Skurin is here,' announced Stepan grumpily. He didn't see why he had to crawl to some bloody Russian. 'He wants to see you. Dripping all over the hall he is.'

'Show him in, please. Oh, and Stepan, would you light the candles and make up the fire.'

It's no good, thought the old man, she'd get round Satan himself with that smile. 'Bloody Russians,' he said aloud to give himself courage. Last time they came here they cleaned out half the cellar.

'Colonel Skurin! How very nice to see you again.' Kasia half rose from her chair. For God's sake, I hope Henryk is polite, she thought as she held out her hand.

Henryk nodded his welcome.

'Have you ridden far? You look as if a hot fire wouldn't do you any harm.' Colonel Skurin smiled, and it was more of a smile than the last time.

Stepan reappeared followed by a spotty youth staggering under a huge basket of logs. They were dry and very quickly the fire was flying up the chimney. Stepan brought candles in large brass holders; he drew the curtains, shutting out the rain. He brought in a tray of drinks : vodka, mead and beer.

'Will there be anything else?' He stood looking defiant.

'No, thank you, Stepan.' He gave a small, imitation bow and withdrew.

'A faithful servant,' said Colonel Skurin. 'In these days you are fortunate.'

'In these days we are fortunate to have anything at all,' said Henryk. Don't let him be bitter, Kasia prayed.

Skurin regarded the damp toes of his long boots, then he cleared his throat.

'I hope I may speak as a friend,' he said. 'If I give offence by what I say then I am very sorry.'

'Before you start you had better have a drink. Vodka?' Henryk gestured at the jugs and decanters.

'Please.'

Henryk filled three glasses.

'And how is your father?' Skurin asked.

'I'm afraid he is dead,' said Kasia.

'I am sorry. You—and Poland—will miss him.'

'Yes, we do.' Henryk remembered his father the first time they had ridden out to meet Major Skurin. Dressed in all the barbaric splendour of another age. No mincing Western dress for him, he used to roar.

After a pause Skurin asked after Henryk's brother; a pleasant young man, he remembered, but quieter, with a certain hesitant shyness that was lacking in Henryk.

'Adam's in Warsaw. It's strange really, though trained as a soldier my brother has always had the idea that all problems can be solved by peaceful means.' He laughed shortly.

'What a pity he is not right.'

'Perhaps one day,' murmured Kasia softly, 'oh, not in our time nor our children's, but some day he may be proved right.'

'I wish I could believe that, darling,' said Henryk earnestly. And Colonel Skurin, the professional, nodded. Then the two men swallowed their vodka in one swift movement; Kasia took a sip and put down the glass on the little marquetry table that had been a gift from Catherine of Russia.

'Come and sit by the fire. Henryk, a chair for our guest.'

'No thank you,' said Skurin. 'After nearly four hours in the saddle I would rather stand.' His green uniform tunic began to steam gently. Henryk refilled the glasses.

'So you've ridden far today?'

'From Zhitomir.'

'But surely that's not a four hour ride.' Henryk looked surprised.

'Normally, no, but I had to make many detours to avoid the Austrians.'

'The *Austrians*?' Kasia's needle hung poised in mid-air. 'What in Heaven's name are the Austrians doing between here and Zhitomir?'

'My dear Countess, did you not know?' She shook her head in bewilderment and he noticed how the sheen of her hair caught the play of the flames; like the reflection of campfires from polished black armour, he thought. He also noticed a few threads of shining silver. She must be in her early forties yet her beauty was unimpaired, if anything

2

heightened by maturity; in common with the Empress, who was in her forty-second year, Kasia Barinska became more desirable every time he saw her. Skurin shifted uncomfortably and gazed fixedly into the fire.

'I knew,' said Henryk bleakly. 'At least I had a very good idea that something like this would happen as soon as we were beaten.'

And I helped to beat them, said Skurin to himself—these proud people whom he had hated so fiercely when he first rode across the frontier of Poland but whom he had now come to admire, to respect—to love. Skurin's eyes glanced quickly sideways at her soft profile.

'But, darling, why didn't you tell me—w-whatever it is that's happening?' Sometimes, even after all these years, the stammer which had afflicted her since the night she watched the burning of her home, Volochisk, the great white house of the Radienskis, lying across the river, bordering Lipno; Volochisk now a broken, charred ruin covering the blackened bones of her parents. Ever since that night when a Turkish horseman had taken her across his saddle-bow and they had ridden past the prone figure of Henryk Barinski, his face a mask of shining blood; had ridden hard and fast until the Turkish border post where she had to endure the horror of watching what they did to her brother, and afterwards, during the weeks, months, years, what they did to her—ever since that terrible time the impediment clamped down on her speech if she was tired, ill, in any way upset or worried.

'If you knew then w-w-why—' She stopped, flushed with agitation, seeming to have forgotten Skurin's presence.

'I did not want to worry you,' Henryk said, topping up his glass. 'You had enough to cope with. The fever Jacek had, Katushka taking to her bed, you being unwell,' he broke off somewhat lamely. It did not sound as if Jacek was particularly sick now, thought Skurin wrily as he heard childish yells of laughter and the scampering of small feet. In the silence that followed there was the sound of an old woman's angry voice from upstairs and the Russian officer felt suddenly unwanted, out of place and very sad.

'In a short time I must leave,' he said, loath to ride back through the rain to the responsibilties of his Regiment; the arrangements for their return to Petersburg. 'Allow me to tell you what I know,' he said. They waited. 'It seems there has been some sort of conspiracy among Frederick of Prussia, Maria Theresa of Austria and—'

'Don't say it,' burst out Henryk harshly. 'Your own Empress, I think.'

'Yes.'

'It is not Colonel Skurin's fault,' said Kasia. She turned to the Colonel.

'And what exactly is this conspiracy?'

'Put very shortly, it is to divide up your unfortunate country among the three of them.'

Kasia stabbed savagely at the canvas.

'But they c-can't.' She had gone pale. Until that moment Skurin had never believed that human eyes could literally flash with anger.

'Some twenty to thirty thousand Austrians have already crossed the frontier and are marching to occupy Krakow.'

'So we will be under Austrian rule, is that it?'

'Unless Russia challenges them, yes,' Skurin replied slowly and deliberately.

'And in the north the Prussians will pour in like disciplined locusts.' Henryk drained his fourth glass. 'But you, Colonel, what will you do? Tell us that before you go.'

'Henryk!'

'No,' went on Skurin, 'let your husband speak. I understand how he must feel, how you both must feel.'

'Do you? Do you really understand? For four years we have fought you and have lost. Don't you think that perhaps we want just a little peace to be with our wives, bring up our children. But how can we? While there is one foreign soldier on Polish soil how can we?'

'Yes,' said the Colonel, 'in your position that is how I should speak. But', he went on, 'the Austrians will not bother you. Unless provoked, of course. Not that there is much comfort in that if you still have to live under the domination of a conqueror.'

'They never conquered us,' Kasia flared in fresh anger. 'They are coming in for the pickings.'

'The Russian army has strict orders to avoid any sort of an incident with the Austrians.' He watched the poplars begin to sway in the rising wind. 'So tomorrow I leave with my regiment for Petersburg. After six years I am going home.' He did not sound overjoyed at the prospect, Kasia thought.

'Supposing,' said Henryk, 'you meet Cossacks on your way, what orders does the Russian army have to meet such a situation?'

'Ah, well, that is different. We'll just have to see how things turn out.'

'I expect you know them as well as we do, Colonel, but take care with them, they're treacherous brutes. They'll approach you, grinning and shouting welcomes and before you know it you're spitted to the ground like a stuck frog, and they'll still be grinning.'

Colonel Skurin took a deep breath. The time had come. He picked up his cloak from where it had been drying and slowly put it round his shoulders. The rain rattled on the windows and hissed in the flames.

'Thank you,' he said. 'Thank you for all your kindness and hospitality to someone who was once your enemy. I hope . . .' He broke off, clearing his throat loudly, then tried again. 'I hope I can leave your house as a friend.'

'Of course you leave as a friend,' said Kasia warmly. 'And if you ever come back to Poland—'

'Without your regiment.' Henryk laughed but with no malice in his tone. 'You'll always be welcome as a friend at Lipno.'

Skurin gave his little bow. 'I'll remember those words all my life.' He spoke very slowly, seeming to be having some difficulty with his words. Then suddenly he bent and kissed Kasia hastily and awkwardly on the cheek.

'Why, Colonel, I believe you're blushing.' Henryk's smile was understanding.

'I—er—I—you don't mind? I . . .'

'Mind? Why should I mind? It would be unnatural not to want to kiss someone like her. Here, have a glass for your journey.' Henryk held out the vodka.

Skurin drained it quickly, and turned on his heel.

'Goodbye then.'

In the doorway he turned and said, 'In case of trouble you have the means to defend yourselves?'

Henryk laughed again. 'There's not a villager under the age of ninety who doesn't have at least two pistols, a musket and any number of sabres.'

'Now, at last you can tell me this, and now I am free to be glad.' He smiled, raised his hand in a half salute and was gone.

They listened in silence as he said something to Stepan, then the sound of his horse, cantering from the court-yard.

Kasia stared into the fire.

'Fancy him plucking up courage to kiss you.'

She smiled softly but did not answer.

'Not that I blamed him. You're very lovely, Kasia.'

'Thank you, my darling one.' Her eyes were very bright as she looked up at her husband as he bent to kiss her on the lips.

Stepan came hobbling in.

'Look at this,' he almost shouted, holding up a gold piece. 'Who'd ever have thought a Russian would be free with his money. Pity they're not all like that.' He drew the curtains and shoved some more logs on the fire, highly delighted with himself.

'Who'd have believed it?' He was still muttering away as the door closed.

'So that is the end of our Russian colonel.' But even as he spoke Henryk had the sudden vivid premonition that he and Colonel Skurin would one day meet again.

* * *

In the months that followed the Austrians came twice to Lipno, once in the spring and once in late summer. On both occasions Henryk happened to be away.

But only officers appeared, no men. They were very correct, very polite. In no way did they even hint that they were conquerors. Though how they could be conquerors, Kasia thought, like every other inmate of Lipno village, when they had not fired a shot or used a sword, was rather difficult to understand. However, victors they were and therefore had to be obeyed. They asked a lot of questions, most of them very stupid, in Kasia's opinion, then they left.

'Nothing much to that lot,' said Stepan.

'At least they were kind.' Kasia tried to placate the old man.

'Kind!' He snorted. 'I'd rather have the Cossacks. At least you know where you are with them. Either with them—or damned well dead.'

Yes, she thought, and there he is right.

The Austrians came back to Lipno. This time they asked more questions.

'Where was her husband?' 'How long had he been away?' 'When did she expect him back?'

And so she lied to these very correct officers and told them stories she had made up weeks before.

'Thank you, Madame,' they said as they left, uplifted by her generous helpings of vodka. 'Thank you for your hospitality. You Poles are very charming.' Oh yes, she thought as she watched them ride away. Aren't all of you charming? And do come back—the whole bloodstained lot of you: Austrian, Russian and Prussian. Oh, do come back.'

And those were the only times they came to Lipno.

Chapter Two

THE rain had passed and only a few wispy clouds, promising wind, drifted across the half moon. In the big glazed stove the birch-wood crackled and spat, for there were traces of the beginning of winter in the night air and Henryk lay close to his wife beneath their thick down covers.

They had drawn back the bed curtains for they both liked to watch the bright play of the moonlight on the window panes and, besides, it allowed them to see each other. But tonight he could see the glint of tears in her eyes and could feel the tremble in her body.

'Don't my darling Rasulka, please don't.' Usually she loved to hear him call her by that pet name. Rasulka—in Polish folk-lore the water sprite that lures men to their doom by her beauty in the light of the moon. Ever since that first day in the hollow on the ridge above the river separating Lipno from her home; in the delicate shade of the little birch tree where they had made love and he had picked an ant from between her naked breasts.

But that was before the three Turks had ridden from the shadow of the oak-trees. That was when she was nineteen and he twenty-three. And now she was forty-one and he forty-five with grey showing in his unwigged and unpowdered hair. Even after what he had been through: the battles, the wounds, the years in the British Navy as a seaman on the lower deck; even after all these things his hair was still thick, it still curled though perhaps with not quite such black vigour as when they used to play as children.

As she lay beside him stifling the sobs which threatened to break out into a fresh paroxysm of bewildered grief, she suddenly saw him with blinding clarity as he had stood above her in the hollow, in long riding boots and hunting tunic of faded green, a dagger at his belt and his dark blue Polish eyes dancing with merriment in a deeply tanned face. From that moment as she had woken in the soft grass she loved Henryk Barinski. Throughout the bitter, lonely years of separation, through all the temptations of life with Catherine as her Lady-in-Waiting (to some of which she had succumbed), Kasia had never stopped loving him. She would never stop loving him. And that she did know.

That was why she wept. Because of what he had just told her. Though his words had been a blade through her heart; though she could not really believe what he said, she loved him even more deeply.

And she knew very well what he meant. 'You're going away?'

For a while he did not answer but, being so close to him, both in body and mind, she knew exactly what he was planning; she also knew he had not the courage to tell her the whole truth.

So she spoke for him.

'You're going on with this stupid, pointless struggle.' He lay quite still, staring up at the ceiling. In the moonlight she could see the shadows on his face and that his expression was changing to one of uncontrolled grief.

She had seen this before and knew it would not be long before he turned to her for comfort. Her comfort would not change his mind but at least he would turn to the woman he loved.

'Yes,' he said. 'I am.' She did not say any of the things women should say at these times : 'Don't you think of your wife and child? How, in Heaven's name can you be so selfish?'

She knew it was hard enough for him without her reproaches and entreaties. If she flung herself upon him, screaming and crying, hysterical and pretending madness, then she might have some hope of changing his mind.

But one thing stopped her: she knew that, in his heart, he would never forgive her. So she held back her tears and waited for him to speak.

'I have got to go,' he said. 'You of all people, must see that, my love.' He calls me that and yet he goes. Her cheeks were wet with tears.

'While there is still a chance, however faint, of saving Poland, then I must go.'

'Yes,' she said flatly.

'Henryk?'

'Yes, sweetheart—Rasulka.' He tried to laugh but it was not very successful.

'Where are you going?'

Again there was a short pause. The cloud vanished and the room was lit with silver.

'You remember that once I told you about a monastery called Novo Vada?'

'On the ridge? In our hollow? Yes, I remember.'

He nodded. She could see he was near to breaking point.

If ever a woman was torn apart it was Kasia Barinska: half proud, the rest of her dead with grief and disbelief.

'Do you remember our hollow? After all these years, do you remember the hollow by the birch tree?' His voice was tight but still under control.

'It's fully grown now,' she said. 'A lovely tree.' From next door she heard Jacek cry out in his sleep.

'God,' she asked silently. 'If You are there, please help us.' Henryk did not move beside her but she knew what he was suffering.

'That is where I am going. There I think I may find a man with the same ideas as mine.'

'A man who wants to continue the bloodshed?'

'I know you, Kasia. You know how to wield a sabre and

a musket, pistol—anything.'

'We have a son,' she said. No hysterics; just the truth. She had to say it.

'Yes, we have a son.' He paused. 'Perhaps it's for him that I'm going.'

'Perhaps.' Her voice was dead. Never in her life had the moonlight seemed so cold. 'Very well then, your mind is made up?'

'Yes, my dearest love—it is. And do you think I enjoy it?'

His answer was the shaking of her body and the sobs drawn from the depths of her heart.

'I'm sorry, my love, I'm so very sorry—'

And that was all he could say.

* * *

That night he made love to her, arousing her to a peak of pleasure that she had forgotten could exist.

She begged for this combination of love and lust again and again, for she knew, in the brief pauses between the wild storms of passion, that he was saying goodbye.

And long after he had fallen asleep, Kasia lay awake, unable to sleep because she was terrified of the future; of what lay beyond the endless steppes of Russia.

Chapter Three

JUST after midnight the blizzard that had suddenly come upon them died away, leaving the night soft with gently falling snow and the hard glitter of stars visible now and then, thrown carelessly across a pitch black sky.

Henryk still kept his heavy cloak wrapped close across his face, for the cold was intense. From head to foot he and Rasulka were plastered so thickly with snow that they resembled a white marble statue moving very slowly, trying to follow the road among the drifts.

From the inn they had travelled perhaps six miles in close on nine hours and the mare was fast approaching the point of total exhaustion. Her head hung down; she stumbled and weaved about like a drunken man, no longer able to place her steps where she knew, by a strange instinct, the road was hidden.

'Come on, Rasulka. Keep going. Just for a little longer.' Henryk talked to her through the frosted snow stuck fast to his beard, and she, like him, blew out great clouds of misted breath.

'There! What did I tell you? It can't be far now.' He had heard the faint sound of a bell from not far ahead. Something to do with the monks of Novo Vada, he thought vaguely; the bell tolled again. Whatever it signified, at least a guide for lost travellers. Rasulka pricked up her ears.

Sooner than Henryk had expected the great mass of the monastery loomed out of the darkness. By now the clangour of the bell was deafening. Huge timber gates studded with patterned ironwork filled the massive archway.

He pulled at the chain by the gates. Nothing happened. The big bell stopped its infernal din. Snow began to fall more heavily. He banged hard on the wood with the butt of his whip. Then he shouted, 'You in there! Open up!'

At once a small grill appeared filled with the vague image of a face.

'Yes, what is it?' asked a grumpy voice.

'Shelter. I have ridden far through a blizzard. I am exhausted and so is my horse. All we want is somewhere to sleep and something to eat.'

'Wait,' grunted the voice.

'I thought this was a refuge for travellers. Hurry it up—or d'you want the cold to finish us?'

There was the rumble of great bolts being withdrawn; the screech of a key and one gate swung slowly open a few feet. Once they were inside the watchman shoved back the bolts. A lantern hung above a small hut; the man held another above his head as he examined Henryk.

'Well, and where are you from, eh?'

'Does it matter where I'm from?' Henryk's hand dropped to the hilt of his sword. The watchman, noticing the gesture, put on a whining tone.

'I meant no harm,' he said. 'It's only that so many ruffians and vagabonds come to this place—well, you see how it is, I have to take care or—well, I have to take care.'

He was a dirty looking creature dressed in a shaggy fur jacket and torn breeches tied into bandages wound untidily round his legs, like a Cossack. Even in the freezing air Henryk could smell the foul stench of the man.

'Can you find me a place to sleep?' His tone was sharp. 'And a stable with some hay for my horse.'

'Yes, yes, of course. But for how long?'

'Does it matter for how long? I don't know. A week maybe. A month. I don't know.' This stranger was no beggar, thought the watchman. Not by the way he spoke. His Russian held a Polish accent. There might be money to be made here.

'No matter, Your Honour—'

'And don't you ever address me as "Your Honour". Understand?' The watchman caught the quick glint of steel as the sword was drawn half from the scabbard then rammed back.

'Yes—no, I mean, not "Your Honour", never again. Come this way, Your—please to follow me.'

Henryk followed the man, flickering, almost crawling in the light of his lantern, as they crossed a rough, cobbled square surrounded by towering walls whose summits vanished into the darkness. The only sound was the muffled clip-clop of Rasulka's hooves on the snow-covered stones. Then the deep tones of a bell rang out; a small door opened and for an instant Henryk caught a glimpse of smoky, golden light, the glint of ikons, a figure in rich robes; he heard the chanting of the monks then the door closed.

'They're always at it,' said the guide. 'Day and night, always at it. Here, this way, sir, up these stairs if you'll follow me.'

The wind swirled the snow round the court-yard and up the creaking wooden stairway. They made their way along an open balcony lined with closed doors; up more stairs to another balcony. At the tenth door they stopped.

'In here. I will show you a bed.' The old man held his lantern high and a voice shouted drunkenly.

'Get away, you dirty old fool. Clear off, d'you hear? We want to sleep.'

The guide swore obscenely as he stopped by an empty bed.

'Don't expect too much, sir. This monastery is poor. We feed these wretches and few of them ever pay.' He waved his lantern above the long row of beds. 'We have to chain the collection box. Oh, you've no idea the sorts we get here.' He waited expectantly while Henryk fumbled with frozen fingers in one of his deep pockets.

'Take this.' He held out the coin. 'See to my horse well and there might be another.'

'Thank you, Your Honour. May God bless you, Your—sir.

Yes, I will take care of your horse as if she were my own wife.' He backed away as though leaving the presence of royalty, muttering his thanks in an exaggerated whine. The door shut.

Henryk checked his pistol in the dull light of a candle stump still burning on a table in the middle of the great, vaulted room. The smell of the place was vile and he did not examine his bed too closely, but flung himself down, still in his long riding boots, pistol and sword by his side.

The dormitory rang to the sounds of sleeping men : snores and grunts, sudden loud cries and groans, the mutter of voices talking in their sleep. And all round him, stifling like a marsh fog, the smell of animal dirt, stale sweat, stale tobacco smoke, rancid grease and the foul exhalations of men's breath.

It was like the gun-deck in *Huntress*. What was he doing here? Why was he lying alone on these filthy rags when he could have been in Kasia's arms. His loneliness gripped him like a vicious twinge of physical pain. He closed his eyes and saw her vividly behind his eyelids.

'Oh, God,' he prayed silently. 'Please God, keep her safe, and our son, and let me get back to her.' He felt the grief building up and the tears squeeze slowly from his closed eyes, then, mercifully, exhaustion engulfed him in its black arms and he fell into a feverish, dream-ridden sleep.

From a bed on the opposite side of the room a man lay awake and watched the newcomer from bright, slitted eyes. He smiled to himself as he drew the heavy Cossack cloak up to his shaggy black beard. He had heard the man speak and knew that this was no ordinary 'Kazak', or freebooter, as the original Cossacks had been called; this was no ex-serf nor escaped convict from the Ural mines. What would a man such as this be doing at Novo Vada? Well, tomorrow might bring the answer. He smiled again. Possibly fate had sent the very man he needed. Through the rush of the wind along the steep, timbered roofs of the monastery, the man heard very faintly the chanting of the monks, the occasional tolling of the bell.

The day would dawn when the priests and the landowners would lose their iron grip on Russia; there would be no more floggings, branding and hangings; no more chanting. On that thought the man drifted into sleep.

The blizzard renewed itself and swept across the bitter steppes of the Ukraine, blown by a north-east wind from Siberia. Whatever the future held for Russia the blizzards would always blow.

* * *

Tomorrow came and the storm was at its peak, the wind rising to a scream as it drove the blast of snow against the ancient walls of the monastery. Even in the court-yard Henryk found it was impossible to be sure of his way except by keeping to the walls and the huge black and white pillars supporting the balconies and the stinking dormitories. He reached the stables. Rasulka whinnied when he came to see her. She was warm and provided with a feed of hay which, if not the quality of Lipno hay, was at least edible. The old villain of a gatekeeper was trying to earn another coin!

Then Henryk went back to the dormitory. They lay on their beds, arguing, sleeping, gazing silently at the thick black beams. Some sat round the tables playing cards or dice or simply emptying the jugs of raw vodka and smoking pitch-black tobacco stuffed into their clay pipes. Though it was early afternoon the candles were lit on the tables, small islands of light in the semi-darkness divided from each other by shadowy grey daylight that crept in through the little, snow-covered windows.

Many were Cossacks. Henryk could see that. Many others could have been anything. Most were dressed in an amazing mixture of clothing ranging from fox-fur jackets and pointed fur caps of lynx or squirrel to padded coats and strange leather skull-caps; there were men swaddled in thick layers of rags with barkskin shoes.

They were all provided with a liberal coating of dirt and many wore long knives at their belts.

As he had entered the room complete silence fell. Every eye followed his slow, steady progress towards his bed. The only sounds were the measured tread of his boots and the heavy breathing of those already affected by the vodka they had been drinking since dawn.

They saw the pistol in his belt and the short cavalry sabre swaying against the worn green tunic; they saw the dreadful scar cutting across his face from the forehead, between the eyes, down the cheek to vanish into his beard. They saw the dark blue eyes and the long fingers resting on the hilt of his sabre; they watched, they saw and they said nothing until he reached the middle table.

'Why not join us, friend?'

Henryk stopped by the table. In the smoky candlelight he looked into two bright black eyes above a thin nose and teeth gleaming in a thick black beard. A lambswool cap was perched at a rakish angle on his thick, grizzled hair.

'Get up and let our friend sit down.' The man gestured at one of his companions who leapt to his feet without a word. Henryk took the empty seat on the wooden bench.

'A drink.' The jug was pushed towards him. He drank, choking over the fiery brew, like swallowing naked flame, he thought with watering eyes and burning chest.

'Too strong for the gentleman?' A small man with massive shoulders looked across the table contemptuously. 'Perhaps he is not used to Cossack vodka.'

'I have drunk worse than this and done nothing more than lose my temper,' said Henryk quietly. The bearded man laughed.

'Well, Chumakov, and what do you say to that?'

The man looked down at the table to hide the hatred in his close-set eyes and said nothing.

'And what brings you to Novo Vada?'

'My horse and I were tired. We needed rest and food.' Henryk smiled at them. 'So here I am.'

Henryk looked round at the men at the table. They looked back at him and their eyes were not friendly.

'We do not own this place,' said the bearded leader with a smile. 'It is the home of priests and, whatever else we are, we cannot call ourselves priests.' At this there was some laughter. Henryk studied the man more closely. About forty-five, he guessed, and a man born to lead. There were a few strands of grey in his beard and the tough brown skin of his face showed signs of sun and wind and snow; the lines running from his eyes deepened when he smiled. A man used to riding with eyes narrowed against the snow-glare and the blizzards; a man of the steppes. The leathery face reminded Henryk a little of old Mishka, the Cossack groom at Volochisk, who had died in his last solitary charge against the Turkish scimitars on the night he himself had received the wound that had opened his face from forehead to chin.

They gazed with undisguised curiosity at the scar. In some strange way it did not disfigure his face but gave it added distinction.

'You are not Russian, my friend,' said the bearded man. Henryk saw the trace of a twinkle in the lively dark eyes; eyes that were never still; always watching, darting this way and that, full of expression beneath thick black eyebrows that met thickly above his nose.

'No, he is not,' said Chumakov, without looking up. 'A Pole perhaps?' he asked softly.

'I have Polish blood, yes.'

'Ah.' It was like a sigh from round the table. The bearded man scratched reflectively inside his dirty red shirt.

'You speak good Russian. But can you speak our Cossack tongue?'

Henryk shook his head.

'Have you ever seen the Don?'

'No.'

'But you have seen many other places. I can see that in your bearing and your look. A man of exprience. Am I not right?'

'Yes.'

'But one of few words,' put in a tall, gaunt man who sat stooped across the table, the pallor of the mines still on his skin.

'When you meet strangers,' said Henryk, 'I've found it better to listen than to talk.'

'Our gentleman friend is too grand to dirty his tongue in talk with the likes of us,' sneered a voice from another table where the vodka jugs were passing with great rapidity.

'A nobleman sits down with peasants?' One of the others spat; they all laughed.

'And since when have Cossacks been called peasants?' demanded the bearded man, jumping to his feet, his face flushed with sudden anger. His deep voice had risen sharply in tone and it seemed as if his eyes were suddenly flecked with red; a pulse beat quickly at the side of his temple and his powerful hands were clenched.

Excited conversation broke out.

'He did not mean it.' 'He's drunk, that's all.' 'Sit down, Pavel, unless you want a knife across your throat.' The man was forced back into his seat.

'Miserable scum,' shouted the bearded man, his voice echoing about the smoke-blackened roof.

He sat down and banged the table. 'Bring food. Or what these beggarly monks call food.'

Two men left the table.

'And you,' he pointed at the escaped miner. 'Another jug of vodka.'

'But where—how shall I—?' He stood, stooping even more, a bewildered look on his grey face.

'God in heaven, do I have to tell you how to get vodka? Find it, steal it, drag one of those bloody priests from their caterwauling and make him fetch the stuff. If you come back without any I'll twist your head off that scrawny neck of yours.'

The tall bent figure hurried out of sight into the shadows, almost running. The bearded man winked at Henryk, his good humour restored as quickly as it had vanished.

'They jump, eh? When I yell at them, they jump.' He threw back his head in a great bellow of laughter. Other men went off to collect food for their tables. It was just like the lower deck of *Huntress*. He remembered as if it were yesterday the terrible journey to and from the galley laden with buckets of salt pork and crawling biscuits, clinging on for his life as the ship rose or plunged to a heavy sea. Gasping and soaked the ration party would get back to their mess-table with the food cold and sodden. His memories were broken by a voice.

'When we've eaten, Mikhail will play and we shall sing. Then we'll watch while Dmitri dances the *gopak*. Brothers, this is a gloomy hole in which to sit out a blizzard. We'll liven up the monastery, whatever God may think.' Laughter and cheering and a thunderous stamping of feet.

'Friend, you will see the *gopak* danced as it is danced in the villages of the Don. Perhaps after a few mugs of vodka you might even try it.' When his laughter died away a voice from somewhere at the far end of the room called out.

'In Christ's name I would rather cut a Pole in two than watch him dance.' There was sudden silence.

'While a man is at my table or in my house he is my guest and so under my protection; whether he's a Turk, a Russian or a Pole, he is my guest.' The bearded man paused, peering down the room, trying to see beyond the candles and the deepening darkness. 'Come forward, whoever you are. Come forward and answer to me.' As he entered the circle of light someone drew in his breath sharply as he took in the size of the stranger.

He must have been at least six feet six with shoulders and

body to match. The steel-shod heels of his Cossack boots rang on the wooden floor; he wore a sleeveless sheepskin jerkin and stained scarlet trousers and at each hip swung a curved Turkish dagger. Without a word he reached the table, stood utterly still for a second then, with the speed of a striking snake, his right hand drew a dagger and threw it so that the weapon stuck quivering in the wood skewering the ace of spades to the table.

He glanced round the group of men from his narrow, slanting eyes.

'Whoever takes up that knife will fight,' he said.

The bearded man reached for the hilt, but Henryk was quicker. With the dagger in his hand he said quietly, 'Thank you, but this is my affair.'

The big man saw the pistol in Henryk's belt, and the sabre. 'Knives,' he said, hardly moving his lips half hidden under the long drooping moustache.

Every eye at the table watched unwinkingly as Henryk unbuckled his belt, laying his weapons on the table. Very carefully he stuck the dagger back into the card.

Nodding his head in a slight bow at the bearded man he said, 'If anything should happen then I would like you to have them.' Then he turned and faced his opponent, quite unarmed.

'Well?'

Behind him they sat open-mouthed. Only in the eyes of Chumakov there glinted a trace of pleasure.

'Stand back,' ordered the bearded man with loud authority. 'Get back. Clear a space!'

Both men stepped into the open space. The giant stranger drew his other knife and slowly began to circle Henryk who moved almost imperceptibly so as to face him. He had fought men with knives in their hands on the mess-deck and, under the tuition of Yorston, a bosn's mate, had learned how to beat them with his bare hands. But this was different; his opponent topped him by at least half a foot and had arms which looked capable of crushing a bear. 'Watch the knife,' Yorston had said. 'Never take your eyes off the knife. Not his feet, not his body nor his eyes, just the knife.'

Henryk never took his eyes from the curved, gleaming blade; he did not hear the heavy breathing of the spectators, nor the shuffling sound of the big man's boots on the floor.

Then, with amazing speed the huge Cossack leapt forward, the dagger flashing in the candlelight as the blade swept up in a vicious arc cutting through the cloth of Henryk's coat. Only the quickness of his reaction saved him from being ripped open from crutch to chest.

With all his strength he brought up his knee deep into the other man's groin as he was partially off-balance from the lunge forward. With a yell of agony he doubled over clutching his lower stomach and Henryk hit him once, twice, full in the mouth and on the chin. And that was something else Yorston had taught him: how to hit with every ounce of power.

As the knife clattered on the floor, Henryk hit him again, this time right over the heart. He saw the man's eyes glaze and knew it was finished and that except for a slashed coat and a thin warm trickle of blood running down his skin, he was alive and safe. He watched dispassionately, though his heart was bumping violently and sweat ran into his eyes, as the man sank slowly to his knees and then toppled over with the crash of a stricken tree. He lay utterly still, his eyes showing white.

With exclamations of excitement, astonishment, disbelief, the crowd pressed forward to stare down at the crumpled body of the giant Pavel.

'By Christ,' swore a voice. 'How in God's name did that happen?' They looked at Henryk with amazed respect. As Pavel regained consciousness he began to groan and roll about the floor, clutching his groin as the pain struck home.

Henryk bent and picked up the knife; he wiped off the narrow rim of blood. A mug of vodka was thrust into his hand and he drank deeply, wiping the sweat from his face. His legs felt shaky and he sat down abruptly, hearing from a great distance the applause.

He stuck the knife beside its fellow in the table.

'My friend,' said the bearded man. 'I do not think you will be insulted again.' He chuckled. 'I would not like to fight you with a weapon in your hand.' Henryk wiped his split knuckles with a handkerchief.

Pavel began to regain his wits; the groaning grew fainter as he slowly heaved himself to his feet. Henryk watched him warily; the men who had crowded close drew back. Using the edge of the table the big man dragged himself to his feet, his eyes still not focusing.

'Here,' said Henryk, holding out his hand. 'I'll help you.' The man shook his head angrily but accepted the offer. He stood, swaying on his feet, now and then wincing with pain.

Henryk took the daggers from the table and held them out.

'Take them,' he urged. 'They are yours.' Pavel stared at him vacantly. 'Go on, take them.' When the knives were safely sheathed Henryk held out his hand.

'We will be on the same side,' he said. 'I hope we do not start out as enemies.' Slowly, like a suspicious animal, Pavel's great hand reached out.

'I don't know how you did it,' he said. 'I don't know—' He shook his head as he took in Henryk's slender size.

'A drink,' said the bearded man. 'A drink for everyone. Our friend, our friend with Polish blood in his veins, and on his clothes,' at this there was much raucous laughter, 'has spoken truly. One day I hope that all of us here will be on the same side. There will be no room for enemies.'

Pavel sat down at the table, still half stunned, still looking at Henryk as if he could not believe him to be real.

'I don't know where you learned to fight,' he said thickly. 'But, by all the Saints in Heaven, you certainly know your job.'

Chapter Four

THE food came : a kind of watery vegetable soup stiffened by a few scraps of stringy meat. Complaints rose from all sides but to Henryk it was better than salt pork and rancid cheese.

'If we were in our homes we would be eating boiled beef—'

'And suckling pig,' said Mikhail drooling saliva. 'Baked fish in vine leaves.'

'Great steaming bowls of *bortsh*.'

'Oh yes, full of beetroot and cream.'

'The time will come when we shall eat even better,' said the bearded man. 'Ten times as well. You'll see.'

The miner had returned with two large jugs of vodka, a lot of which he appeared to have sampled on the way.

'Drink up, friend. You deserve every drop. God in Heaven, I never saw a man go down so hard, not even with a musket ball in his brain or his head split in two like a watermelon.' Henryk found the shaking of reaction was subsiding. He tossed down another mugful, not even blinking.

The noise around him was terrific. Singing, shouting and roars of drunken laughter. Little Mikhail was playing the *baikal*, bent over the strings, totally absorbed, and words of the song made the huge roof-beams shake.

'Along the beaten country road
After the bloody invasion
Don Cossocks are returning home—'

Kasia had told him how they used to sing this song as the men rode into the village of Zimoveskaya, laden with plunder from the Turkish lands or the rich pickings from the merchant barges of the Volga.

> 'With proud souls and gay songs,
> And all are happy,
> And all are proud.'

His eyes smarted from the pipe-smoke, his throat burned from the rawness of the vodka, his brain was spinning under the noise. But it was not only the noise. He was getting very drunk; he knew that. Drinking with his enemies, the enemies of Poland. But tonight he did not care; these were men with whom one could drink and fight—not against, but side by side. That was why he was here. He knew he would find Cossacks at Novo Vada, and yet he had come. He leant across and shouted above the din into the ear of the bearded man.

'Us together, the Poles and the Cossacks, we could take on the world.'

'Yes, friend. And beat the world.' His teeth gleamed in another mighty laugh. Sweat poured down into his beard. He raised his mug. 'To a stranger with Polish blood in his veins who can fight like a Cossack.' Henryk raised his own in return.

'To a man who—' But the bearded man had turned away, clapping his hands and calling for Dmitri.

The call was taken up. 'Dmitri! Dmitri! The *gopak*!'

The other inmates crowded closer, standing on the beds so as to see the better.

Dmitri, the tawny-haired young Cossack held up his hand for silence. 'Music, Mikhail.'

Another man joined Mikhail with an ancient fiddle and mugs banged on the tables in time to the wild music as Dmitri whirled and leapt with amazing skill; he sank lower and lower on his spinning heels, twirling with folded arms, shouting in a sing-song voice above the excited cry of the *baikal*, the frantic wail of the fiddle: *'Ahi, dou, dou, dou!'*

The candle-flames bent and danced as though in time with the music. The boy grinned as he danced; some eyes that watched him were merry, some sad as the men thought of their villages and their wives or sweethearts whom they might never see again if they followed the man in the red shirt; the man with the heavy black beard who was to lead them to . . . To where? That they did not know.

But they clapped and applauded the end of the dance as Dmitri leapt to his full height with arms held out at shoulder height, welcoming their cheers. Wiping the sweat from his face with the back of a slim, brown hand, Dmitri acknowledged the applause with smiles and laughter as he poured a mugful of vodka down his thirsty throat.

'He dances the *gopak* well, that boy.' Henryk had been thinking of the time when Kasia had danced for him.

'That is how they dance it,' she had said. 'But much better,' she added. Better perhaps but not with more grace. Henryk remembered the way she had made love that night: the passion, the ecstasy—the love. It had been incredible, wonderful, yet he had felt a flicker of jealousy. Kasia and he had loved each other for—for how many years? He tried to control his mind which came and went on waves of sound, mounting and fading, mounting and fading. A hand poured more drink into his mug. For how many years was it? He tried to count on his fingers but could not find them.

The candle-light and the gently swirling smoke were filled with memories, visions. The gun-smoke of Quiberon Bay and Rossbach; the ship-to-ship fight with the *Richelieu*. Always gun-smoke, always the sounds of killing, of dying: the horrible sounds of war. Kasia was right. He had earned a rest from war. Tomorrow he would go back. Adam and he would look after Lipno and protect it as their father would have wished.

Shouting voices; singing voices: the burning taste of the vodka, the hazy swaying of faces, to and fro, to and fro, like a ship's battle-lanterns. All he wanted was to let his head fall forward on the table and sleep, like so many round him were doing, but there was the monstrous din of a voice in his ear.

'Your name. What is it that they call you?' He blinked at the man. It was Chumakov. Desperately he sought for the name Kasia and he had chosen.

'Borodin,' he said, as though from miles away. 'That is my name. Borodin.' There was something wrong with the man's eyes, he thought. They were tiny and sharp and shifting all the time like pebbles on the tide-line.

Tomorrow he'd ask the man his name. There was much to do tomorrow. By now it must be tomorrow. The pebble-eyes disappeared. In their place the bearded man in a red shirt was standing on the table above him and the little weazel called Mikhail was waving his hands for silence. His words came to Henryk from a great distance but they reached him all the same.

'And now, brothers, we'll drink to a great Cossack.' A sort of silence fell, broken by bursts of song, snores and hiccups, the ugly sound of retching and angry bickering.

'Quiet!'

Henryk recognized the man who shouted as the giant Pavel. Even after his defeat at the hands of the strange 'nobleman' he seemed to wield a certain restraining influence for the noise slowly abated.

'I repeat, a great Cossack.' Mikhail swayed on his bench but did not fall.

'As great as Yermak.' Loud shouts of agreement rose from all sides. 'Yes. Yes. As great as Yermak Timofeyitch.' 'The man who conquered all of Siberia, far beyond the iron mountains of the Urals.' 'The hero of the Don.'

'And now we have a new hero of the Don.' Mikhail paused. Now what's he going to say, Henryk thought as

Chumakov refilled his mug, smiling his sly smile.

'Now I say, brothers, let us drink to the man who will lead us to Moscow, to St Petersburg itself.' He held high his mug. 'To Emylyan Pugachev, Cossack of the Don.'

Hearing the sounds around him through a sudden sobering drench of ice-cold water, Henryk sat open-mouthed, his mug half-way to his lips.

And from the table, as the bearded Pugachev responded to the gale of sound, he looked down at Henryk and winked again.

* * *

They rode out through the gates and up a winding path that led among the wooded hills surrounding the sprawling, red-tiled monastery. The two men rode in the silence of the windless morning, disturbed only by the dull scrape of their horse's hooves on snow frozen hard as polished stone. The iron shoes just bit into the surface, leaving a faint imprint. The sky was heavily overcast and now and then an occasional flake floated down. In the middle of a long shallow valley, well away from any trees or folds in the ground where listeners could be hidden, Pugachev halted. Huddling deep in his thick fur jacket, he began to speak.

'I have brought you here because I have certain things to say which are for your ears alone, friend Borodin.' He chuckled. 'That is your only name? Borodin? No first name?'

Henryk smiled back. 'Borodin,' he said.

'Very well then, let it remain that way.' Pugachev watched a little party of roe-deer making their way delicately in single-file towards the shelter of some trees. When they had disappeared he said casually.

'You came to Novo Vada for some purpose. I should like very much to know why a man such as yourself should come to be among a gang of cut-throats and villains. *Why*?'

'For various reasons,' Henryk answered cautiously. 'Because I fought for the Confederates. Because we were beaten—'

'And you would like your revenge. Is that it?'

'Partly, yes. My home was destroyed and my family killed by Russian soldiers.'

'You had a wife then?'

'Yes.'

'I too had a wife. Two wives. One was a laundry maid I met during the campaign in East Prussia nearly twenty years ago. She died of the spotted fever. Then—' He broke off, lost in thought.

'The second one vanished from my village in a snowstorm. I don't know why she left me. I was good to her. In the Cossack fashion, you understand?' He had often thought of the Polish girl with the bearing of a Princess whom he had taken from the Turks at the town of Kerch in the Crimea. Kasia Something or other. Funny, he could never remember her surname.

'We had a son,' he mused. 'But he died.' He sighed. 'She was a very lovely woman. A Pole but every bit as spirited as one of our Cossack women. I missed her.'

Henryk thought he saw the trace of tears in the large dark eyes but it might only have been the cold. He missed her too, he thought, studying the other man closely from the corner of his eye. So this was the man who had held Kasia in his powerful arms and taken her body 'in the Cossack fashion, you understand'. Strangely, Henryk felt no jealousy. He was secure in the wonderful knowledge of Kasia's love. Not jealous, merely curious in a detached sort of way, as to what her life on the Don must have really been like.

'The likes of you and I,' said Pugachev, 'were not born for wives and squalling brats. You and I are too fond of roving and fighting.'

'Sometimes I'm not so sure about the fighting,' Henryk said and they both laughed.

'You'll never stop fighting.' Pugachev regarded him shrewdly. 'Not until the Russian armies are scattered and the German bitch toppled from the throne. And then ...' Henryk saw the same red spark in his eyes as he had last night. 'Then I, Peter the Third, rightful Tsar of All the Russias, will sit in her place. The jewelled and sable cap of Monomachus shall be placed upon my head.' He rose slightly in his long stirrups, gazing fixedly to the North as if he could see beyond the snow clouds to the throne of the Tsars. 'And you, my friend, will help me. You will be my chief adviser, my second-in-command who will lead our armies to the gates of Moscow and then Petersburg itself.'

Henryk listened, amazed yet fascinated.

'Can you not see, Borodin, that when the Cossacks are joined by the angry men from the iron mines, the runaway serfs and the wild tribesmen of the Bashkirs, the Khirghiz and the Chuvash, the descendants of the great Khans who ruled Russia in "The Time of the Tatar" for over two hundred years, can you not see how the flames will spread like a steppe fire from the Volga to the Neva?'

'Yes, but—'

Pugachev brushed aside the doubt with an arrogant wave of his hand. Even his big bay horse, snorted with distended red nostrils and pawed at the hard snow.

'Think of the *golytba*, the naked ones, the hundreds of thousands of ragged ones, the people of Russia, stirring in their chains. All they need is a leader and they will follow.' Into the flaming muzzles of the Russian guns, Henryk thought.

'But,' he began again, and this time Pugachev let him speak, 'You must know that Peter is dead. He's been dead for eleven years.'

'Murdered with the knowledge and blessing of his wife,' said Pugachev angrily.

'That's what people whisper,' Henryk replied calmly.

'Soon it will not be a whisper, it will be a shout, becoming louder and louder until it can be heard within the walls of the Winter Palace itself, so deafening that Catherine will find nowhere in the whole of Russia where she can hide from it.'

'But she knows he is dead. Many thousands of people, nobles and peasants, know that Peter is dead. They filed past his coffin; they looked down and saw him lying there, dressed in his Holstein uniform.'

'Ah,' said Pugachev, a crafty expression coming over his face, 'but how did they *know*—the peasants, that is—it was the Tsar lying in the coffin. It could have been the body of a common soldier or officer. Have you ever seen the real Peter?'

'Yes,' said Henryk. 'I have.'

'Where?'

'At Court.'

Pugachev's expression turned to one of complete astonishment. 'You have been to Court? You have seen the Empress?'

'Yes.'

'And spoken to her?'

Henryk nodded, smiling to himself, remembering the time when for political reasons, as the French diplomat de Bonville, he had been chosen to share Catherine's bed. Yes, he could claim to have spoken to her.

'What is she like?' Pugachev could not restrain his curiosity. 'As a woman, not only as Tsarina.'

'Unfortunately, I have to admit Catherine has great personal charm.'

'Not for her serfs and slaves. But enough of her. One day you will tell me about your experiences at Petersburg. It will be a great help when I come to form my own Court.'

The horses were becoming restless in the cold and the men let them trot along the floor of the valley, between the white walls of small scrub-oak, spindly black skeletons made beautiful by the snow outlining every branch.

'And Peter, what was he like?'

Henryk remembered the long, thin face beneath the wide, bulbous forehead; the popping blue eyes, now cruel, now cunning; sometimes pitiful, sometimes completely vacant. His body was puny, his face pock-marked with the ravages of small-pox.

'He was rather like those trees without the snow. Small and very ugly.'

'But the great mass of the people do not know that. He could be large and bearded and,'—here Pugachev paused—'and he could have escaped the plot on his life and reached southern Russia where even at this moment he is busy planning a triumphant return to his throne. What do you think about that, friend Borodin?'

If Kasia could see the two of them, thought Henryk. If she could be here to listen to this arrant nonsense. And yet, was it so fantastic? For centuries Tsars had been murdered or imprisoned and throughout their realms men had appeared claiming to be the missing Emperor. Most had ended in the torture chamber or upon the scaffold in the Red Square.

'I would gather a good following from this part of the Ukraine,' said Pugachev confidently. 'For Peter supported the *Raskolniki*, the Old Believers. Novo Vada is the monastery of the Old Believers, the sanctuary for those of us who will not submit to the power of the Orthodox Church which has tried to alter all the old forms of worship and bring in a lot of new rubbish. And what are you? Do you believe in Christianity?'

'Yes, but not in most of those who administer it. I suppose, if I'm anything, I am a Catholic.'

'So you are a Pole?'

'I said I have Polish blood.'

'A word of advice, friend. Do not mention the part about being a Catholic. Some of my friends haven't the same understanding as Emylyan Pugachev.' He grinned his sly grin. 'Especially Frol Chumakov. That is one you will have to watch.'

'He has a nasty limp.'

'We grew up together in Zimoveskaya.' It sounded strange to hear the name from Pugachev's lips after Kasia had spoken of it so often. 'He stole something when he was a boy and they broke his leg with a wooden paling stake. A Cossack punishment,' he added, as though it meant nothing.

'We had a fight with long whips, another custom of our people. It was over my wife, the one who ran away. I beat him, but only just; for a fortnight she nursed me back to life then she went. Funny animals, women. I still trust him though.'

At the end of the valley they turned and walked slowly back along their tracks.

'So you'll join me then?' Henryk thought for a while in silence.

'I must have time to think it over. It's a big decision.'

'Revenge and glory,' said Pugachev. 'There can be only one answer. A week then.' He held out his hand and Henryk grasped it.

'A week,' he agreed.

'And no word of what I have said. Not in front of the strangers in the room. Within the next few days we will meet in a secret place where only the monks are supposed to go and you will help us to prepare my proclamation to the people. The proclamation of Peter the Third, fugitive in his own Empire.'

He laughed, throwing back his head.

'Now there will be six of us. Six of us to take on the might of Catherine's armies.' The thought amused him vastly for he went on chuckling while Henryk rode in a kind of daze. Did the man really believe all this, or was he mad? The way in which he spoke was not mad for, though uneducated except through the hard schools of war and Cossack cruelties, he was obviously a man of some considerable intelligence and natural ability.

As they came in sight of the dark-brick monastery walls, thickly plastered with patches of snow, Pugachev asked one last question.

'Tell me, Courtier—' that made him chuckle again. 'What will the nobles do?'

'Fight,' said Henryk with no hesitation.

'Against us, or with us?'

'Against.'

They waited in silent thought as the great gate swung slowly open and the two men rode into the courtyard.

* * *

The six of them sat round a table in a small white cell. Henryk, Pugachev, the little man with the pen and paper; the limping Chumakov and the bent miner from the Urals who did not seem to have a name. By the door, leaning against the wall and biting his nails was the enormous figure of Pavel. He seemed to bear Henryk no ill-will as a result of their encounter.

It was only Chumakov who steadfastly refused to be friendly, going out of his way to avoid Henryk as far as possible and answering in surly monosyllables or not at all.

He was speaking now, angrily, emphasizing his words with fist on the table. 'This is meant to be a proclamation to the people,' he said. 'Not a begging letter. I say we leave out the promises and the rewards and tell them what is intended, namely to fire a rebellion against Catherine and her nobles which will not be put out until she and all her Court are rotting in the prisons of Siberia and the landowners and Jews are hanging from their own roof-beams. Tell the serfs to rise and join our banner or else—'

'Or else what,' put in Henryk. 'Surely it's unwise to put the peasants against us by threats?'

'It's all they understand. The thought of the branding iron or the gallows is more powerful than kind invitations,' he growled sullenly. 'Besides, what use will they be with their pitchforks and sickles against bayonets and musket balls?'

'There I agree with Frol,' said Pugachev, puffing out a dense cloud of smoke from his blackened pipe. 'But there will be hundreds and thousands of them.'

'Yes,' said the miner between his harsh, racking coughs. 'And they will be desperate. Desperation gives men courage. That I know.'

'However many are killed by the Russian soldiers, there will be three times as many to take their places,' squeaked Mikhail in his thin, reedy voice.

'Read what you have written so far, Mikhail,' ordered Pugachev. Mikhail stood up, pushed his wire-rimmed glasses to the top of his sharp nose and, with an important flourish of the paper, began to read.

'A Royal Proclamation to the People of Russia.' He paused, drew another deep breath and continued. 'I, Peter the Third, by the Grace of God—' He was interrupted by a loud clearing of Henryk's throat.

'Well, what is it,' demanded Mikhail testily, peering furiously through his spectacles. 'Do you have an objection to God or what?'

'None whatsoever. But I think it should be "We" and not "I".'

'We? Why "we"? There aren't three Peters, are there?'

There had already been three men who had been secretly executed for their false claim to be Peter, but Henryk thought it wiser to forget the fact.

'He's right,' said Pugachev. 'I remember hearing a Royal *ukaze* read out in the village square once when I was young and it began with "We, Elizabeth, Empress"—and a lot more like that. So alter that, Mikhail.' Mikhail made a noise like an angry rat, and his pen scratched violently across the paper.

'By the Grace of God, Tsar of—'

'Almighty God,' Henryk corrected quietly.

'Who is writing this? You or I?' Mikhail was beginning to stutter with rage.

'He is right,' said Pugachev, enjoying himself hugely. 'It is important that such a document should be properly written.' More loud scratching of the nib.

'Go on then, Mikhail. Almighty God—'

Mikhail wiped his misted spectacles on a dirty rag, muttering.

'Of Almighty God, Tsar of All the Russias, who escaped death by murder at Ropsha on the Seventh of July, 1762 at the hands of foul assassins appointed by the German usurper, Catherine, who now sits upon our rightful throne.' The little fellow paused to wipe his glasses again.

'Excellent,' said Pugachev cheerfully. 'Don't you agree, Borodin?'

'So far,' said Henryk, and Pavel rumbled his agreement. The miner coughed a fine spray of frothy blood into his hand. Chumakov said nothing.

'I—We—declare upon this twenty-fifth day of January, 1773, that I—We—intend to reclaim my—Our—throne from the unlawful grasp of Our wife, the said Catherine Romanovna, if necessary by force of arms, if all peaceful overtures should fail.'

Pugachev looked like a cat bathing in cream, Henryk thought with quiet amusement. As if he himself had composed every last word.

'And so,' Mikhail continued, 'We desire that every subject loyal to their lawful Tsar should come forward to join the banner. If they do not do so then the most dire punishments shall befall them : they will have their noses cut from their faces; their tongues ripped from their mouths and their women will hang from high gallows.'

'No,' said Henryk firmly. 'That is wrong and I advise you to take it out.'

'And who are you, Pole, to dictate to Emylyan Pugachev?' Chumakov's eyes were narrowed.

'I am not dictating,' said Henryk mildly, disguising his rising temper. 'Your leader asked that I should help compose this—this *ukaze*. That I have done. But I shall go on arguing against the last paragraph.

'Fear is the best goad,' repeated the miner.

Pavel moved slowly towards the table, as he had done once before, but this time he stood behind Henryk protectively, one of his daggers naked in his hand.

'He is right. Start a war with words like these and who knows where it may end.'

'Thank you, Pavel.' Henryk looked up and smiled.

For a second or so Pugachev hesitated then he said, 'Strike out the words, Mikhail. And write instead, "To those who come to join your Tsar We have this to say: you will be liberated from the endless darkness of serfdom; the lands held for all these years by the land-owning tyrants will be divided among you equally and you will be your own masters, free from the oppression of the nobles, the officials from the great cities, and from the blood-sucking Jewish money-lenders.

' "These things We promise you. But you must be ready to help yourselves. When the time comes, and that you will be told, and the place—and that you will also be told, then lay down your instruments of slavery and beat them into weapons of war and march with Us to overthrow the false Empress." '

Henryk gazed at Pugachev in amazement. This was an extraordinary man; one who could not read nor write but yet could string words together and make them sound great. The Cossack was sweating heavily as if he had undertaken some feat of exertion. His eyes held a strange look, almost of exaltation.

Henryk nodded silently. Mikhail put down the paper and pushed his spectacles to the very tip of his little, spiky nose.

'Emylyan Pugachev,' he said sincerely, 'that was magnificent. The words of a true Tsar.' The miner coughed and wiped his hands on his thick breeches. Chumakov said nothing.

'And now I sign it.' Then for a moment, Pugachev's face crumpled. 'You will sign it, Mikhail, in my name.' His moment of exaltation had gone; he was once again the illiterate Cossack with the dreams of the Great Khans.

'There are two questions,' said Henryk. 'One, how is this to be copied into hundreds, even thousands of copies? Two, when are they to be spread among the people?'

'One,' answered Mikhail promptly. 'There are all the monks here who can write. In how many months?'

'Two, three, we don't know yet.'

'Very well then, in two months many hundreds can be copied and distributed. They will be passed from hand to hand, from village to village. So they will reach the far corners of the Empire.'

'Good God,' thought Henryk. This snivelling little clerk might be Stenka Razin himself. He had a second thought: if the men who followed men like Razin and Yermak had been half the calibre of their leaders then the rulers of Russia would have been Cossacks.

'And the date when this pamphlet—I am sorry—this *ukaze* is to be let loose among the Russian people?'

'When I think the time is ripe,' said Pugachev. When he spoke like that he would be a hard man to cross. Henryk wondered briefly what he might be like in battle.

'But not too soon. Not before the spring thaw.'

Pugachev was on his feet holding up the mug of raw vodka that Henryk still found almost undrinkable.

'A toast, brothers,' he roared, flushed and heated.

'To the Tsar!'

'To the Tsar,' they echoed, each man hidden in his own thoughts.

To the Tsar, said Henryk, a stab of fear piercing his heart.

To the Tsar, and whatever that may bring us all.

That night he sat by the light of a guttering candle, among the snores and cries of nearly a hundred men, and wrote to his wife, wondering, as he spelt out the words of love and longing, how she was ever to receive this letter.

PART TWO

Chapter One

THE morning was hard and clear and bright. The blizzard which had shaken the house throughout the night had vanished leaving a pale sun in the cold, blue sky. Underfoot the snow was crisp and spiked with ice, and white crystals hung among the branches of the bare birches.

A group of children waved to her and shouted a greeting as she rode through the village. She raised her silver whip in reply, smiling down at them as they ran alongside kicking up the powdered snow that covered the ice.

After leaving the village behind she took the same path as she had done the day when her horse had stumbled and fallen and she had lain very close to death with Henryk allowing no one near her except the priest as she hovered on the brink.

On that day they had gone out after wolves: Henryk, Adam and herself. Today she rode alone. These days she always rode alone. It wasn't that she did not like Adam, it was just that she preferred to be by herself with the thoughts and memories.

She let her horse follow the track they both knew so well, winding through the clumps of scrub-oak, up and down the gentle slopes of the hills; as she rode she let her mind wander where it would. As always it went to Henryk. Where was he? What was he doing? And, more than anything else, was he safe?

There had been rumours in the village that a band of Cossacks had left the monastery heading for the east;

another story had it that a huge army under a man calling himself Peter the Third was even now marching on Moscow.

'Don't you believe a word of any of it,' grumbled Katushka as she drew back the curtains one morning. 'Where do these crazy stories come from—where do they come from? Carried by the birds I suppose, or the squirrels. Cossacks!' The old woman snorted. 'I'll give them "Cossacks", God rot their black hearts and red sabres.'

So deeply was she buried in her thoughts that she did not notice the man riding slowly towards her up the slope until she felt Kinga break into a brisk trot and heard her whinnying note of greeting to another horse.

The man had obviously been waiting, hidden in the copse below in the valley, and now rode to meet her. As he came closer she could see he was a Cossack and instinctively her gloved hand went to the hunting knife at her belt. No ordinary peasant rode a horse and this was not an Austrian; besides she knew enough about the Cossacks to recognize the small rough pony as an animal of the steppes.

About ten yards away he reined in and sat staring at her. He wore a sabre but carried no lance, and he swayed in his saddle from fatigue.

'Is this Lipno?' he asked in a weak voice.

'Yes.'

Kasia could see he was no more than a boy, perhaps twenty but no more.

'I have a letter—' Her heart leapt for he had ridden from the east and there was only one person who would write. Unless—This time fear escaped in a little gasp.

'Oh, no!' She rode towards him. 'Give it to me. Please.' He did not move but looked at her suspiciously from bloodshot eyes.

'Give it t-to me,' she ordered angrily. 'Or you'll feel this across your face.' She raised her silver riding whip, but he did not flinch.

'I come from Borodin,' he said steadily.

'Borodin? Oh, thank God. You have seen him, spoken to him?' She let the whip fall to her side.

'How is he? He's not sick or wounded?'

'Not when I last saw him.'

She smiled at him and he felt confused, agitated, for never in his short life had he seen such a beautiful woman. Her face was flushed with the cold and the joy within her; her long blue eyes were soft as the sable cloak round her shoulders and the hat of silver fox perched jauntily on the gleaming black braids of her hair. He just sat and stared, his mouth slightly open, everything forgotten except the wide warm smile and the outstretched hand, very slender in its doeskin glove.

'Please,' Kasia said again. 'The letter.'

The wary look came back to his eyes.

'I don't know who you are. He said I was to give it to the first person who could read and they would know what to do. Go to the big house, he said. Do not stop in the village. Some of them do not like the Cossacks. Why should I care if they like me or not?' he added fiercely. 'Peasants!'

'They are good people who live in the village,' she replied, striving desperately to be patient.

'I can read,' she said. With almost unbearable slowness he fumbled inside his thick sheepskin coat. She smiled her encouragement, tapping the whip against her riding boot. At last he found the letter and held it out to her. Kasia could see, in Henryk's scrawly writing the one word, Rasulka. She looked down to hide the tears threatening to spill over. He watched her as she tucked the letter away under the fur cloak.

'What is your name?' she asked gently.

'Dmitri.'

'Dmitri. That's a nice name. But not so usual for a Cossack.'

'My father was a Russian soldier.' He wondered vaguely

how she knew he was a Cossack or that Dmitri was an unusual name.

'I must ride back,' he said abruptly.

'How far have you come?'

'Two day's ride, perhaps it was three, I can't remember. The snow was bad.' His speech was beginning to slur from exhaustion. To the east the sky was blackish yellow, filling with fresh snow-clouds; a few small flakes were already falling.

'You have done me a very great favour, Dmitri, by bringing me this letter.'

'So it was for you?'

Kasia nodded.

'Please let me repay you in a small way. Come back with me to my home where you can eat and sleep for as long as you like. Then we can see.'

Before deciding he glanced over his shoulder and saw the approaching storm, felt the icy blade of the rising east wind on his cheek and the heavy panting breaths of his little horse.

'Thank you,' he mumbled.

They rode through the thickening snow. Kasia skirted the village and reached her home by the back way. When he saw the bulk of the house looming ahead Dmitri exclaimed in amazement.

'Is this *all* yours?'

'Partly, yes. Lipno belongs to my brother-in-law. He is Borodin's brother. And I am Borodin's wife.'

All Dmitri could say as he dismounted was, 'But you could put the whole of my village in here.'

* * *

If Dmitri's arrival caused excitement in the village, in the house it caused a minor earthquake.

'What on earth induced you to bring him back here, Kasia?' Adam paced the floor of the sitting-room. She sat by the fire, quite composed as she listened to her brother-in-law's complaints.

'Because,' she said, 'he brought me a letter from Henryk.'

'Henryk?'

'Yes, Adam. Your brother. My husband.'

'But how—how could he—?'

'Does it matter how? He did. I have it here.'

Adam poured himself another drink and sat down.

'What does he say? How is he? Surely there are some parts of it you can read to me,' he said with a trace of a smile.

'Of course.'

Adam listened in utter silence as she read the extracts: the sentences to be heard by his own brother.

'... I am here, at the place where we talked about. It is not easy to write except of the things ...' Here she stopped and silently left out a few lines, not daring to look at Adam's face. 'Ah, yes, here we are. His writing's not as good as yours, he's always been a bit hurried. And as for his spelling, even after those years at the wonderful Konarski Academy—'

'All right, Kasia. Do we have to go into all this?'

'No, Adam, I am sorry.' She found the place in the letter. '... I may be away for some time, but do not worry, darling, it will only mean that I have gone further away ...' Further away! It was not going to be easy to bear.

'What does he mean by further away?' Adam was sitting opposite her by the fire.

'Away from Poland.'

He twirled the drink in his glass.

'I see. Go on.'

'... There is much to say and very little time ... I send this letter with Dmitri, whom I trust. He is young, he is a Cossack, but is to be trusted.'

'Trusted,' Adam asked coldly. 'And since when have the Cossacks been trusted?'

'If that is what Henryk says.'

'Very well, so this one is to be trusted. Go on.' Adam's voice was rough.

'I shall go on.' Very soon he would have had too much. Well, we'll meet trouble when it comes, and however it is disguised.

'. . . You and I have often thought of improving the Lipno stud-farm . . .' Adam snorted. Exactly like an angry stallion, Kasia thought but without laughter. '. . . why don't you and Adam build up the Lipno herd into something that will make money for the place?'

The fire crackled happily into the wide chimney. Any snow-flake that penetrated that far was melted to oblivion.

'Shall I go on?'

'Yes, Kasia.'

'. . . Dmitri knows as much about horses as all of us put together. All you have to do is ask him . . . He loves horses; . . . And now a different matter . . . You must need a change . . .'

'Do you think I need a change, Adam?'

He looked at the fire through his glass, slowly, reflectively. 'Yes, I do.'

'You think I haven't enough to do here?'

'I think a change would do you good.'

'And where do you propose that I go?'

'Pulawy.'

She put down her embroidery and searched for a new thread.

'Why Pulawy?'

'They are your family. Remember, Kasia, you are the cousin of the King of Poland.'

'You think that fills me with joy?'

'No—well—but—'

'I should stop, Adam. Because it would not make Henryk burst himself with laughter. Now, can we continue with his letter?'

'I am sorry,' he said humbly. 'I did not mean anything, well, you know what I mean?'

'Yes.' She picked up the letter.

'... Dmitri is to say nothing. And please do not ask him. I rely on this ... And now to another matter. You, or Adam, or both, please get in touch with Jan Dombrowski and Sergeant Nym ... ask them to Lipno ...' Adam was staring fixedly into the fire.

'Why should they come to Lipno?' His question was bewildered, almost desperate.

'You know the answer, Adam, as well as I do.'

The flames spurted high, giving him the answer.

'Yes, I do.' He poured himself another drink. 'At last, I do.'

Kasia said, so quietly it was almost a whisper, 'Thank you, Adam, thank you from all my heart.'

'Go on,' he said in a muffled voice. 'Please go on.'

'Yes, ah yes, here we are.' The fire was very obscure through her tears.

'... see if they can gather a few horsemen, some of the Confederates; any of them who are willing to carry on the battle ... tell them to go to the monastery of Novo Vada, in small parties, so as to avoid the eyes of the Austrians. When they get there they will be told what to do and where to go ... And you? Why not go to Pulawy? I know you didn't want to in the old days, but now—well, my dearest ... You may not agree with this idea, but at least think about it ...'

This next part she did not read to her brother-in-law. '... it will not be easy for Adam, and I do not like to think of you being left on your own at Lipno. But, at least, you do not have the Russians to deal with, only the Austrians who are not quite so bloodthirsty. Anyway you have every

him back single-handed.' Kasia gave a little husky laugh. 'And we'll call him Dmitri.'

'I will stay,' said the young Cossack with shining eyes.

'Good.' Adam held out a glass of vodka. 'We'll drink to the new Lipno stud farm.' They drank.

'Before you go,' said Kasia, 'we should get one thing clear. Should you want to leave us and go back to the Don we shall not try to stop you, you have our word on that. Oh, and another thing: don't worry about Stepan and Katushka. They have been here most of their lives, they are old and a bit grumpy. Keep out of their way for a while, don't be cheeky and they will soon come to accept you.'

'Now, go and find Zagorski, the head groom, and tell him to find you a place to sleep and that I shall speak to him about you tomorrow.'

'You can trust me,' said Dmitri. 'I'll even grease the wheels and bang in fence posts.'

When the door had closed behind him Kasia said, 'I think he'll be useful here. Don't you, Adam?'

'Ye-es.'

'You sound doubtful. What is it?'

'He's a high-spirited young devil. It'll only need some stupid insult in the village and that damned sabre of his will be out in a flash. There'll be bloodshed and people will end up dead, including him.'

'He'll calm down.'

'I hope so, Kasia, I sincerely hope so.'

This was the sort of man with whom Henryk was riding once again to war. His brother fought for Poland and did not care about the origins of his comrades-in-arms. At that moment Adam felt more envious of his brother than ever before. And Kasia, looking at him, understood how he was feeling. And yet she would give anything she had—except for their son—here she paused and wondered, was that true?—to have Henryk standing, unharmed, in this quiet, safe room.

'Already he has had a fight with Stas in the village—and won. The girls are excited, they want more. If he is to remain here then he must work hard, and quietly, not fight.'

'I agree, Adam. You are quite right.' He glanced at her suspiciously.

'Very well then, but at the first sign of trouble, out he goes.' He moved towards the drink table. He was moving towards it too often these days, using larger glasses or mugs.

She remembered a song of Mishka's; the Cossack who had given his life for Volochisk and her family.

> 'I don't drink from any glass—
> Nor out of any beaker—
> I drink deep from a bloody great pail.'

'What will happen?' She asked.

'I don't know, Kasia. I wish to God I did.'

'All I know is that there'll be more killing, more suffering, more hunger and disease before this is over.' She steadied herself, drawing deep breaths and willing herself to calmness.

And Adam gave her a very unexpected answer.

'Because my brother is, in many ways, a very remarkable person. He loves you more than anything else in this whole mad world, yet he leaves you, and your son, to follow some fantastic dream in which Russia is beaten into the ashes and Poland rises from the grave into another Golden Age. That's his dream, Kasia. You are his reality. You have always been his reality.' Adam started to pace the room again. 'And for that I envy him.' He stood before her, his eyes telling her what he felt, but made no attempt to touch her.

'Thank you, Adam. I thank you from my heart.' She got to her feet. 'And now I shall go to my room.' In the doorway she turned.

'At last I see. You understand Henryk as well as I do.' She was gone and he was left alone.

He refilled his glass once more, emptied it then hurled the

glass into the dying fire.

'Oh, my God, please help us all.'

Upstairs, in her room, Kasia sat by the stove in her dressing gown gazing unseeingly at the glow of the heat, Henryk's letter in her lap. Now and then she picked up the crumpled paper and re-read certain passages. '. . . life without you, my dearest love, is so unutterably lonely, so horribly empty and cold . . . like a deserted house . . . And yet it was my decision . . . I cannot run away, even to come home to my woman, my love, my wife . . .'

Oh, Henryk, my heart, my life. You stupid, brave stubborn fool, come back to me. If somewhere there is a God then let Him protect my husband.

She shivered as the snow swirled round the house; for she knew only too well what such weather was like on the steppes.

And, once again, she allowed all her pent-up grief and longing to escape in a flood of hot tears.

* * *

Dmitri lay, warm in the hay beneath two blankets. It was like the long room in the monastery, except for the sounds round him. Instead of the ugly snoring and hawking and the muffled talk of sleeping men, he heard the occasional stomping of hooves or the soft, crackly noise of horses moving in their straw. He was content, but for one thing. Or rather, two things. Stepan and Katushka. Grumpy! Old and grumpy. That's what Borodin's wife had said. But who was she? What did they call these kind of people in these parts? What should he call the grand lady?

Who were they? They were so rich and lived in such a huge house, and yet Borodin was content to sleep under the open sky or in a leaking tent. It was all too much for him. But, whatever happened, he was not going to be driven away by a shrill old bitch like that Katushka thing, nor by Stepan, however long he'd been here. Sour as a bloody quince, and no more juice in him. He turned over in the rustling hay. Bloody old fools!

And yet, perhaps one day, he might get old. If he lived long enough, he thought with a chuckle.

That had been a close thing in the village. The fellow had been strong; he had fought well but—well, he wasn't a Cossack. But the Master had been right—you see, Dmitri, even after this short time you think of him as your Master. Ah, but that was because of the lady, the woman. She had a way with her. You did not argue with her. If she had killed one man, two men, a hundred men, then what would one more mean? Capture a wild stallion, she had said. Bring it home single-handed. As he slipped slowly into sleep he thought of the words. Single-handed. Yes, for her, he would do it—or at least try.

* * *

'So I will go to the Potockis and see what they have got in the way of stallions.' Kasia and Adam strolled in the sunshine of the orchard. Spring of 1773 was turning to summer. The eerie cries of the wolves were giving way to the soft blandishments of the turtle doves and brown was turning to green all around them.

The thaw was nearly over; the swollen rivers and streams were subsiding to their normal size, the roads were passable and no longer a sea of mud.

For perhaps six months life was becoming possible again.

'And you'll take Dmitri?'

'Yes,' said Adam with no hesitation. 'He has worked hard, he's caused no trouble except for that small fracas over Simeon's daughter.'

'But Simeon is one of the village elders. It was only through your influence that quite a nasty misunderstanding was avoided.' That must have sounded pompous, she thought. But not to Adam.

'At least he did not use his sabre.'

'Otherwise heads would have flown,' she said, remembering very clearly the slicing of the pumpkins stuck on stakes at Zimoveskaya. Every green vegetable a human head.

'D'you think he likes Simeon's daughter?' she asked.

Adam looked at her with hard eyes and a tight mouth.

'No, Adam, you are very wrong. You think I have a fancy for that young man, don't you?'

'I never said that.'

'No, but you thought it? Didn't you?'

'Of course not,' he mumbled. 'What nonsense you talk.'

'All right, I admire him. I admire him for sticking to the tasks you gave him. And has Zagorski complained?'

'No.'

'Well then, the boy has passed the test you set him.'

'Yes.'

'Then he stays and helps us with the Lipno stud.'

'Yes.'

'Very well. He stays. And I want no more insinuating remarks from you, Adam. When,' she bit back the word 'if', 'Henryk returns, I don't suppose you will make any more suggestions like that.' This time her eyes were not fire but ice. 'And now I am going to Jacek.'

Adam continued to walk in the orchard. He had been a fool. He was wrong. But she was not a difficult person with whom to make things right; she did not harbour resentments.

A bumblebee swooped close past his head.

'For God's sake, get away!' he shouted quite loudly.

He was very touchy these days, he knew that; he flew off the handle at the slightest thing. And he knew the reason.

It was the problem growing ever deeper into his mind: whether or not he should join his brother. Jan Dombrowski had said he would go and Sergeant Nym was willing. though unhappy at the prospect of leaving his wife, Maryshka.

'Count Henryk needs us to look after him among all those heathen devils.'

Chapter Two

THOUGH the sun was low in the western sky the spring sunshine was hot and the horses in the paddocks were badly plagued by the flies.

'Poor animals,' said Kasia.

'At least we can swot the little pests.' Dmitri laughed.

They were walking slowly along the fences, looking at the mares and foals. Then they came to a wide field occupied by a single horse. A chestnut stallion with light blond mane and tail. A horse by the name of Satan.

'And you brought him back alone,' she said. 'As you promised.'

Dmitri watched the horse as he tossed his head and began to trot towards them. 'Yes, I brought him back. And he'll be the making of this stud. He's a true wild stallion of the steppes.'

Kasia did not answer for she was thinking of Henryk. The horse reached the wooden rails and took the crushed oats from Dmitri's hand.

'You see, he likes me,' he said without boasting. 'We're friends—unless I try to ride him.'

'The Cossacks sometimes ride without saddles.' Kasia had plucked a length of grass and was chewing it with great concentration.

The stallion trotted along the fence, hoping for more food.

'Do you mind if I ask a question?' the young man asked.

'Of course not.'

He took a long breath. 'How is it that . . .' He stopped, seeming to lose his confidence.

'Yes?' Her voice was very gentle.

'How is it that, well, that a great lady like you knows the customs and the language of the Cossacks?'

Before answering she pretended to watch the antics of a foal: the movement of the clouds, anything. They both leant on the rail, watching the horse. There was beauty, real beauty. In the sunset the heavy fall of his tail was pale fire.

'I'll tell you, Dmitri. Once, long ago, when I was a young girl my home was—'

'Yes,' he said very seriously. 'I know about that. They have told me about it in the village.' He called to the stallion, holding out his hand.

'No one except our two peoples seem to fight the Turks.'

Kasia watched the horse eating again from Dmitri's open hand.

'And what happened after that?' he asked. 'I mean no impertinence,' he added quietly.

'I know that.'

'And what happened then?' He pushed away the questing muzzle. 'That's enough now. Off you go!'

The stallion cantered off tossing his head angrily.

'I was taken captive by the Turks.' Two years with Diran Bey whom she came, if not to love, at least to like and respect.

'And?'

'Then your people came, and I went with them.' She smiled. 'I didn't have much choice.'

'Did they treat you badly?'

'No.'

She watched the evening clouds gathering round the sun.

'During your time with my people—with the Cossacks—did you ever hear of a Don village called Zimoveskaya?' He held his breath. How was she going to take this?

'Yes,' she answered quickly. 'I spent two years there. I had a son there. I buried a son there. Oh yes, I know Zimoveskaya.'

The hills were outlined against the sunset in sharp, black contours.

God, he thought, what a damned mess. He turned back to the horse for comfort. So that was why Borodin—Count Barinski—had made him promise not to mention the name of Pugachev. The thought kept coming back to him.

'Dmitri?'

'Yes.'

'I think we both know what we have been talking about.'

'Yes.'

'Can I rely on your word of honour that what ...' For a long time she watched the sunset and chewed her piece of grass 'that what we have spoken about is never repeated to anyone, anyone at all?'

He held out his hand.

'I don't know what you think of the Cossacks,' he said hesitantly, 'but, if they give you their hand then ...'

'I do know that.'

The stallion watched them depart into the dusk and snorted again, this time with disgust.

* * *

So it had come at last. The moment Kasia had been dreading.

Jan Dombrowski and Sergeant Nym sat eating in an embarrassed silence.

'And when do you suggest we leave?' asked Adam

He did not look at his sister-in-law. For many days they had talked of this decision. At first she had tried to dissuade him but, at last, she had understood that he now felt himself a man trying to equal his brother.

'But what will happen to Lipno, to your home, Nym, and yours, Jan, if they are left empty? The Austrians are correct;

they do not behave like the Russians but with this revolt seething all round us what—'

'If Dmitri remains in charge here,' said Adam firmly, 'you will come to no harm.'

'And Maryshka?'

Sergeant Nym pushed the remains of the baked fish round his plate.

'I—we—were wondering, that is if you don't mind—'

'Don't mind what?' Kasia rang the little silver bell beside her and one of Stepan's harassed underlings appeared to remove the plates.

'If you would think of—' Again he stopped, as if hit in the mouth by a lump of iron.

'Oh, come on, we have known each other long enough surely? What is it you want to say?'

'Well, it is this. My wife, Maryshka, would be very grateful, Countess—and so would I—if—'

'He would like his wife to come here, to the protection of Lipno, while we are away,' said Adam impatiently. 'Isn't that the answer, Nym?'

'Yes, Your Honour.'

'But of course.' Kasia's smile would have melted a block of ice. 'Could you have had any doubts?'

Sergeant Nym stared fixedly at his plate. 'No,' he mumbled, 'none at all. And thank you.' He plucked up his courage. 'Do you wonder that we follow Count Barinski when he has a wife like you?'

'Yes,' said Jan Dombrowski, getting to his feet. 'He's right.' He lifted his glass. 'To the bravest woman in Poland!'

She averted her eyes to conceal the tears.

'And to very brave men,' she said. And yet, as she said the words, she thought, 'This is madness, surely this is madness.'

* * *

'I have spoken to Dmitri,' Adam said. 'He knows what to do.'

'Of course he knows.' Kasia continued with her embroidery. If she were waiting her turn on the scaffold, she would still work at her embroidery : it was very soothing.

Then Jan asked the room in general, 'So you trust your wives and lands to a Cossack?'

'Yes, we do,' said Adam. 'And this is my home, my land, and so, if I leave it all in the hands of a Cossack then that is my affair.'

Kasia had never heard him speak in such an authoritative tone.

'Don't forget,' she said, 'we have over sixty men in the village.'

'Very well then,' he spread out his hands in a gesture of submission.

Kasia looked at him in the candle-light; the evenings were cool and the young lads, under the sharp instructions of Stepan, had built up the fire and drawn the heavy, brocaded curtains.

Outside, the village was very quiet. Even the pigs had stopped their grunting chorus and lain down to sleep under the cherry trees.

'Anyway, it won't be long before we are home,' said Jan. His freckled cheerful face had aged, but not all that much, since the first time she had met him fifteen years ago. He had a scar across his forehead—nothing to equal Henryk's—but something to be proud of, and his eyes were different: just as blue but not so warm: wary, more calculating.

And Sergeant Nym? A professional soldier. War was his trade. A true mercenary who would offer his sword first to Poland but, if she would not take it, then to the highest bidder. Like a shoe-maker, a carpenter, a builder—it was the only trade he knew. Perhaps Henryk was like that, she thought. He did his best to settle down; to be a husband

and father, but always the lure of the guns drew him away. Yet, she would have him no other way, for then he would be living out a charade.

Rather a dead hero than a quiet, ordinary man of peace: was that what she wanted? No! No!

'The Austrians,' said Jan. 'Have they been here?'

Kasia nodded.

'Twice, yes. They were very correct, very polite and not very interested in what was going on.'

'No poking about in the straw with bayonets to find rebel Poles?' Jan laughed mirthlessly.

'The bayonets were not even unsheathed. A few of the senior officers came into the house. I gave them some wine. They bowed and clicked their heels and apologized for any inconvenience—they also put in some nasty remarks about both the Russians and Prussians, then retired, with more bowings and clickings, and that is the only experience I have had of the Austrians.'

'Not as bad as the Russians?' asked Sergeant Nym.

'No, Nym, not as bad.'

'Would they come to your help if needed?' Jan's eyes were hard, his mouth twisted.

'That I do not know, Jan.' Then Kasia looked round the table slowly.

'Could I say something?' she asked.

The men nodded.

'As I think you all know, I can talk about the Cossacks with as much knowledge as any of you. No, Jan,' she held up her hand, 'please listen.'

'If they are your enemies then you can expect no mercy . . .' How very lovely she is, thought Adam, and at that moment how very much he envied his brother. I would be proud to claim her as my wife, thought Jan Dombrowski. By God, she's a woman all right, thought Sergeant Nym.

'But, if they are your friends then be very thankful, for they will do anything for you, including die.'

Adam looked up and, for the first time since she had known him, Kasia saw tears in his eyes.

'I believe you,' he said.

Sergeant Nym lumbered to his feet. 'I believe what you have said. But—but—if this Dmitri proves to be false then, as God is my witness, I will come back and tear him to pieces with these two hands. And that I swear.'

'And I will help you,' said Jan Dombrowski.

* * *

In the morning they left: the three of them.

'They have courage, those men,' said Dmitri, as Kasia and he and all the villagers watched Count Adam Barinski, Pan Jan Dombrowski and Sergeant Nym, ride slowly out of sight of Lipno.

'I will look after you,' said Dmitri. 'I promised your husband and I will do all in my power to keep that promise.'

'I know you will, Dmitri, and thank you.'

* * *

The three men stayed at the monastery of Novo Vada for a week. During that week two hundred and six Polish light horsemen joined them, in small groups, all ex-Confederates, all longing to continue the war against Russia.

At the end of the week the whole body of horsemen rode to the east, to where Pugachev led his revolt, helped by Henryk Barinski and his remaining Poles.

Chapter Three

CATHERINE, Empress of Russia, sat at the head of her council table. It was not a full meeting; only four men sat with her on that spring morning in 1773.

Count Panin, her chief political adviser, a small, sharp-faced man with a slight cast in one of his little brown eyes, was dressed in simple clothes. He should have a quill-pen sticking out from his bird's nest wig, thought Alexis Orlov maliciously, and that would make him a real clerk.

Alexis, the second of the five huge brothers, sat at the Empress's Council in his capacity as High Admiral of the Russian Fleet. Although knowing nothing about ships or fighting at sea, he was still high in favour with Catherine, some said because he was brother of her former lover, Grigori, now replaced in her favour—and bed—by the loutish but brilliant Potemkin. Others whispered that it was owing to the part he had played in the coup of 1762; the coup that put her on the throne and caused the hideous death of her miserable husband, Peter the Third. Many thought it must be owing to the successful battle of Chesme Bay, three years before, when the Fleet, supposedly under the command of Orlov had defeated the Turks.

In actual fact the victory could have been even more decisive but for the inexperience and impetuosity of Orlov. It was only made possible by the presence of Admiral Spiridov and the two Scottish officers, Elphinstone and Greig. But that fact was not mentioned too often at Court.

The other two men were dressed in the uniforms of

generals. Field-Marshal Suvorov, thought of as Russia's greatest soldier and his subordinate, General Rumyantsev; both summoned back from the Turkish War to explain why it was taking so long to defeat the Ottoman Porte.

'And how is our son this morning, Count Panin?'

As well as being her adviser, Panin had been tutor to her son, the Grand Duke Paul, for eight years. Now that the young man had reached the age of eighteen, the politician had taken on the task of teaching him the rudiments of government and monarchy—that is, as much as Catherine would allow.

She was at her most regal this morning, he thought. Care would have to be exercised; even that swollen-headed Orlov would be well-advised to watch his step. Instead of her quilted dressing-gown and mob-cap pushed to the back of her head the Empress was dressed in a rose-coloured gown magnificently embroidered with silver birds and flowers; her hair was swept up, powdered and shining with pearls; diamonds glittered on her fingers and round her smooth white neck.

She was not beautiful, thought Alexis, she never had been, but supremely attractive yes, and never more so than now in her early forties. Her skin required little or no artificial colouring. Not like many other ladies of the Court who hid behind ridiculous quantities of rouge and powder. It still held the same lustrous sheen as it had when she was the young Grand Duchess Sophia of Anhalt-Zerbst, pledged in marriage to her half-deranged cousin, Grand Duke Peter.

'Very well then, now that we know from Count Panin that the heir to the throne enjoys good health today, we can proceed with the business in hand.'

Alexis drew little pictures of cannon and muskets on the paper before him; he was unlikely to be disturbed in his capacity of High Admiral, unless of course she suddenly decided to send the Fleet to sea in pursuit of the Turks. He hoped most sincerely this would not be so. But if she commanded he could not risk refusal; if she asked then he knew he would succumb to what someone had called 'the sheer magic' of her personality which could bring enemies to her side as devoted friends and could win over men and women of every description and class.

'I have decided,' she said firmly, 'to disband the Dnieper *Setch*.' The men gazed at each other in amazement. 'The idea came to me in the night.' Her smile was radiant and faintly mischievous as she sat back, toying with her ivory fan.

'But, Ma'am—' began Suvorov.

'No ifs or buts, Marshal Suvorov. My orders are to be carried out. Is that understood?' The colour was rising to her cheeks; her hazel eyes under their thick black crescent eyebrows hardened slightly. 'Russia has been pestered enough by these Cossack wretches. For too long they have spurned the commands of their rightful Tsars.' She banged her small hand on the table.

'I'll have no more of it, gentlemen. The *Setch* will be disbanded. The horse-tail standard will be lowered before the eagle of Russia.'

'Your Imperial Majesty,' Suvorov was on his feet. 'I beg you to reconsider this decision, at least until the Turks are defeated.' He noticed her fingers drumming on the table edge and hesitated. He did not look like a soldier, she thought. Thin, with the pale, aesthetic face of a man more suited to a life of reading and meditation than the horrors of a battlefield. He wore no wig to cover his thinning hair. He should have been a priest. Yes, she decided, definitely a priest.

'Yes,' she said, no longer smiling, 'please continue.'

'In the Dnieper *Setch* there are more than six thousand Cossacks. We all here know how they can fight. To subdue the Zaporozhian Horde—'

'*Zaporozhia*,' she interrupted with the sting of contempt in her tone. 'The wild lands lying beyond the rapids, where thieves, murderers and fugitive serfs have hidden themselves behind palisades and earth ramparts in a fortress they call the *Setch*. And we cannot defeat this handful of barbarians with our trained and disciplined soldiers?'

'Six thousand barbarians,' murmured Panin, lowering his eyes before her imperious gaze. But he continued resolutely. 'If we succeed in destroying their *Setch*, their home—for which they will fight till not one of them is left alive,' the others muttered their agreement, 'then, Ma'am, we will have made the most bitter enemies of those who could well become the true allies of Russia. It will build up such a legacy of hatred against Moscow and Petersburg throughout all the Cossack lands that—'

'Enough!' Catherine turned to Suvorov. 'I want a straight answer. Can you or can you not destroy the *Setch* and burn out this nest of vermin?'

Suvorov looked doubtful and confused; he would rather face an army twice the size of his own than the anger of this one small woman.

'It will take more troops than we can afford to draw from the Turkish front.'

'Have we no reinforcements? In the whole of Russia, in the Eastern provinces, are their no more soldiers to be found? What about the Guards Regiments?'

Suvorov glanced quickly at Orlov. The Guards Regiments! Alexis Orlov had been an officer in the Preoprashensky, the *élite*.

'What about them, Count Orlov?'

'I think you know the answer to that, Field-Marshal.' Orlov looked the soldier very straight in the eye. 'You may remember Zorndorf?'

Suvorov nodded slowly. They all knew about Zorndorf—the battle in which the Russians had fought the Prussians under Frederick for twelve long and bloody hours; the field where Grigori Orlov had been wounded three times and become a legend in the Army.

'I think, Ma'am,' said Alexis Orlov,' that you can trust the Guards Regiments.'

Catherine looked at him for a moment. 'Yes, Count Orlov, I know we can. Therefore they must be used.' She leant back in her chair and smiled.

'I think that the Empress can be guarded by ordinary soldiers.' After a short pause she said, 'Very well, that is settled then. The Preoprashensky and their comrades will leave the luxury of Petersburg and go back to war.'

Suvorov made a note on his papers. Alexis gazed fixedly at the ceiling. Count Panin turned towards the sound of the opening door.

The officer bowed to the Empress who nodded her head in answer. He handed Panin a sealed note, bowed again and withdrew. They all watched as Panin, using his paper-knife very meticulously, slit the folded paper.

Catherine suddenly thought of Kasia. There had been a moment like this when Panin had opened a letter in just such a fastidious fashion; like an old maid opening what she hoped might be a *billet doux*. That time they had both got the most terrible giggles.

This time no one was giggling. She missed Kasia; she often missed her. Now the Confederates were defeated, the Polish forces scattered and armies from Russia, Austria and Prussia marching across Poland unhindered, Catherine wondered what it must be like for a proud woman who loved her country.

Beyond Panin's bowed wig she watched a merchant ship making her slow way upstream against the wind, the brown sails filling and emptying as they altered to the changes of the wind. In the background the crooked spire of the St Peter and Paul fortress leant across the light spring sky. Unwillingly she came back to the present.

'Well, Count Panin?'

For a long moment he kept his gaze on the open paper. 'Trouble, Ma'am.'

The others looked up together as if their heads were jerked by the same string.

'May we ask if it is trouble that can be dealt with?'

'Yes, Ma'am, it can—with no difficulty.'

'And what is this trouble, Count Panin?'

In answer he passed her the letter. After reading it the Empress pushed it from her.

'A small, unimportant revolt in the province of Orenburg. Are we all to tremble in our shoes because of a few disaffected Cossacks?' She rose to her feet, followed by the men. The little ship was having difficulty in beating against the wind. Catherine got so engrossed in the struggle that only a subdued clearing of the throat from Panin reminded her of the problem.

'Some stray rebels, one small fort taken. Does that mean the end of the Tsars?'

'No, Ma'am, but—'

'But *what*, Marshal Suvorov?'

'The Turkish war, Your Majesty.'

'The destruction of the Dnieper *Setch*,' said Alexis Orlov, with a trace of arrogance in his voice.

'We have sufficient forces in the Eastern provinces to put down a minor escapade.'

'There you are right, Your Majesty.' Suvorov consulted his finger-nails. 'But if it were to spread then—' He paused.

'Then what?' She knew he was right, but she wanted to hear the answer from his own lips.

'Then, Your Majesty, we shall have a lot of trouble on our hands.'

'Nothing our fortress garrisons on the river Yaik cannot deal with,' said Orlov firmly.

'That is what they're there for,' added Rumyantsev, his voice quivering with martial ardour.

'Quite,' said Suvorov, without conviction.

'Your Majesty,' said Rumyantsev earnestly, 'allow me to go. There are enough trained troops in Petersburg and

Moscow. Let me lead one of the Guards Regiments, some cavalry and two batteries of cannon and we shall finish the business within a week or two. I pray you, Ma'am, to grant your gracious permission so that I may begin preparations this very hour.'

Pompous fool, thought Catherine. She saw the undisguised amusement on Orlov's face, the darkening of Suvorov's brow. There was no love lost between the two men, that she knew well.

'We thank you, General, but it is really up to your superior officer.' Suvorov acknowledged her decision with a grim little smile. Catherine resumed her seat and they all sat except for the Field-Marshal.

'As I said, Ma'am, the Turkish campaign must have every priority.'

'I agree,' said Panin. Orlov nodded. Only Rumyantsev remained silent, staring down at the table.

'I have reason to believe that the Porte is about to open negotiations for peace at any moment. They—'

'Excellent, my dear friend,' cried Catherine happily. 'Oh, that is the best news we have heard for many a day. Wonderful, Field-Marshal. But'—a small cloud hid the animated smile—'are you certain of this? I have heard nothing of a Turkish surrender.' Her fingers began to tap on the table and her eyes darkened.

'Why was I not informed?'

'Because', answered Suvorov calmly in his slow, deliberate voice, 'I did not wish to risk disappointing Your Majesty by speaking before I was sure.'

'And now you are sure?' Panin gave him a short, piercing glance.

'Yes,' Suvorov said, 'I am sure. The Turkish armies are in confusion, their casualties have been enormous. The cost of the war is becoming too much even for the wealth of the Sultans.'

'It has not been cheap for Russia,' said Catherine soberly.

'Neither in lives nor gold. But, gentlemen, at least we are victorious.'

'Yes, through your iron will, Ma'am, and the courage of the Russian soldier we are victorious.'

'Not to mention one other small fact,' she said, smiling. 'Your skill in the field.' Suvorov thanked her with a stiff bow to hide his intense pleasure. When Catherine of Russia smiled and spoke like that there surely could not be a man in the whole of her vast Empire who would not lay down his life for her. Orlov could feel her amazing charm wafting over them; Panin also. They all could, even the sullen Rumyantsev. For him she had a special smile.

'I am in your debt, General, for your generous offer to leave the scene of our approaching glory and take yourself to the gloomy wilds of Orenburg.' They knew she was teasing but her words were said so kindly, so warmly that his sullenness was swept away.

'Your Majesty—'

'Field-Marshal Suvorov will naturally want you with him to sign the preliminary peace terms.' She turned to Suvorov. 'When these terms are drawn-up to your satisfaction you will bring them to me with your own hand. I wish to receive them from no one else. Is that clear, Field-Marshal.'

'Yes, Your Majesty.'

One of the palace pigeons alighted on the window-sill, calling throatily as he marched up and down.

'You see, gentlemen. We have another sentry.' She laughed gaily. 'And look, his lady-friend has come to join him. 'The two birds advanced towards each other, then retired, rubbing their beaks together and their blue, sunlit breasts, cooing and puffing out the feathers of their throats in an ecstasy of spring love.

Soon she would be in the arms of her new love; the man she loved not only with her body like the previous men in her life but also with her mind. She yearned not only for his hands and his coarse, uninhibited words of love, but to talk with him and explore that amazing mind of his. She glanced at the gold and marble clock on the mantel-piece: the clock given to her by Stanislas Poniatowski, the gentle, adoring Pole whom she had also loved, though in a different way, for his good looks and cultured wit.

'Your Majesty.' She realized from his tone that Count Panin had tried to attract her attention twice.

'I am sorry, I was lost in my thoughts. It is such momentous news about the Turks I—please go on.' Orlov smiled to himself; he had often seen her look like that during the years his brother had been her lover. And now she shared her bed with this one-eyed savage, half Tatar, nearly always drunk.

A pity that he and his brothers had not put out the other eye, Alexis thought viciously, listening with half his mind to what Panin was saying.

'This trouble on the Yaik,' said the neat, precise voice. 'It should not be ignored.'

'As Count Orlov mentioned, the river garrisons can surely deal with this matter.' She glanced again at the clock; the gilded hands seemed to be stuck fast at five to eleven. Why did her whole life have to be cluttered up with niggling, worrying affairs of state when all she wanted was . . .

'Someone must be in overall command, Ma'am.'

'That I leave to Marshal Suvorov.' The minute hand advanced imperceptibly towards the magic hour. By the first crystal chime of eleven this business must be concluded.

'General Bibikov, Ma'am, or—' He inclined his head towards Count Panin. 'Your cousin brother. Both are capable soldiers. Will you leave the final decision to me, Ma'am?'

'Of course, Field-Marshal.'

'And now, gentlemen, if there is nothing else, we shall meet again this afternoon at four.'

'The Dnieper *Setch,* Ma'am.' She could see by the slight trace of insolence in his grey eyes and the curl of his lip that Alexis had added this final question on purpose. Very well, *Count* Orlov, she thought as the clock-hand hovered just short of the hour, very well, this you have done to annoy me. Because you and your brothers hate the man who has taken your places. Be careful, Alexis, not to go too far, as Grigori did. Russia owes you a lot, Alexis. *I* owe you a lot, but be careful.

With a tiny whirring sound the clock prepared itself to strike.

'Until the Turkish campaign is officially ended and the Orenburg nonsense under control, we will place the plan in abeyance. But only in abeyance.'

The clock was striking.

'And now, gentlemen, if you will excuse me. I have my private papers to attend to.'

They bowed low as the small, very regal figure, walked from the room. No one said a word. For many years Catherine's routine had seldom varied, not if there was a man in her life. Up early, about six, she worked until nine in her dressing-gown; then, after coffee and something to eat, she would dress more formally and receive people in audience. Then, between eleven and twelve the Empress would vanish to her private rooms for a period of relaxation with her lover. Private papers in her private rooms! Her whole Court, from the most powerful Prince to the lowliest scullery boy, knew what that meant.

The four men said nothing as they gathered up their papers, but they all knew.

Catherine was on her way to Potemkin.

* * *

Once beyond the bowing heads and the closing doors Catherine ran towards the only door that mattered: the door to her private apartments.

And she, the Autocrat of Russia, hurried towards this door.

On the other side she faced an unshaven giant of a man with a black patch over one eye; dressed in a dirty kaftan; bare feet and huge hands, thick with tangled black hairs, long, dirty nails.

'My darling, my golden pheasant, my glorious tiger.' She ran to him, calling out absurd names. But that was how she had always been with him. No words were too fantastic—not between Catherine and her lover, Potemkin.

'My bird of paradise—'

'Come here, woman.' He stank of cheap spirit and unwashed flesh yet she did not mind. Nothing that this man did was wrong. The others? Beside this one they were chaff in the wind.

She went to the day-chair where he lay, stuffing grapes into his mouth and pouring vodka down his throat like so much water. She knelt beside his head, kissing the thick stubble on his face, murmuring words of love and lust.

With a free hand he tore the beautiful dress from her shoulders; he pawed her breasts whilst still cramming his mouth with grapes so that the purple juice trickled down her half naked body.

Catherine began to moan, her hands to move, more and more frantically. They tore open the kaftan.

'Yes,' he said thickly. 'Yes, go on!'

He was strong, terribly strong, and utterly ruthless. His great hands hurt her body, bruising and squeezing the breath from her, but she did not mind.

'Oh, my dearest angel, my heart of hearts—' She gasped and cried out, not caring who might hear. By now her clothes were crumpled on the floor and he took her like an animal, but that was how she enjoyed it.

'You're a woman, all right. By Christ, you are.' They both lay panting. 'You may be an Empress but you're a woman that every man would want to—' He used an obscene word but she did not care. It simply began to excite her again.

* * *

They sat opposite each other. She in a dressing-gown; Potemkin still lounging on the day-bed, eating the grapes.

'God,' she said, 'you're wonderful.'

'And you, my Empress,' he answered with mock reverence, 'are a fairly remarkable woman.'

'Thank you, Grigori.'

'How many times did you say that to the man who had you before me?' He belched loudly. 'Excuse me, Your Majesty.' They both laughed. 'Tell me this: how many times did you tell the other Grigori the same thing?'

'You don't believe me,' she said, 'but never in my life have I really meant it as I do now. Never have I loved any man as I love you. Not only physically but—' She hesitated.

'But—well—' She tapped her head. 'Mentally—in every way.'

He sloshed vodka all over her little Louis Quinze table as he refilled his glass.

She shook her head.

'No, my horn of plenty,' that was a favourite between them, 'no. In an hour's time I have to appear as Empress again, not as a woman wildly in love.'

'What did they have to say, those miserable worms in there?' He gestured angrily towards her official conference room.

Catherine told him. And never before with her other lovers, Saltikov, Poniatowski, Orlov, had she ever mixed love with politics or sovereignty.

'So they're frightened of the Cossacks. That's what it comes to, isn't it? They're scared of the bloody Cossacks.'

He swallowed another large vodka and flung the empty

glass at the wall where it smashed into the middle of a picture.

'Rotten painting, bad colouring, better out of the way.' It had been one of her favourites, but Catherine said nothing. He could do no wrong.

'And this revolt near Orenburg? What about that, my angel-heart?'

She glanced into the gilt mirror above the mantelpiece and patted gently at her hair.

'Nothing there that a few trained men cannot deal with.' His answer made Catherine feel quite secure.

'And now,' she said, 'I must go.' She bent and kissed him on the forehead.

'Until this evening,' she said.

'Yes,' he answered, helping himself to more grapes. His single eye was bleary, his speech very slurred.

This was one of his bad days, she thought. But, at other times, when he ignored the vodka, his mind was one of the best she had ever met. It would take him half a minute to grasp the root of a problem that would cause others, including herself, hours of worry and indecision.

As she walked slowly towards the doors Catherine pulled herself together and changed from the woman to the Empress.

Chapter Four

PUGACHEV'S continued successes were causing the beginnings of alarm in Moscow. Not panic, of course—after all, what had anyone to panic about? But certainly uneasiness. Even the Empress herself was not entirely immune and summoned her Council every day to discuss the situation.

'What must give us cause for concern are not his military victories, they are of small account—'

'But, Your Majesty, the villainous creature is successful. That we cannot ignore; the fact is known to every serf in the land, Count Panin, and that is what worries us. This is no longer a minor Cossack affair. The whole country between here and the Yaik river is seething with unrest. Peasants flocking to join this rebel, serfs running away from their masters. Attacks on the great houses; burnings and murder. An utter collapse of law spreading across Russia. Are we to witness another "Time of the Tatar"?'

None at the table answered.

'No, gentlemen, we are not. This business has got to be stopped. And stopped *now*. So you, Marshal Suvorov, will go to the east and take overall command in place of the unfortunate Bibikov whose sudden death could not have come at a more unfortunate time.'

'Ma'am.' Suvorov bowed.

'You will destroy the forces of this man Pugachev and bring him to Moscow, alive or dead, preferably alive, for an example must be made.' Her small face was white with controlled rage.

'We shall show this Cossack murderer who rules over Russia.'

That night Suvorov rode with his staff and a bodyguard of cavalry on the road to Kazan and all round them the countryside was red with the fires of burning villages and the mansions of the landowners.

Behind the horsemen, marching at their best speed, followed the regiments of the Guards and the Smolensk Regiment under Colonel Skurin.

With drums beating, and bayonets glowing like red-hot steel in the stained, flaming night, and the heavy rumble of artillery wheels, they marched towards the distant city of Kazan, unmolested by the wild, drunken bands lurking in the forest edges watching the disciplined columns marching east to meet the hero, Pugachev.

But the Guards, the guns, the cavalry and Marshal Suvorov were too late to save Kazan.

* * *

They were too late to help the many noble families who had been too proud to run for the safety of Moscow or who had trusted their own people to help them to hide or escape.

Even on some of the estates where the serfs did not actually turn on their masters or run away to join the rebels, they were surly and rude, knowing well that they would not be flogged or branded through fear of Pugachev and his men.

The Cossack was regarded as some sort of a saint, bringing freedom from the tyrants who owned them, body and soul, and did not need to answer to anyone but God for their brutalities.

So, in the name of freedom—and revenge—the most appalling cruelties were inflicted upon men, women and the smallest of children by half-crazed mobs urged on by men and women mad with hate.

Burning alive; crucifixion with pitchforks; slow drowning, hanging, disemboweling : the mobs, drunk with blood-lust, used all these methods, enjoying every last horrific moment. The stories that reached Kasia and Maryshka made their blood freeze.

'If they reach here then we must kill them,' said Kasia, as the two women stood looking down at their sleeping children. Maryshka did not answer.

'Do you agree?' Kasia asked gently.

'Only when there is no possible hope left. When they are in the next room, battering at the door.' Jacek murmured in his sleep. In the next little bed Marya Nym clenched and unclenched her small, fat hands.

'It would not be easy to watch,' Kasia said. 'You and I tied-up and forced to listen to—to them—subjected to some unspeakable horror.'

'Could you kill your own son?'

'To save him from that, yes. At least, I hope I would have the courage.'

'But, God willing, we may escape unharmed,' said Maryshka. 'Count Adam and that young scoundrel, Dmitri, have done a good job over the defences of Lipno.'

'Yes.' Kasia imagined Henryk here at Lipno. Then they would have nothing to fear.

But Adam had done enough. Through him the men of the village knew how to shoot; they had built defences: trenches, spikes, hidden pits in the ground; high earthen walls and sharp-pointed palisades; they had stretched tight wires between the trees. Somehow, from somewhere, guns had been brought to Lipno, big enough to blow apart a dozen men.

In the distance they could hear the crackle of musket-fire and the savage shouts carried on the warm, summer wind.

'The defences are manned,' said Maryshka. 'He may be a young dare-devil, that Dmitri, but he knows what he's about, and the people of the village have taken to him, especially some of the girls.' For the first time that evening she saw the slight glimmer of a smile on Kasia's face.

On a chair between the small beds the pistols and daggers shone in the light of the single candle, deadly as coiled snakes.

'Listen!' Kasia held up her hand. 'D'you hear it, Maryshka?' The sounds were closer now.

'It's like animals,' Kasia said.

'Wolves don't sound half as bad.' A sort of awful, baying howl, growing louder every minute.

Kasia glanced down at the sleeping children. She had killed before in her life and, by God, she would kill again: to save these two little children so happily asleep in their safe, comforting beds, she would do anything, however ghastly.

They were woken from their sleep by the crash of a gun; the loud spatter of musket-shots. Both women ran to the window. In the light summer darkness they could see the flash of guns and the sparks of the muskets. They could hear the angry shouts of their attackers; the screams of the wounded.

For an hour they watched, pistols in their hands, as the battle raged in the woods and on the outskirts of Lipno.

Then, suddenly it was over. Flames still licked the sky; an occasional shot scarred the night; the hard rattle of hooves in the village. After that, nothing but the deep red of distant fires.

'They've gone.' Kasia sank down on to the bed, the pistol falling into her lap.

'My God, they've gone.'

The door burst open. 'Yes, they've gone.' Dmitri stood bare-headed in the door. A thin thread of blood ran from his temple to his mouth.

'And they won't come back.'

He walked over to the children. For a while he looked down at them.

'They are safe,' he said. He pointed his blood-stained sabre at the window.

'For the moment they are safe. You are safe. We are all safe. Because of the peasants, the men and women of Lipno who fought.' He strode to the window, saying nothing. He gazed over the excited scene in the village.

'Yes, because of Count Adam's training, and perhaps a little of mine, they learned to fight, not just with sickles and pitchforks, but with real weapons.' He turned from the window. 'Do you realize, Countess, how much these people owe to you? And you to them?' She avoided Maryshka's eyes.

'How did you do it, Dmitri?' Kasia asked.

'Without Count Adam's advice, we would never have held them. Drunken men are hard to stop.'

'Never mind about that,' Kasia said, the relief bursting out in her angry answer. 'How *did* you stop them?'

'Discipline.'

'Discipline?' Maryshka sounded incredulous.

'Yes,' said Kasia.

'And something else,' said Dmitri. 'The loyalty and . . .'—he paused—'and the love of your people in Lipno.'

Kasia stared very hard out of the window.

'Without that,' he went on, 'you would be dead, I would be dead and—' he nodded at the children—'they would be dead.'

'You and your husband, and his father, were good to them; you treated them as human beings. For that they stood by you. Lipno would always have been defended.'

'Thank you, Dmitri. Thank you for everything you have done for us.' They heard one more shot, a scream in the night, then nothing.

'Does this have to go on all our lives?' Kasia asked.

Dmitri shook his head. 'That I don't know.'

The night was filled with the triumphant cries of the villagers.

'The answer lies down there.'

Unashamedly Kasia allowed the tears to run down her cheeks. The children snuffled in their sleep. There was a bang on the door.

'Is it all right?' cried Katushka. 'Is it safe? Can we go to our beds?'

'Yes, Katushka, of course you can.'

'You see,' said Dmitri, 'they trust you.'

And in the distance Kasia heard the fading voices of the people who had come to murder her children and herself in an orgy of horror.

'Thank you, Dmitri.'

'Yes,' said Maryshka. 'Thank you,' she smiled, 'Cossack.'

* * *

In the morning they counted the cost: twelve villagers dead; fifteen wounded, the worst of which Kasia had brought into the house where she and Maryshka and old Katushka staunched the wounds with moss, cleaned, bandaged and comforted. Those who died closed their eyes without the last rites, for their beloved Father Brodowski lay dead with a pistol ball in his heart.

Of their attackers over fifty were dead, scattered about the woods and in the village street.

'And wounded?' Kasia asked.

'There are no wounded,' said Dmitri flatly, and she understood what he meant.

'And now I must go and see to the horses. They had a disturbed night and Satan will be in a filthy temper.' He swaggered off, grinning and whistling to himself.

PART THREE

Chapter One

THICK brown dust rose behind the hooves of the two horses. Above them the hot sun blazed down on the Orenburg steppe. The marmots popped out of their burrows, sitting up and whistling as they watched the riders gallop past. A buzzard wheeled slowly across the cloudless sky.

One man, with a black beard and wearing a red shirt, rode a white horse; beside him Henryk felt the mare, Rasulka, moving easily beneath him. She ran eagerly with pricked ears.

When they reached a small hillock within cannon-shot of the town, they reined-in and sat in silence staring at the wooden palisades and earthern ramparts of Orenburg. In the hazy sunlight they could see soldiers moving behind the top of the fortifications, their blue uniforms blending well with the sky.

'Well, friend Borodin, what do you think?' Pugachev slapped irritably at the swarming horse flies. Henryk considered the question carefully, his eyes taking in every detail of the undulating steppe, already waist-high in feathery grass; where the grass did not grow the little clusters of flowers were strewn thickly in patches of yellow, violet and scarlet. The air was heavy with the scent of sage and wild thyme. He was working out a possible approach for large numbers of men, an approach that would give cover until they reached the belt of ground razed flat by the garrison.

There was a mighty bang, then a loud whistling sound, followed by a crashing thud and a trembling of the earth.

The iron ball glanced off the hard earth and spun away, bouncing through the grass until it finally came to rest about a hundred feet from the two men.

Rasulka, being well-accustomed to such sounds, did not move, but Pugachev had to hold in his magnificent white horse.

'Hold still, you devil!' When the dust had settled he said, 'My men inside the town have told us the soldiers have six cannon capable of reaching this spot. Not like the other miserable little places we have taken.' He laughed. Then, drawing his sabre in a bright flash of steel, he shouted with all the great power of his lungs: 'Come out from behind your walls, you pack of cowards! Come out and fight or join your lawful Sovereign Tsar.'

A chorus of jeering laughter and insults came back faintly from the soldiers. Pugachev's face, deeply tanned by the sun, darkened further.

Henryk saw the puff of black smoke as the gun fired again. He had acquired throughout the years, both on land and at sea, a high respect for artillery fire, and did not relish sitting as the main target with the only cover some beautiful but ineffectual grass.

This time the ball screeched briefly in the air as it passed above their heads to land some fifty yards behind them. The next one, Henryk thought with professional detachment but with a tightening of his stomach, will land almost exactly where we are sitting. If they have a skilled gun-captain, or whatever they called it in the Russian artillery, he will find a pure white horse in the sunshine an excellent target.

Pugachev sheathed his sabre. 'Well, what do you think? Is it possible to attack this place successfully and without losing too many men?'

'Yes, I think it is.' Henryk wheeled Rasulka to face their camp, hidden in a wide valley unseen from the town. 'Now that we have discovered the range of their guns would it not be better to continue this discussion elsewhere?'

'So my brave friend with Polish blood is afraid?' Pugachev's eyes were twinkling, without the wild light Henryk had noticed on occasions, to his dismay—the light that hinted at madness and which shone savagely when Pugachev, with a click of his fingers and a careless laugh, would give the signal for torture or death. But he turned his horse.

'You fought in what is called the Seven Years War,' said Henryk, his whole body tensing as they heard the gun fire for the third time. The ball made no sound until it landed between them, showering them with dust and making the horses rear in fright. Without a word they dug in their spurs and followed the shot as it ploughed its way through the grass.

In the protection of the hillock, out of view of Orenburg, they halted. Pugachev brushed the sweat from his eyes. 'They are better marksmen than I had expected.' He was breathing quickly and rubbing his thigh where a small splinter of stone had struck him. Henryk saw the dull circle of blood spreading on the thick woollen trousers.

'You surely learnt during that war the stupidity of risking your life for no good reason? Yes, I was afraid. If I have to fight then I hope I can still do it as well as any man. But I see little object in risking a cannon ball in the belly for—well, for nothing.'

Pugachev listened, stroking the long white mane of his horse. 'You are honest, friend Borodin. I respect your military judgment, but . . .' His eyes began to smoulder, 'but, do not presume too much on our friendship. Do not argue with me before others or question my leadership, because I am your Tsar.' My God, thought Henryk, he really believes that he is Peter.

'And a rope will stretch your neck as far as another man's.' Then Pugachev leant across and slapped Henryk on the shoulder. 'Don't worry, I am only joking. I need my adviser too much.'

They rode slowly back towards the camp where five

thousand Cossacks, Tatar tribesmen and a riff-raff of camp followers, lay contentedly in the heat, enjoying, for the time being anyway, the leisurely pace of the war.

Their women cooked for them; they drank large quantities of *kumass*, the fermented mares' milk that kept out the cold and increased the heat within them. They smoked their rank tobacco and told and retold the stories of legend going back to the days of Ghenghiz Khan, Batu Khan and the limping Tamerlane.

The tribes of the Khirghis, the Mordvins, the Bashkirs. Warrior peoples who had rallied to the call of Pugachev, attracted by the bait of killing and plunder like bees to the summer flowers. What did they care what he called himself? If he led them to war and riches and proved himself a bold and just leader then they would follow him into the inferno of Hell itself. Were they not, after all, Tatars, the creatures from Hell?

'Soon,' said Henryk, 'they are going to demand war. That is why they joined you.' He heard the high, whining sound of their music rising from the valley ahead. 'At the moment they are happy, but these people are changeable, never forget that. One minute they are your friends, the next they will slit your throat without a qualm. Don't hold them back for too long.'

He remembered the men in *Huntress*. They longed for a fight with the 'Frenchies' to relieve the harsh monotony of their lives—and, when they fought, there was no one in the world to beat them. It was like that with these barbarians from the East.

'Let them go,' he said. 'I suggest a night attack. But wait for the winter.'

'The winter's five months away.' Pugachev frowned. 'First you tell me to let them loose, now you say, not until winter. What exactly do you mean?'

'I mean this. Leave a holding force round Orenburg. Go to Samara, south down the Volga, north to the Ural Mountains where you'll find many thousands to join you.'

They had reached the summit overlooking the valley. Below lay the countless goat-skin tents; the smoke of a thousand fires vanishing into the mid-day heat; the lazy hum of an army at rest among the thickets of mulberry bushes. High above the smoke, two steppe eagles swung in long, lazy arcs across the sky and Henryk heard partridges calling.

'One day,' said Pugachev, 'this army will be three, four times as large. And as we march towards Moscow it will grow, and grow, till half Russia is behind me.'

Henryk had a sudden memory of Kasia telling him about Pugachev. 'Russia's not a country,' he had said. 'It's a world. A world I am going to see—and to conquer. To the furthest corners.' That is what had been shouted exultantly at Novo Vada. 'Into the wastes of Siberia and beyond the Ural Mountains.'

Something like this had made the Confederates fight on when they had no more hope. This is what made him ride with Pugachev. Somehow he would try to avenge the rape of Poland.

'I agree,' Pugachev gazed down on the camp. 'Fools,' he said placidly. 'No sentries, nothing . . . Very well,' Pugachev agreed, turning to him, 'your plan is good. We will ride to the eastern steppes and find men. Orenburg will be contained by the Tatars, who are experts in this type of warfare. Agreed?' He held out his hand to Henryk.

'I agree. But for one thing.'

'Yes?'

'There will be no attack on the town until the winter. In the summer the chances of success are very small. You need darkness and snow.'

'Yes,' said Pugachev, 'you are right. We'll wait until the blizzards come to blind the sentries of Orenburg.'

They rode down towards the restless camp.

* * *

'So we don't attack until the winter.' The man was tall and heavily built; his eyes were blue, his hair very fair for a Tatar. His name was Nazar.

'I have listened to the words of Borodin.' His voice was scornful. 'I have heard how he wants to put off the attack on Orenburg till the winter storms can hide himself and his few Polish horsemen.'

Henryk sat without speaking. The tent was hot, almost overpowering with the smoke and smell of rich food. His head ached from the thunder in the air. For God's sake, why couldn't the man stop talking? Surely they all understood what he meant.

'I am Nazar.' All right, thought Henryk. So you are Nazar. Does that mean the end of the world?

Above him the hide tent shook slightly in the warm night breeze. Cherry vodka flowed like water to help swallow meat, pork and the soft, sweet taste of partridge and quail.

Pugachev lay back among coloured cushions, dressed in a kaftan of rich, embroidered silk and satin, bright scarlet and vivid with golden eagles. He wore the soft leather boots of the tribesmen. Surrounding him were his six favourite concubines. Their hair shone with bright lustre and speckled jewels; their mouths were red and moist; their breasts hard against the transparent silk that covered their shining, perfumed bodies. All the time he turned to fondle them, to make them gasp with lust. Then he would leave them, disappointed but quivering for his return.

'I am Nazar.'

Pugachev took his hand away from a warm, firm breast. 'Yes,' he said.

'My ancestors came from the north, from the lands of the Swedes and Danes. Hundreds of years ago. They were conquerors. No one could stand against the Vikings as they fought and traded down the Volga; they reached Constantinople and trod the bazaars of Baghdad, many centuries before the coming of Ghenghiz Khan.' There was an angry murmur among the Bashkir chiefs.

'The Vikings feared no man. They joined with the great tribes of the Bashkirs and the Khirghiz.' The Tatar chiefs appeared somewhat mollified by this last remark. They married your women who bore them sons, half Norsemen, half Tatar and, when these sons grew to manhood there was no one on the steppes nor in the mountains who could stand against them.'

Turning to stare straight at Henryk, he said: 'I say we should make a night attack on the town within the next two weeks.'

There was a low rumble of agreement from the chiefs. Their people were getting restless; they wanted fighting and plunder and white women. Some were even talking openly about returning home. They all looked at Pugachev. For a while he sat in silent thought, pulling slowly at his beard. Then, pushing away the girls gathered round him, he got up and went to the entrance of the tent, and stood gazing up at the night sky.

'I agree,' he said, not turning round.

'But,' protested Henryk, 'this afternoon you agreed to starve them out and attack in winter when the garrison will be weak and unwilling to fight.'

Pugachev came back to his bed of cushions.

'It is the privilege of a Tsar to change his mind.' He smiled as the girls crept back to his side. One of them, a black-eyed *houri* with a slim, tawny body, gave him a dish of his favourite food—dipping the pieces of cucumber into the sour milk, she put them into his mouth.

'Another privilege of a Tsar.' He pinched her hard so that she gave a little squeal of excited pain. All the men laughed except for Henryk.

'It's you who're in command,' he said, controlling his temper with an effort.

'Yes,' agreed Pugachev equably 'There, friend Borodin, you are quite correct.' Nazar's expression of triumph equalled his swaggering assurance. For the first time he had humbled the Pole. And before the others.

'Very well then,' Henryk said. 'I do not agree with the decision but if you all think that Orenburg should be attacked now then all I can add are a few suggestions.'

Pugachev nodded in agreement.

'Let him speak. He knows much about war.'

'And we do not?' Nazar's eyes narrowed.

'He knows the war of big guns and disciplined soldiers. You—' he gestured round the tent—'know the war of the steppes, of quick, daring raids : the war of your ancestors. Harassing, outriding your enemies and cutting them down with a rain of arrows. Therefore we must harness these skills to defeat the guns and muskets of Catherine's soldiers. This is what I propose. One, that we attack on a cloudy night, preferably with no moon and with rain.' Henryk waited.

'Then our fiery arrows will be extinguished,' protested a voice.

'The burning bushes and brushwood will not set alight the palisades.'

Pugachev, quite impassive, listened closely as Henryk spelled out his plan for the attack on Orenburg.

'Very well, not heavy rain,' Henryk continued, 'but a night of misty drizzle and bad visibility when the sentries will be wrapped in their great-coats and thinking of home.' He saw he was winning them over. 'There must be a slight wind to rustle the grass and hide the sounds of our approach and'—Henryk paused—'above all, there must be ladders. Use whatever you can find, but there must be ladders of at least twenty feet. Tent-poles, branches, lances, anything.'

'And how many of these precious ladders does Your Honour require?' Nazar's tone was venomous.

A voice said angrily, 'Let him speak, then we shall decide.'

'At least thirty.'

'Thirty? Ai-yai-yai!'

'Yes, thirty.' Henryk knew he had got them in the palm of his hand. 'And at the top of each ladder there must be two loops of rope to hook round the spikes of the palisade.'

He continued to outline his plan. '... horsemen to ride round the front of the town firing arrows, as you say, tipped with flame, making as much noise as they can ... as close to the palisade as possible for then the big guns cannot be used against them ... the storming parties to make their way to the back of the fortress ... brushwood to be placed against the timber in the front and set alight ...'

Though this kind of attack had never been known among them before, the chiefs nodded and murmured agreement. They liked the sound of it.

'But can you persuade your people to attack on their feet, carrying ladders, instead of on horseback? They may not like the idea.' There was a whispered consultation.

'They will agree to whatever we order,' said the oldest of the Bashkir chiefs. His beard was white but his voice strong; he was dressed in a long black *kaftan*, a red hat trimmed with fur and the crumpled leather boots of the Mongols.

'Yes, they will do as we say.'

'That's all I've got to advise.' Henryk accepted a glass of the cherry vodka from one of the girls. As she offered it, she gave him a long, provocative look then lowered her black eyelashes. His mind was elsewhere but his body stirred as, involuntarily, his eyes followed the slight tremble of her breasts and the rounded sway of her hips.

At that moment a commotion became louder outside the tent. Pugachev looked up angrily as a Khirghiz tribesman stood in the doorway, glancing round nervously.

'Well,' said Pugachev to the chiefs. 'One of you ask him what he wants?' The man answered quickly, obviously wanting to get out of the place as soon as possible, and with a whole skin.

'He says, Your Majesty,' the voice was fawning, 'he says

a man has been brought in who claims he comes from Orenburg. He claims—this man—that he carries a message from the Commandant of Orenburg addressed to Your Majesty.'

Pugachev preened himself like a peacock at the words 'Your Majesty'. His smile widened.

'Bring in the fellow.' He allowed his smile to play slowly over all six of his women. Although Henryk mentally spat in disgust he could not banish from his mind the look in those black, smouldering eyes.

There were shouts and the sounds of jostling as a man was pushed into the light of the tent. He was a Russian soldier.

'That's a fine uniform,' said Pugachev. 'It suits you. Yes, definitely it suits you. Why do you wear it?' This last question was said so softly and so kindly, that the man took courage and replied.

'Because I am in the service of Her Imperial Majesty, the Tsarina of Russia who—'

'*Silence!*' Pugachev leapt to his feet, scattering his women in a shower of filmy garments and shrill complaints.

'Who are you to speak of an Empress when you address your rightful Tsar?' The soldier gawped at him, open-mouthed, shaking at the sight of Pugachev's darkened face.

'Give me that paper!'

The soldier held out the folded sheet in his hand.

Pugachev began to read.

> To the Commandant of the Byelorsky Fortress.
>
> I hereby inform you that the fugitive and dissident Don Cossack, Emylyan Pugachev, having committed the unpardonable insolence of assuming the name of the deceased Emperor, Peter the Third, has collected a band of evilly-disposed persons, and has started a revolt in the settlements of the Yaik; already he has taken and destroyed several fortresses, looting and murdering on all sides. Therefore, on receipt of this . . .

Pugachev flung down the paper. By now his face was almost black.

'Who sent you? How did you escape from Orenburg?' With his heavy boot he ground the paper into the earth.

'Answer me, or by the Christ above, I'll have your tongue torn out.'

'I escaped over the walls, Your Honour—Your Majesty—and brought this to you. Can't you see, I've had enough of the knout and the terrible discipline. I want to join you and serve you faithfully—' The man was on his knees, ashen-faced, begging for his life.

Pugachev turned to one of his women and whispered something in her ear. At her answer he smiled slightly and nodded.

'Take him to the almond tree.'

The soldier was hauled to his feet and stumbled from the tent, blubbering in his terror.

The moon was full that night. The almond tree stood, black and silver in the hard, white light.

'The almond tree! The almond tree!' The cry had gone round the camp and men and women came hurrying to the tree.

One branch stuck out straight and strong in the moonlight and the glare from flaming torches.

'Bring the rope!' Pugachev's order cut through the loud hum of the crowd gathering round the tree.

'No. No. Oh, please God, no! I meant to—I meant no harm to His Imperial Majesty, I—'

'More wood on that fire.' Eager hands threw branches on the nearby fire and at once the flames leapt into the sky.

'Bring me the loop.' Slowly, almost tenderly, Pugachev placed the hempen sentence of death round the man's neck. He was no longer crying for mercy; he seemed to have accepted his sudden finish with life.

Henryk turned away. He had seen death in many forms but still did not like to watch it happening. All he saw, as the rope was flung over the branch, was the glitter in the slanted Mongol eyes; all he heard was the horrible sounds of a man choking to death, the sudden heave for one last breath, the crackle of flames from the fire lit to illuminate this brief entertainment.

* * *

A man hung at the end of a rope. The fire had died away, but the moon still shone down.

Henryk walked alone, beyond the light of the fires. The moon had escaped the drifting clouds and the steppe grass gleamed like the gentle swell of the sea. He reached the summit of a small hill and saw, in the distance, the lights of Orenburg.

What was it going to help if they captured the town? A small victory, hundreds of miles from Petersburg. What would it cost? Many lives; many widows and orphans. He had been present when that poor man had been hanged, for no reason, but to satisfy the sadistic whim of a man who thought himself the rightful Tsar of Russia. Was this what Henryk and his sixty horsemen had ridden from Poland to achieve?

The stars twinkled as brightly as did diamonds in firelight. Once beyond the sound of the camp, the silence of the steppe was disturbed only by the marmots—don't they ever sleep, he wondered curiously—and the whisper of the breeze in the grass.

Sixty horsemen. What could they do among these thousands of Mongol tribesmen?

He sat down in the shadow of a tall bush. If only he had Nym with him, and Jan Dombrowski and two hundred more of the men who had followed him throughout the Confederate Wars. Then they could do something. They could begin to dictate to these arrogant tribesmen—and to their leader—the man who pretended to be Peter the Third.

He sat in the swaying grass, watching the moon appear and vanish between the drifting clouds. Whatever happened, the moon would still shine and the clouds still drift. The breeze was warm on his face. He lay back, his arms under his head. And Kasia? Why the hell was he here when she was hundreds of miles away. And he did not even know whether Dmitri had reached Lipno with his letter.

He had not told the young Cossack to come back. He was mad : he knew that. But he had to go on. What would she be doing at this moment? Giving Jacek his bath; she loved that and would not allow Anna or Katushka to scrub him till he shrieked with laughter.

She loved his gurgling, infectious laugh. Henryk used to sit on a stool by the tub and pretend to enjoy the showers of soap-suds.

Oh, God, he asked himself again, what am I doing here?

The wild songs of the camp came to him. The distant sounds of the town also came to him. Soon these two sounds would be merged in a screaming, howling hell.

Kasia! Rasulka was close and ready. They could ride away, to Poland. Pugachev was fully occupied with his women. He could go, and the Poles would ride with him, for they too were angered by the taunts of Nazar. One day, Henryk thought, as he chewed a stem of grass, I shall have to kill the blue-eyed Nazar.

He got to his feet. But I cannot fail them, Kasia and these Poles who have come with me. I cannot fail them.

* * *

The thirty storming ladders were ready, rough affairs of twisted branches; tent-poles lashed together with thin leather thongs. The arrows to be fired into the town had their points dipped in pitch.

The whole camp rang with the sound of hammering and the rasp of sharpening steel.

'We are ready,' urged Nazar. 'Why don't we go, now, tonight?'

'Tonight,' said Henryk, 'the moon will rise just after midnight. There are no clouds. We'd be spotted before we got half way. We know they have at least six guns, and skilled gunners.'

'No one can ride like the horsemen of the steppes,' boasted one of the Bashkir chiefs.'

'Agreed,' said Henryk, 'but can they ride faster than a cannon-ball?' This amused Pugachev immensely. His roaring laughter filled the tent.

'That was good, Borodin. Very good. Faster than a cannon-ball!' He repeated the phrase two or three times.

Then, quite suddenly he stopped laughing and ordered, 'Be prepared to attack on the first dark night.'

* * *

It came within three days. A sky heavy with cloud, a slight drizzle and enough wind to sigh in the long, feather grass.

Ten men to a ladder: three hundred miners, serfs and ex-convicts. Each with a knife or an axe in his belt. Eight hundred Cossacks on foot with blackened faces, and muskets, sabres, pistols.

'Cover the touch-hole with a rag,' Henryk ordered, remembering the guns in *Huntress* as she swept into Quiberon Bay shipping water through the gun ports.

Five hundred Tatars to shoot their flaming arrows over the walls and into the town. Sixty Poles, on their feet, dragging great tangles of brushwood to set alight by the main gate while the ladders were carried to the rear wall of the town.

'Excellent,' said Pugachev. 'You have planned well. It cannot fail.' He was already fairly drunk.

The last trace of moonlight vanished behind the thickening clouds. Henryk imagined the sentries on the ramparts. They would be wet, tired and deadly bored, longing only for their reliefs to appear.

He went through the plan once again. 'I will go with the ladder parties . . . fifteen round the right of the town, fifteen to the left . . . on my signal, the first burning arrow . . . ladders against the walls and light the brushwood . . . then every man for himself, and God help us.'

Nazar gave an elaborate yawn, very long and very loud. Pugachev held out his silver goblet to be filled. Henryk had a sickening premonition of impending disaster. But, to the devil with the whole lot of them! He was sick to death of the eternal jealousies and bickerings. They were supposed to be fighting for the same cause, weren't they? Pole. Tatar. Cossack. Peasant.

'Don't expect it to be too easy,' he said very coldly. 'These are trained soldiers we are up against and they will fight.'

'For centuries we have met trained soldiers, as you call them, and defeated them.' Nazar spat and turned his back on Henryk.

The latter glanced at Pugachev. 'I think it is time,' he said.

'Friend Borodin says it is time.' He got to his feet, swaying slightly. 'So we go.' He strapped on his sabre, assisted by two of his girls.

'You'll be waiting for me when I return.' He pressed their bodies to him, stroking up and down the silken skin, till their eyes were velvet black.

And if he does not come back, Henryk thought, to whom will they turn with the same ardour?

'Now,' Pugachev shouted. 'My horse.'

He mounted his white horse. The men picked up the ladders; the horsemen checked their arrows; the Poles moved forward into the drizzling night, dragging the piles of damp brushwood, and the attack on Orenburg had started.

* * *

If it had not been for the dead on both sides the whole sorry business would have been a farce. And all because a Russian soldier called Dubrovsky going on sentry duty fortified himself too liberally against the cold and wet. He reached his post all right and went through the motions of taking over from his friend, Andreyavitch.

'Anything to report?' he inquired.

'Look for yourself. How could there be anything to bloody well report on a night like this?' They both looked out between the sharpened points of the protecting stakes.

'Only another night in this God-forsaken desert.'

'Never mind,' said Dubrovsky with a small hiccup. 'Two more weeks and we'll be back in Petersburg.'

'Doing bloody guard duty outside the Winter Palace with Her Imperial Self watching out of the window to see that we don't get out of step.'

'Better than having to watch these Mongol bastards tearing up and down firing arrows at us. Doesn't anything ever make you happy?'

'Not much. Is the Sergeant asleep, and where have you hidden the vodka?'

'Yes, snoring like a hog with a cold in the head. The drink's in the usual place.'

'That's something.' Private Andreyavitch disappeared into the darkness. Private Dubrovsky settled down to his two-hour spell.

Below him, not thirty feet away, men were inching piles of brushwood closer to the gates. Every word on the ramparts had been audible to them even above the gentle hiss of the rain.

The wood was sodden by now and they knew it hadn't a chance in hell of catching alight.

Round both sides of the town crept the ladder-parties, tripping and stumbling in the soaking darkness. At the main gate at the rear Henryk waited. Beside him the Bashkir who was to fire the signal arrow sat his pony trying to work out what could possibly be going on. He had done a lot of fighting in his life but never anything like this.

Henryk crouched over his pistol, trying to keep it dry. 'Come on!' He kept saying to himself. 'For God's sake, *come on*!' At last the leading ladder appeared. By now the rain was very heavy indeed.

He should certainly call off the attack. But how? Somewhere Pugachev was riding round on his white horse—or perhaps he had very sensibly gone back to his women. God, how Nazar would crow in the morning.

Another ladder, and then another, until they were all beside him and ready. All right then, perhaps this heavy rain was just what they wanted.

He prodded the leader of the carriers and nodded upwards. The man wiped the rain from his eyes and gave the pre-arranged signal, passed by touch. The ladders began to go up. It might work, there was just the chance that it might work, as long as the distractions at the front of the town played their part.

The ladders were up. The only sound was that of the rain pouring from the roofs.

'You think you can do it?'

The leader nodded, patting the axe at his belt. He put his mouth close to Henryk's ear. 'Yes, we will do it, have no fear of that.'

Henryk turned to the horseman. 'Now!'

The arrow arced into the rain, flaming red and plunged down into the middle of the town.

The miners, the ex-convicts, the serfs swarmed up the makeshift ladders yelling all kinds of home-made battle-cries. They found three sentries whom they cleft with their axes; they then dropped into the town from the walls and went hunting other prey. Now their turn had come.

Henryk followed them in an effort to avoid the killing of women and children. And to get through to the main gates where the Poles were supposed to be.

Pugachev had agreed to no slaughter of anyone, man, woman or child, unless absolutely necessary. But Pugachev, on his white horse, was drunk. A drunken Cossack, holding complete power in his hands.

He must reach that front gate. He was not going to have his countrymen blamed for a massacre at Orenburg.

But fortunately, owing to the sudden awareness of Private Dubrovsky, made even more urgent by the call of nature, the massacre was averted. The man was made aware that something was wrong by the sudden hiss of a flaming arrow which stuck into a wooden stake about a foot from him.

Leaping to his feet he yelled something like, 'The Devil's here! The Guard, call out the Guard!'

In the guardroom his friend, Andreyavitch, thought, 'God in Heaven, he's finally broken.'

But the Commandant of Orenburg thought otherwise. Dishevelled, half asleep, he asked, 'What's going on?'

'They're attacking us, sir.'

'I can hear that, I'm not a complete idiot. What are we doing about it?'

'Well, sir. They seem to have got in over the back walls but—'

'The ones who've got in over the back walls—get the men out and deal with the swine. Well, go on, don't stand there gawping. Are you a soldier or not?'

'Yes, sir, at once, sir.'

The Guard was called out. They lined the wall above the main gate. Dubrovsky, dead sober now and frightened to death, aimed his musket at the unshapen mass directly below him.

The Commandant of Orenburg had another idea.

'Artillery?'

'Yes, sir.'

'Ready to fire?'

'Yes, sir. Ready to fire.'

'Well—*fire*!'

Six large cannon fired as one. A few hundred yards out in the rain-swept steppe, a group of Tatar horsemen waited impatiently for the signal that would send them riding round Orenburg, discharging their deadly arrows. But it never came. Unfortunately, the horsemen were in the direct line of fire. The cannon-balls arrived through the rain with a rising whisper and landed among them. The horses and riders disintegrated—or the fortunate ones did—in a wet, bloodstained spray—the others screamed their lives away.

The soldiers of the garrison ran, half-asleep, to man the walls. Some of them clubbed, shot or bayoneted the men who came up the ladders; others simply pushed the ladders away from the walls so that they fell backwards with men clinging to them like desperate flies.

Throughout the town the men with the axes butchered everything they could find, all their pent-up hatred concentrated in the axe blades. Screams and shouts mingled with the steady thrash of the rain, accompanying the flash and bangs of muskets and, at regular intervals, the roar of the guns.

The fire arrows came plunging down on Orenburg by the score, turning the rain to gleaming red threads.

The Poles tried vainly to set alight their piles of brushwood. The Bashkirs rode round and round the town, loosing off arrows without flames that arrived in the little streets and gardens. A large pig ran squealing round the main square with a broken arrow shaft sticking from his hairy back.

And, except for the slaughter of some unfortunate children and the rape and death of their mothers and sisters, that was about the limit of Pugachev's success.

The men with the axes were cut down by the fire from the defenders above them on the ramparts; targets well-lit by the flames of burning thatch. And they became the hunted, spitted on the long bayonets of the angry Russian soldiers.

'Fire!' The artillery officer yelled, and again, *'Fire!'*

The horsemen withdrew out of range, frustrated by the cannon balls which came whispering and skipping among them, tearing the heads from their shoulders and the legs from their horses.

It was useless. Henryk knew that. Keeping close to the walls he ran round to the front gates.

'It's no use,' shouted one of the Poles. 'We'll never get this stuff to light.'

'I know. Get back to the camp while you can.' Thankfully they obeyed the Count's orders. In small parties or singly Pugachev's men also made their way back to the camp, soaked, wounded and dispirited.

Only Pugachev himself, his courage considerably bolstered by his usual cherry vodka, galloped all over the place on his white horse, the rain streaming in his beard, his eyes mad with failure.

'I am your Tsar,' he raved at the shadowy figures flitting by through the rain and darkness. 'Get back, I say, get back!' But not a man obeyed; they had all become stone-deaf.

For one last time the guns bellowed, their muzzles spouting long crimson tongues. My God, Henryk thought. It was like a broadside. They'd never take the town until these gunners were dead or too weak from hunger to load the guns.

He glanced back at Orenburg. The light from the burning thatch was dying away, drowned by the ceaseless rain.

And, as Pugachev rode back, slumped in his saddle, the tears streamed down his cheeks; cherry vodka ran from his eyes as he heard faintly behind him the derisive jeers of the Russian soldiers.

* * *

For days after the abortive attack a cloud of gloom hung over the camp. Everyone blamed everyone else. Nazar accused Henryk of everything short of cowardice. Henryk remained silent, refusing to be drawn into furious argument.

As for Pugachev, he remained with his women and saw no one; half a dozen men were hanged for no reason, except that he was permanently drunk during this time and it amused him to see the almond tree put to good use.

Many of the Bashkirs vanished in the night, until very few were left and the rebel army had shrunk to something like three thousand men. Some of the Poles disappeared and Henryk was strongly tempted to follow them. But he had shaken Pugachev's hand that day by the monastery and, for some crazy, quixotic reason, he knew he could not break his word and creep away in the night. Not even for Kasia.

'I'm mad,' he told himself. 'I *must* be mad.'

Chapter Two

SO, after the failure at Orenburg, as summer turned to autumn, Pugachev rode with a large part of his force to the north-east, to the Urals and the iron mines where he hoped to bring recruits in hundreds to his banner from the bitterly oppressed miners and convicts who had escaped from Catherine's prison camps in Siberia.

Nazar led another force of Khirghiz, Mordvas and Chuvash to the south along the banks of the Volga to win support for the 'deposed Tsar, Peter the Third', and to exact tribute from the rich merchant caravans on their way to and from Moscow and Astrakhan.

And Henryk remained with a mixed army of Bashkirs and the few Poles who had gradually joined Pugachev—mostly ex-Confederates—to carry on the war against Russia or simply for adventure : to continue the only life they knew.

'Yours is the most important task of all,' said Pugachev, looking down from the silver-edged saddle. 'You have got to hold these Orenburg men inside their fortress and starve them out, until we return from the Volga.'

'That was the idea we agreed upon,' Henryk said with a cold smile. For a moment Pugachev frowned, then he too smiled.

'You are right. By God, Borodin, you are right.' He held out his hand.

* * *

With the onset of winter the deep ravines or *balkas*, which split the steppes into gullies wide enough to hide a village, were frozen hard as iron. They were bounded by high, ice walls, glazed by blueish lights. Into these walls Henryk ordered his men to hack holes for themselves, in which they could escape the winter blizzards, and where they could light candles and oil-lamps. If a blizzard came then these little shelters would afford some kind of protection.

The way between the *balkas* was signposted by the bare bones of horses. Or, sometimes, the frozen corpses of men, women and children pointed the way with stiff, outstretched arms—the remains of those who, in small parties as little families, had tried to break out of the besieged and starving town.

Soon, as the weeks went by, the holes in the frozen walls were enlarged and slowly became a labyrinth of tunnels and chambers furnished with rough benches and tables, lit by the smoky light of pitch torches.

When the first bad storm came in late October the inmates of these rabbit warrens were snug and warm, sitting round home-made clay stoves and sleeping, wrapped in their thick woollen cloaks, on beds of dry steppe grass cut during the summer.

All day the Tatars rode round the walls of Orenburg, now and then shooting a few arrows at the soldiers shivering on the ramparts, lashed by the icy blast of the *chorny vetier*, the black wind of the steppes.

At night the men of the Mongol horde would leave their horses and creep close to the palisade, listening with their ears pressed to the ground for the distant vibration of wheels or marching feet which would mean the approach of reinforcements or food.

'They must be eating their own dead by now,' said a Bashkir chief, spearing a large lump of bustard flesh on his knife. Grease trickled into his beard. The interpreter translated Henryk's answer.

'We have about four thousand men,' he said, 'counting twenty-four Poles.' The Tatar laughed. Since the departure of Nazar, Henryk and the chiefs had come to know and respect each other.

'We were sixty but now some have gone home, some are dead.'

'Many of my people have gone home, too.' The Bashkir poked around in the pot searching for more meat. 'This is not what they came for, to sit round all day, ride out and shout insults at some miserable Russians, or fire a few arrows. Where is the fighting, they are asking, where is the killing, the plunder and the women. We are warriors, not rats to sit skulking in holes. However warm and comfortable.' He laughed.

'I know,' Henryk said. 'I understand.'

'But, do you?' The chief belched loudly and continued 'Why don't we attack tomorrow, the day after, as soon as a blizzard comes? Smash the palisades with axes, tear them down with our bare hands. Get into the place. And then—' Henryk thought he had never seen a smile so cruel.

'Those are not my orders.'

'Orders! Since when were battles won by orders?' The interpreter raised his eyebrows in agreement. What stupidity!

'Sometimes,' said Henryk, thinking of Captain Primrose as his ship was swept by a scything swathe of iron and he still kept his crew under command.

'This was what we agreed with Pugachev,' he added.

The Bashkir snorted. 'And d'you think he would be so loyal to you? No, he would not. If it suited his purpose he'd slit your throat—or mine—just like this.' He drew the back of his knife across his throat before wiping it on the grass. 'No, I say, attack, seize everything we can and vanish, you to your country and the Bashkirs back to their true home. Let this imitation Tsar and any who care to follow him march on Moscow; let them carve the Tsarina into a thousand little pieces and feed her to the ravens but let us get what we can from this pathetic business and ride home.'

Henryk heard the faint howl of the wind above the *balka*; he hoped the sentries were at their posts and had not gone below to join their comrades round the fires blazing beneath the small chimney-holes, or to lie snugly with their wives or sweethearts. The soldiers and women of Orenburg might have reached the stage when they would leave the shelter of their walls and attack simply to get food. He thought of Kasia and Jacek inside the starving town. And, at that moment, he made up his mind, but said nothing except, 'I'll think about your idea.'

* * *

On a grey day in mid-November Henryk rode out of the *balka*. Beside him one of his Polish horsemen carried a large white flag. Both men were unarmed and were watched incredulously by the Bashkirs gathered on the open steppe.

They rode slowly towards the distant town.

'Will they surrender?' asked the Pole carrying the flag of truce.

'Would you?' Henryk's voice was grim.

'Not with those devils waiting, no I wouldn't.'

'I got their word that if the garrison laid down their arms there would be no bloodshed.'

'And do you believe that?'

'We can only hope.' he said.

'And if we hope wrong then there's not much we can do, is there? Twenty of us against three thousand heathen savages.' The man spat into the snow. By now they were within musket range.

'Wave that damned flag,' Henryk said. 'They might not see it against the snow.' The man waved it vigorously, very conscious of the muskets aimed at them.

Some fifty yards from the palisade, they halted.

'Is there an officer on the ramparts?' Henryk's voice echoed in the quiet morning.

'Yes.' A blue-clad figure held a sword above his head. 'I am Lieutenant Shrabrin. What do you want?'

'I wish to speak to your Commandant, please.'

'Who are you?'

Henryk simply repeated his request.

'Very well. Wait there.'

For perhaps half an hour they waited under the muzzles of forty to fifty muskets. Then, to their intense surprise, the gate opened slightly and a voice shouted, 'Come on in! Quickly now, and if there are any tricks you won't live to see them.'

'Try and take in everything you see,' whispered Henryk from the corner of his mouth.

The gate crashed shut behind them and they heard the thud of the great cross-bar going down.

As they followed Lieutenant Shrabrin slowly through the narrow streets Henryk observed the state of the town, and the people. Here and there a house gaped open, struck by a ball from one of Pugachev's ancient cannon. A few roofs were scarred and splintered; some garden fences smashed. The church tower leaned crazily and he saw the cracked bell hanging askew. There was the same smell he remembered from the siege of Bar: filth in the streets, smouldering ashes and the thick stench of blood and disease. A few women and children watched them apathetically, skeleton creatures with grey faces, almost all bone, many obviously in the last stages of dysentery. The soldiers looked stronger, but not much. Their uniforms were ragged, their faces unshaven and dirty but their weapons and equipment were still well cared for. They regarded the two Poles in their thick fur jackets and thick felt boots with undisguised hatred.

Henryk wondered how long it would be before the white flag was ignored.

They came to a house set in a small garden. There were a

few withered apple trees, one of which had been cut in two by a cannon-ball. The frozen head of a pig stuck up through the snow, eyeless and black.

'Emissaries from the rebel Pugachev, sir,' said the young officer, ushering them into a small room stinking with tobacco.

The Commandant was tall, elderly and very dignified. White-wigged and with a heavy white moustache, slow and deliberate of speech, he reminded Henryk of Colonel Skurin; the same pale blue eyes which looked at him very coldly; the same ram-rod figure. But his face was very thin, the skin blotchy and drawn very tightly over the high cheek-bones. The lines of worry and strain were deep and dark.

'And what could you possibly have to say to an officer in the service of Her Imperial Majesty?' The contempt in his voice stung Henryk to anger but, realizing what this old man must be enduring, he answered politely.

'I come to offer terms for the surrender of Orenburg.'

'You—you have the effrontery to come here from that vile rebel and offer—' The Commandant sat down abruptly, the unhealthy blotches in his cheeks a darker hue.

'Who are you?' With a trembling hand he reached for his jar of tobacco, almost empty, and his long-stemmed pipe.

'My name is Borodin.'

There was a stifled exclamation from the young Russian officer.

'So you are the Borodin we have heard so much about,' he said. The Commandant slowly filled his pipe, and lit it with a splinter of burning wood from the remnants of a fire burning in the cracked stove.

'They say you are partly Polish. Is this true?'

'Partly.'

'And partly what else? Renegade? Traitor—?' The old man began to wheeze in short, sharp breaths.

'No Pole who fights for his country is a renegade or a traitor.'

'Even one who fights at the side of a butcher?'

'We are wasting time,' said Henryk harshly. 'Out there, as you know only too well, are many thousands of Tatar tribesmen. Their only wish is to capture this town and put every single inmate to what will be a very agonizing death. I have seen their methods, and they are not pretty to watch, or to hear. Call me what you like, traitor, butcher, but for God's sake listen to me. It is your only chance.'

'We can hold out,' said the Commandant proudly. 'We are the soldiers of the Russian Empire. We shall not be defeated by a pack of barbarians.'

'It has happened before,' said Henryk drily. 'Do you want to watch your wives and children die of hunger? Because, and I promise you this, no food will reach you unless you give up Orenburg.'

'But my orders—' The old man's pipe had gone out. He gazed helplessly from Henryk to Lieutenant Shrabrin. 'On no account is the fortress of Orenburg to be given up.'

'Look,' Henryk said, 'already the buzzards and the ravens are hovering over the town. There's probably not a rat left alive. The children's bellies are swollen. Those men out there, and their women, are filled with food. They can afford to wait. They know there is nothing you can do against them.

'Did Pugachev send you,' asked the Commandant, gazing at his dead pipe.

'No. I came of my own accord.'

'Why?'

'To save useless slaughter.'

'See if there's any more wood, Shrabrin.'

'Yes, sir.'

'What is your offer?' The cold in the little room was becoming bitter. 'I hope he finds a few sticks,' said the Commandant. 'It is hard to think clearly in the cold.' He opened the stove.

'The damned thing's almost out again. A good officer,

young Shrabrin. He hadn't bargained for this when he was sent to Orenburg.' He paused, then added quietly, 'Perhaps none of us had.'

Outside the small window the afternoon was darkening. The Pole with the white flag whispered, 'We haven't much time.'

'The terms—my terms—are these : that you should surrender the Fortress of Orenburg in exchange for a signed promise of safe conduct for you, your officers and men, and every man, woman and child in the town. See, the terms are set out here.' Henryk handed the old man a sheet of paper.

'Safe conduct? Where to? How do we leave? These tribesmen, have they given their word?'

'No. You will leave by the rear gates and follow the river to the fortress of Ufa. You will wait until the moon is down and go. You may take what weapons you need to defend your women and children and whatever you have left in the way of food. Your heavy guns must be destroyed. Is this understood?'

The Commandant did not answer. Then he asked, 'And you think that this will save you when you climb the scaffold in Red Square?'

'If you refuse this offer how many of *you* will be saved?' Henryk glanced out of the window. 'The weather is breaking. The wind is getting up and bringing snow. I suggest you leave tonight.'

Lieutenant Shrabrin came in with an armful of charred planks which he began to smash with his boot.

'Should you try any kind of ambush or trick, then the Bashkirs will be given permission to sack this town. Should you, on the other hand, decide to accept the terms and slip away under cover of the snowstorm then light a fire on the ramparts.'

'If I were to accept these terms what undertaking have I from you that we will be allowed to get away in safety?'

'My word,' said Henryk. 'Even though it is only the word

of a renegade.' He smiled. He heard the wind rising over the roof.

For what seemed a hundred years he waited for the Commandant's answer as the old man strode slowly up and down the little room, backwards and forwards, pulling at his moustache, frowning deeply.

'I could keep you here,' he said.

'Yes, you could. Two more mouths to feed.'

'You do not have to eat,' said Shrabrin, hatred in his voice.

'Nor do all your women and children,' put in the Pole who carried the flag. Henryk thought of the ride back to the camp through the blizzard. He did not want to die from a Tatar arrow fired through blinding snow.

'I'm afraid I must have your answer.'

For a last few seconds the Russian officer struggled with his conscience, his sense of duty. Then he faced Henryk. 'I trust you and I accept.'

'Thank God,' Henryk held out his hand. Listening to the wind he made up his mind.

'It must certainly be tonight. There will be danger and deaths but it must be tonight. Do you want my signature?'

'Yes.'

Henryk scrawled the name 'Borodin' across the paper. 'One day perhaps you will know my real name and—' he looked away, 'and perhaps not think so badly of me.'

'I thank you, Borodin. We all thank you.' He coughed and tried to relight his pipe. 'I hope we never have to meet again as enemies.'

'It is beginning to blow,' said Henryk, 'and this wind will bring snow. We must go.' As the two Poles went towards the door, he asked : 'Have you any Cossacks in the garrison?'

'A few dozen,' said Shrabrin. 'Why?'

'Once you are beyond the gates then let them lead. A Cossack just shuts his eyes against the snow and allows his pony to find the way among the drifts. But—' he smiled briefly, 'tie at least two of the Cossacks to your men on short leading-reins. You never know, they might take it into their heads to vanish in the blizzard.' He touched his fur hat with the tip of riding-whip.

'Good luck, Colonel. Good luck to you all. Especially the children.'

* * *

The howling grey smoke of the blizzard swept round the two men, tearing with claws of ice at the skin of their faces visible above the frozen white collars of their jackets; ripping through the thick fur as if it were so much paper. They rode with bowed heads, barely able to breathe against the choking ferocity of the storm.

The high scream of the wind across the steppe was like the Atlantic storms, Henryk thought but only dimly, for it was impossible to think in such conditions. It was all he could do to help Rasulka; she was not a wild steppe horse, used to such appalling conditions, and stumbled frequently or sank to her belly in drifts.

The white flag had been torn from the frozen hands of his companion who was gasping and crying from the icy, solid blast. At least at sea there was a compass, a wheel, a Captain, even a damp hammock, but here, in this wild mad wilderness—nothing but blinding emptiness. Here, he suddenly thought with awful certainty, here in this shrieking hell, we are going to die, and no one will find us until the thaws of spring. Two skeleton horses; two skeleton men, picked clean as ivory by the wolves and the buzzards and the black ravens.

And Kasia would never know. Oh, my God, what a fool I've been, to throw away real happiness, contentment—for this. We all have to go some time, but not like this, like a couple of miserable little insects blown away by a puff of wind.

He wiped the snow from his aching eyes as Rasulka lurched sharply to her left. He noticed there was no longer any feeling in his hands; his face seemed to consist only of eyes in which the tears of cold were beginning to glaze. He knew he must hang on, to his saddle, to her icy mane; if he fell from the saddle then he would lie, sleepily waiting for a death that would not be long in coming. Just let himself slide into the deep warm snow and it would soon be over.

But Kasia would never know. As the swirling grey death struck him, with even more force this time, Henryk cried out—it may have been aloud, it may have just been in his mind, 'Let me see her. Just once more, let me see her!'

Rasulka had stopped, utterly spent, her head hanging down, her muzzle touching the snow. They had been riding back from Orenburg for perhaps an hour and yet it seemed to them all, men and horses, that there had never been anything but this blinding nightmare.

'Kasia!' He saw something ahead of them: a face, a form. Again he shouted her name.

His companion dragged his exhausted horse alongside Rasulka.

'Look! There! A light. It's a light! By God, it is!'

A will o' the wisp light danced for a second in the freezing murk. Then another.

* * *

'There's something out there,' said the Tatar, fixing an arrow to his bow.

'Nothing could live in this, except one of us, or perhaps a bloody Cossack,' he added grudgingly. But he, too, drew an arrow swiftly from his lynx-skin sheath.

They watched warily as the two men came slowly into view.

'They can't do us much harm. We'll take them into the camp.' They sheathed their arrows and rode forward not caring about the storm raging at their backs.

'Another ten minutes and they'd have been carrion-meat.'

'Come on, you,' ordered the first Bashkir, seizing Rasulka's rein. But Henryk did not hear his voice. He knew one thing, and one thing only : Kąsia had brought him to safety.

* * *

In the depths of the same blizzard some eight hundred and seventy persons—men women and children—some in uniforms, still carrying their muskets and ammunition pouches, some in the garments of peaceful folk, left the fortress of Orenburg by the gates unwatched by the Bashkirs in the mounting storm, and set off on the long and dangerous trek to the little fort of Ufa where they might have a chance of another few weeks or months of life.

The sick and the starved they carried in store-waggons; on litters or strapped to horses so weak with hunger that the poor beasts staggered as though drunk.

But with the Cossacks leading and men like the Colonel and Lieutenant Shrabrin riding slowly up and down the column, encouraging, cursing, now and then using their whips, they got the survivors of Orenburg to the little wooden outpost of Ufa built originally two hundred years before to protect the Khirghiz from the marauding Bashkirs.

On that terrible journey they lost 230 of their number to the snow and the cold or by simply missing their way.

* * *

There had never been much love lost between the Bashkirs and the Khirghiz. Mainly because each people considered that they, and they only, were the true descendants of Ghenghiz Khan; and that, to a Tatar warrior, meant more than his life. So it was not surprising that when the Bashkirs rode into a deserted Orenburg and found not even a chicken or a pig, let alone men to hang and women to rape, they were furiously angry. They set fire to the buildings, throwing an old woman who had been left behind in the confusion of the blizzard, into her blazing hut; they piled the corpses into a stiffly frozen heap and tried to burn them without much success, then returned through hard, icy weather, to the camp where they found that Pugachev had returned.

He was half-crazed with the success of his expedition to the Ural Mountains.

'I have cannon,' he boasted. 'I have three, four thousand men. I have coins cast in the name of Peter the Third.' He threw a handful of newly minted coins at their feet. But the Bashkir chiefs were not impressed.

'That Pole,' they said angrily, 'you know what he has done?'

'Yes,' Pugachev answered calmly, 'I know what he has done. He has captured Orenburg and without the loss of *one single* Bashkir life.'

'What do we care about lives? Our men, or any one else's?'

'That is your business.' Pugachev ate some cucumber, swallowed a large mug of cherry vodka, and turned to his beautiful young women.

'The Pole is not here,' said one of the chiefs. 'I thought they were so brave, these Poles, and yet he has not the courage to face you.'

'And why not?'

'Because he knows he has done wrong. On his own, without consultation with you, he arranged the surrender of Orenburg.'

Pugachev looked at him, and the red spark was glinting in his eyes.

'And what did you do, great Bashkir Chief?' The scorn was like the lash of a Cossack whip. 'What did you do whilst I was away?' Pugachev swallowed another deep draught.

'You did nothing. I know. I have heard. You and your people did nothing but lie in comfort and play with your women. Well, I will say something to you, Bashkir Chief. That is all you're fit for.'

The chief half drew his dagger. 'No one can speak to me like that and live.' Behind him were five men.

From nowhere appeared at least twenty Cossacks, pistols and knives in their hands.

'Do you wish to stay and fight with me,' Pugachev asked coolly, drawing a dark-haired girl close to him. 'Or do you wish to ride home, to wherever it is you come from?'

The Bashkirs were tense with hate but, with the Cossacks' pistols aimed at their backs, they could do nothing.

'We will ride home,' said the chief proudly, 'and, when one day your head rolls or you die screaming on some torture rack, then, Tsar of All the Russias, expect no help from us.' He spat on the hard floor of the tent then, nodding at his men, he turned and strode from the tent followed by the tinkling, mocking laughter of the painted girls.

And the Khirghiz who stayed to fight under the Tsar's banner laughed and cheered to see their enemies ride away into the bleak eastern dawn.

'Go back to your bee-keeping,' they taunted, for the Bashkirs were great lovers of bees. 'And mind you don't get stung!'

* * *

'So you allowed a few hundred of Catherine's soldiers to escape.' Pugachev sat on a pile of furs beside Henryk's bed.

'Yes,' said Henryk. 'I did.'

His head was raging hot, the blood pulsing in his skull. The ride in the blizzard had brought on another of the fevers contracted during his time in *Huntress*. He was used to these bouts of conscious madness; they soon passed. It had been the scurvy or, as some called it, the spotted fever. What did the name matter? The results burnt you up like a cinder; every bone hurt as though struck by a splinter; your teeth came loose and your breath stank like a cesspool.

'You have done well, Borodin.'

'Thank you,' Henryk said faintly, wishing he would go away.

'Perhaps we have both done well,' said Pugachev smugly, teeth gleaming in his beard. At that moment Henryk did not care what he had done.

'The Bashkirs, except for a few, have left us.'

Bashkirs? Who the hell were they? Kasia. Now he knew who she was. But Bashkirs? He laughed weakly.

'What do you find so amusing?'

'Oh, I don't know.' Even with the cold outside Henryk felt the sweat hot on his head and chest.

'You know what we have achieved?' Pugachev gazed at Henryk suspiciously.

'I've not been able to understand very much of what has been going on, but I think I have an idea.'

'You are a brave man, Borodin. I am sorry you were not born a Cossack.'

'Why?' Henryk's head was bursting; his senses wavering like cobwebs in a breeze.

'Because then you would have been a *really* brave man.' His great gust of laughter cut through Henryk's head like a sword-blade.

'Together we'll reach Moscow. By the Great Christ Almighty, you and I will reach Moscow.'

He got slowly and unsteadily to his feet. 'Now I'm going to sleep.'

And now, thought Henryk hazily, I am going to sleep. And as in his fever he slipped slowly, amid many extra-ordinry dreams, into a deep sleep, he saw, heard and felt his wife.

Chapter Three

DECEMBER came in. Everywhere was a waste of dry, powdered snow, flying in white clouds before the north-eastern winds. The goat-skin tents shuddered and the flames of the fires flattened, first this way, then that way. Above everything the devil song of the storms raged like demons unleashed.

Pugachev made his plans for the spring. Henryk's fever had gone. When he was not thinking of the future—and to him the future meant the defeat of his enemy, Russia—he thought only of his wife and son. Then sometimes, he told himself yet again, I must be mad. I must be mad to be here. Which—who—are the most important? And, with the vicious roar of the wind shaking his tent, he would ask himself, again and again, which is the most important?

January came. Now the winds swept up the snow from the steppes in white clouds of drifting smoke—the white spindrift of foam stripped from the huge Atlantic rollers.

What difference was there? Water, snow? What the Hell's the difference? When the elements close in on you, what the hell's the difference? Henryk lay in his tent, the roar of a vicious north-east storm tearing at the flimsy cover over his head.

For two months the winter raged. The real Russian winter. Sometimes the wind stripped patches quite bare, right down to the dead brown grass. Then the winds would die away and the frosts bit deep into the earth turning the clay to yellow iron : everything split and cracked from the intensity of the cold, which often dropped to 100 degrees of frost—a cold that froze the liquid in a man's eye and made his limbs so brittle that they would snap like twigs.

Without the wind it was beautiful, dazzling in the light of a sun hanging low in the sky like a silver orb. When Henryk rode out to exercise Rasulka he was blinded by the glare of the frozen snow-fields stretching in brilliant white folds to the horizon and far beyond.

At nights he lay awake wondering about the future and what he should do, worrying about his wife, his son and his horse. Rasulka would not join the Cossack ponies who grouped themselves in a circle, heads facing inwards, and allowed the snow to cover them until they woke in the morning and shook it off their shaggy backs.

'She's too high and mighty to join the common herd,' Pugachev used to say on their occasional forays into the deserted, decaying Orenburg.

So Henryk and the other few remaining Poles had built an enclosure from branches and snow-blocks for their horses which caused great amusement among the Cossacks and the Bashkirs who had not deserted the 'Tsar'.

It was like expecting Kasia to share a hovel with some peasant slut, Henryk thought in his more bitter moments. Yet, in her life, she had done worse than that. And he had come across many 'peasant sluts' with great courage and loyalty. If he harboured such thoughts then what was he doing, fighting with this man who was supposed to be raising armies in the cause of such poor people?

'A slut's a slut, whatever her position in life.' He remembered someone saying that during his time in Paris. It was said about Amande; Amande de Stainville : the girl he had loved. No, not loved but lusted after. How many years ago was that? And now he rode beside a man he was coming to recognize as being partly mad; risking his life every day in the wastes of Russia when he should be at home in Poland with Kasia and their son.

* * *

All the little houses of Orenburg were buried deep in snow. Here and there a raven rose from some shapeless heap and flapped with black wings to the roof of a house where it crouched waiting until these interlopers had left it to finish its pecking at some newly discovered corpse, preserved by the frost.

Black against white. Very decorative, Henryk thought. Very apt. He glanced at the silent figure riding beside him. Snow was falling softly and the black beard was white. Black against white. If only life was so simple. Good against Evil, and that is all there is to the whole stupid charade.

'We could move in here,' said Pugachev. 'There are still nearly two months before spring.'

'No,' Henryk said, 'once they knew we were here we'd be the target for every gun in Catherine's armoury.'

'You're a good soldier, friend Borodin, and I'm grateful to you.' He suddenly raised his clenched fist and shook it at the raven.

'Get away!' His face had darkened, as Henryk had seen so often.

'Go on, you black devil!'

If there was anger in his voice, there was also fear. Black against white. Very beautiful. Artistically, very beautiful.

'When the spring thaw is past,' Henryk asked, 'what then?'

'Then we march for Kazan.'

'We?' With a loud *plumph*, a large lump of snow slid from a roof and hit the ground.

'You see,' said Pugachev, 'the thaw will soon be here.'

'And after Kazan?'

'After Kazan?' Pugachev repeated the question twice.

'After Kazan, Moscow then St Petersburg. What do you think of that, Borodin?'

'Perhaps it might be wiser to think of Kazan first.'

Pugachev looked at Henryk in silence. The snow gathered more thickly in his beard and on his Cossack hat, covering the red top, the colour of the Don Cossacks.

'The Bashkirs have gone, God rot their stinking souls, but we have three thousand Khirghiz to take their place. As we go to the west we will gather more men. Don't you see, the peasants, the *golytba*, will flock to us—to *me*.'

Dusk was coming down fast. The shapes of Orenburg were vanishing. Only the raven stood out against the sky, and even the bird was hazy through the thickening snow.

They started back to the camp.

'Do you think the Khirghiz are any more trustworthy than the Bashkirs?' Henryk asked.

'Give them fire and death and plunder and they are,' said Pugachev. 'And what is war without that?' He whipped his horse. It was as if he wanted to get away from Orenburg and the raven on the roof. He was a frightened man—and a cruel man.

Since his return from the Urals he had become even more ruthless than before. Now he would order a flogging, a hanging, torture with a movement of his finger. Only the night before a man had tried to escape the icy imprisonment of the camp and return to his family.

'Roast him!'

Pugachev lay back among his cushions, fondling girls aroused by the horror of a man slowly turned on a spit above a glowing fire, screaming his life away.

'Why do you do this?' Henryk had reached for his sword but, at a signal from Pugachev, had been surrounded by the 'Tsar's' Imperial Guard.

'You do not have to worry about such scum as that.' He pointed to the blackened remains of the man, still uttering high-pitched mewing sounds and feebly waving his black claws as the spit continued to turn above the red-hot hell beneath him.

Henryk had stood in the moonlight, sick to the pit of his stomach. He had looked up into the twinkling, starlit sky and said aloud, 'God, if You are there, please help me. What should I do?'

* * *

As was his custom, Henryk rode alone in the February evening. Rasulka's hooves rang hard on the glassy surface of the snow; she tossed her head and snorted as a heron rose clumsily from the reeds of a frozen pond and flew, gaining grace, across the sunset. Thin black bars of cloud stretched across the molten sky, long embers in a dying fire.

'How lucky you are,' Henryk patted her head, 'to have so few problems.' And yet, how could he know? Perhaps she had her own difficulties to contend with.

What he did know was that his own were slowly becoming insupportable. And every day they grew worse. How could he go on beside a man whose cruelties were becoming daily more revolting? A man who was going mad before his eyes. To the five thousand Khirghiz warriors who had come to join the Tsar, Peter, the atrocities were commonplace, part of war. Provided he led them to more plunder, and conquered more cities, what did it matter to them how it was done? They were Tatars, and hell meant nothing to them.

Ever since he and Emylyan Pugachev had ridden from Novo Vada a year ago, Henryk had remonstrated with the Cossack, protesting against the cruelty.

'This is no way to win over the people,' he had argued time after time and, because Pugachev respected him and listened to his advice on other matters, he did no more than laugh and say, 'Stick to military matters, friend Borodin, and we'll get on famously.' But now, after last night's horror,

Henryk felt physically sick again at the memory of that awful, black curling body on the spit.

At first, when they captured the small forts along the Yaik, it had been the gallows. As they took each little settlement with its single cannon blocked with birds' nests or rubbish, the first new thing to appear was the gallows: a long cross-beam resting on two uprights; long enough to accommodate twelve humans. And, as the authorities of the so-called fort were brought before Pugachev, sitting in his red shirt and black fur hat with golden tassel, in the background was the heavy thud of hammers on nails.

They would be dragged before him, one by one: first the Commandant, usually an elderly retired soldier banished to the provinces to finish his life in a position of imagined power, commanding a tiny garrison of half-trained soldiers and treacherous Cossacks.

With some Pugachev was lenient, depending on his mood. No more than twenty strokes of the *knout*. With others a nod of the head and the man, or woman, was dragged to the gallows. They were lifted so that the executioner, sitting astride the beam, could push the noose over their jerking heads, then their bodies were dropped to jump and kick.

Some spat at Pugachev's feet when he asked whether they would join him; some crawled in the dust, licking his boots, crying for life. But whatever they did, the gallows were always full; the sagging beam always topped by the buzzards. In every fort, every village, the bleached bones of the skeleton figures showed through the rotting rags and danced with a mournful clatter in the wind.

And that had only been the beginning. The furnace sunset slowly faded. Henryk heard the sound of ducks' wings and saw the swift dark shapes of the birds as they flew to search out food.

He must be partly to blame. He had, however loudly protesting, connived at these horrors. As always his thoughts came back to Kasia. She had witnessed many horrors in her life but—but if she knew what he was part of? He imagined her contempt, even hatred. Yet that he could not imagine, not hatred, surely.

He turned Rasulka's head for the camp: now a camp swollen to hold some fifteen thousand men. A formidable army, if well-led.

This is what I left Lipno for. This is why I deserted my wife and the son we had always longed for. And yet, with an army like this, which would surely grow larger, they could reach Moscow and then St Petersburg. Was this not why he was here, deep in the steppes of Russia instead of in Poland with his family? Taking part in an attempt to topple Catherine from her throne and untie the noose so tightly drawn round his country's neck?

Chapter Four

KAZAN had fallen. Kazan had been sacked.

For Henryk the question was impossible. Either it was his country that was sacked or it was some town in Russia. In the end, except for the poor innocent people, burned, butchered, raped, what the hell was the difference? And he loved his country. He did not love Russia. Therefore he was prejudiced, filled with hatred? No. But he was human enough to see it happen—if it had to happen—to his enemies, not his own countrymen. After the sack of Kazan he had thought a lot about this. It was not easy. He thought of Kasia in Kazan; he thought of her hanging on hooks in Moscow. It was not easy.

But Kazan still burned. From Kazan still came the shrieks of the tortured and the dying. Kazan.

So the city had fallen to the Tatars. And what were they calling it? The Carnival of Death. They had not changed, not since the days of the Mongol Khans who had so very nearly conquered the whole of Europe, the whole of the world.

He knew the Mongols now; he knew them for what they were : ruthless, skilful in war, arrogant far beyond the feeble demands of Christian Princes; very nearly the rulers of the world.

On their little ponies, with their superb discipline and tactics.

No wonder Kazan had fallen; no wonder it had been sacked. For the Cossacks had joined with their hereditary enemies, the Tatars of the eastern steppes—and nothing could stop an avalanche like that: not all the artillery in Russia.

And nothing had stopped it. Thank God, he had held back the Poles. They had not taken part in the shambles.

* * *

'Let loose the Red Cockerel!'

The gates of Kazan had been breached. The Cossacks and the Tatars were pouring into the city.

'Let loose the Red Cockerel!'

The terrible Cossack cry rang through the town.

Henryk rode slowly on Rasulka through the flaming streets, and what he saw sickened him. He had seen war. He had seen the deck of *Huntress* after ten broadsides. He knew blood and pain. But this, this was different.

At every door where a Tatar arrow stuck, like a guide to perdition, the shaft pointed the way to yet another act of ghastly cruelty.

The Cossacks were not quite so bestial as the little Mongol horsemen, though there was not much between them. The former were after plunder, the Tatars after the twin sports of torture and, if the victims were lucky, death.

At one place a huge wine store had been broken into and the great wooden barrels staved in with axes. Men lay on their faces sucking up the wine as it ran in the gutters; they staggered drunkenly about sodden red from head to foot in blood and wine.

Cossack killed Cossack; Bashkir killed Khirghiz. They fitted their deadly arrows into the powerful bows and roared with laughter as the arrows thudded home in the bodies of old women and small children as they ran or hobbled, screaming, from their burning houses. Flame, dust, ashes, blood and, above it all, the blazing summer sun turned the leaping flames to pale, shimmering gold, hazy in the smoke.

The Poles rode close behind Henryk, saying nothing coherent, just swearing with terrible monotony and obscenity; now and then a man leaned to one side and vomited into the sludge that covered the streets.

The sound that rose among the flames was like that of a swarm of gigantic, maddened bees. Henryk had read accounts of cities being sacked but never in his wildest nightmares had he imagined this.

'Heh, Pole!' Nazar rode from the smoke, surrounded by his men. His long blond hair was tangled, his short belted blouse streaked with blood and ashes; the head of a girl was spiked on the steel point of his lance, her dead blue eyes still wide with fear.

'See that, Pole? There are still plently left, still many women hiding in the ruins ready to be taken, alive or dead. There's wine and vodka running in the streets. But perhaps it's too much for your sensitive stomachs.' He was swaying in his saddle drunk with both alcohol and the sheer lust of killing and raping. Most of his men were in the same shape, spurred on by what they had already done to even more fiendish acts of savagery.

'May God forgive you, Nazar, for what is being done today, for no one else will.'

'God!' Nazar spat out a mouthful of black dust. 'What does God—your God—care about Kazan?'

'Kill them,' yelled a voice from beside the Tatar. 'Kill the whole bunch of them. Cowardly vermin.' Henryk saw the Bashkir slowly fitting an arrow to his bow.

Three shots rang out, almost as one, and three of Nazar's men sprang from their saddles from the force of the musket balls which had shattered their faces and landed, sprawling on the ground. Slowly and calmly the three Poles began repriming their carbines.

'Thank you,' said Henryk.

'It was a pleasure,' answered one of the men harshly.

For a moment Nazar glared at Henryk from blood-shot

eyes, his hatred almost tangible. 'The Tsar will hear of this.'

'Let him,' Henryk said. In the midst of all this carnage what was the death of three drunken men?

With a shouted order Nazar wheeled his pony and vanished into the smoking dust, his men following.

'Filthy, stinking scum,' said a voice.

'Let's get out of this,' said another.

'Yes, into the fresh air—if there's any left anywhere.'

Henryk led his little group towards where he thought they would reach the open steppe. They rode slowly down the narrow street, shielding their eyes from the swirling embers, now and then dodging the charred beams that fell without warning from the remnants of gutted buildings. At one point a pile of bodies lay in the middle of the road, small flames licking all over them; in another, smaller pile, lay their limbs.

Then, on the very outskirts of the town, in sight of the sunlit steppe, they came upon one last horror. On the flattened grass lay the naked, living bodies of a man and a woman, spreadeagled and tied together. Her wrists and ankles were tied by ropes to the saddles of four Mongol ponies, and so were his. The tribesmen were mounted and laughing at the prospect of the slow tearing apart, in no hurry to begin.

Then the leader gave a signal with his whip and the ponies began to move forwards and the strain tightened the ropes. The man began to groan and then to scream; the woman did not make a sound.

'I want every rider killed,' Henryk ordered coldly.

'With pleasure,' said the same harsh voice.

'Ready?' Henryk had to shout above the awful shrieks of the woman as she felt herself being torn apart.

'Fire!'

Again every shot was deadly accurate and, as eight riders hit the ground, the other Poles were cutting the ropes with their knives. The screaming stopped and the little ponies galloped away into the steppe free from the fear and smell of death which had hung over them for so long.

'Can you walk?' The man was speechless with fear and pain, but the woman managed to whisper. 'Yes, I think so.'

'Here,' said a voice. 'Take this!' The Pole threw her a saddle-blanket. 'Cover yourself with this.'

She burst into a storm of sobbing. 'God knows who you are—God knows who anyone is in this hell. What have we done to deserve this? Oh, Your Honour, thank you, from the depths of our hearts we thank you.' She was on her knees.

'Please,' Henryk said, 'not that. Now, can you ride?' She shook her head.

'Do you know the country round here?'

'My husband does, Your Honour. He was born in a village about twelve miles from here.' She pointed vaguely across the steppe.

'Very well then. This is what you must do. Hide somewhere in the steppe until nightfall then go to your husband's village, and don't come back to Kazan.'

'Do you think we would ever come back to this, this slaughter-house?'

'Here,' said one of the Poles, 'take these. You may need them.' He handed her two long narrow daggers taken from the dead Mongols.

'I don't know who you are, nor your men but—' Here she broke down again and, sobbing, pressed her face to his coat.

'Please,' he said gently, 'please don't.' He blinked away the tears forming in his eyes. Timidly the husband came up to him. He said nothing but held out his hand, nodding his head in mute gratitude. Henryk watched the two of them disappear into the long, waving steppe grass.

Then the Poles took what they might need from the bodies of their so-called allies and remounted.

At that moment something inside Henryk snapped.

'God,' he said, hitting his saddle with his fist. 'God Almighty, is this what they call war?' He was silent for a while, then he turned to his men.

'You have seen what has been done here today.' No one answered. A fine film of ash drifted across the sun.

'After what you have seen, do you want to go on? To Moscow? To Petersburg? Well, do you? Do you want to see this repeated, time after time?'

'Well, sir, at least we took care of eight of them.'

Yes, Henryk thought : at least we did that. So whose side are we on? In war, does it much matter? You all end up dead anyway.

'If you would rather ride home to Poland,' he said, 'then it is up to you and nothing will be said. If you want to follow me—and I will go to Petersburg if I can—then I shall be proud to have you with me.' He paused. 'Even after what has happened here today.' Again he paused.

'I swore to myself I would go on fighting for our country —whatever the conditions.'

There was silence, then a rider spoke up, the man who had given up his blanket.

'We understand how you must feel—I think we know how we all feel. But—even after this—' he pointed at the smoking ashes of Kazan—'We still will fight for Poland.'

'Whatever it means?' Henryk asked.

'Yes, sir, whatever it means.'

'Thank you,' said Henryk. 'I thank you very much.'

PART FOUR

Chapter One

'KAZAN has fallen, Your Majesty.'

Catherine did not look up from her desk. In the long silence they could hear the banging and thudding from the Admiralty yards just down the river.

There was only one man in the room with her: Count Panin. She continued to study the papers on her table. After a long pause the Empress asked quietly, 'And why has it fallen, Count Panin?'

'I understand the garrison was outfought and starving, Ma'am, the city taken by storm.'

'In fact, they gave up. Is that it?'

Panin shrugged but said nothing. It cannot be easy to go on fighting, she thought, when you are starving.

'Never mind who was in command,' she said firmly. 'It was not his fault.'

'But, Ma'am—'

'Yes, Count Panin?'

'Well, he should have held off the rebels until help arrived and—'

'Help, Count Panin? And from where was help supposed to arrive?'

'I—I don't really know—'

'Exactly.' She watched the gulls planing above the river, envying them.

'They say,' he began hesitantly.

'Who say?'

For a moment he looked confused.

'Well, who?' She relented. 'I know. *They* : the ones who we never meet, never see.' She laughed but without much mirth.

'They say—' he dared himself a bleak smile—'it was due to an unknown man who rides with the rebel Pugachev.' He saw her mouth tighten. 'A man with a scar across his face. A man who rode with the Polish rebels until their defeat.'

Catherine remembered Potemkin's words, talking about a man in the Polish wars. A man with a scar on his face. Then she remembered further back, to what she had been told about a man—no, she remembered it all herself. A Frenchman, he had called himself. She could not recall the name, but he had a dreadful scar across his face—oh yes, and what a lover he had been. A French diplomat working in the French Embassy.

She wondered but said nothing. Many men must have dreadful scars across their bodies, including their faces.

'What—' he began.

'What,' she said, 'does it matter who helps this murdering rebel? What matters surely is to defeat him.'

'Of course, Ma'am.'

Catherine studied her outstretched fingers. 'Well then, I suggest this is what you do.'

Her orders were terse and to the point.

'Yes, Your Majesty.' As he got up from the table she asked quietly, 'Tell me, Count Panin, have you ever seen this man?'

His look was incredulous, terrified.

'No, Ma'am. Of course not.'

'Not—?' She stopped. 'As you say, of course not.'

Again she looked out of the window. Again she saw a small fishing vessel making her slow way against the wind. That must, she thought, mean something to me, as Empress. A small boat fighting her way against the wind—and the wind could be very strong—and would she do it? Will I do it? And of course at any moment the wind could change. The little boat slowly forced her way into the wind. Yes, thought Catherine, she's got the courage. She turned back from the window.

'If this imposter is captured then there will be no mercy. He will be brought to Moscow, yes, Moscow, as the ancient capital of Russia, and then . . .' She fell silent.

'Yes, Ma'am?'

'Then we will see.'

* * *

There was another meeting of her advisers called by Catherine.

'I hear that this Pugachev has taken to styling himself, "His Imperial Majesty, Peter the Third, Tsar of All the Russias", that he has built up a so-called Court around him giving names to his followers such as Orlov, Panin—' here as she spoke Catherine had some difficulty in concealing a smile, and turned away to the window: her favourite window, overlooking the river and the little ships she had come to enjoy so much. 'I hear too,' she went on, 'that he has adopted the standard of Holstein, the colours of my late husband, as his flag on the battle-field.' Let us hope, she thought, it will bring no more success there than it did when carried at the head of his ridiculous Holstein Guards.

Up till now Catherine had refused to take the threat of Pugachev seriously. In fact, only a few weeks ago she had written to her friend in Paris—a Monsieur Voltaire—regarding the laughable *'affair du Marquis de Pugachev.'*

But now she was no longer laughing.

The fact that one of Pugachev's 'courtiers' had been christened Marshal Potemkin she did not mention, though she knew very well it was common knowledge throughout Petersburg.

'I hear also that he has a military adviser of Polish origin who has helped him to his victories.' She came back to the table. Her eyes were cold. Another bad morning thought Orlov, thanking God he had nothing to do with the Army. At least she couldn't order ships into the middle of the Russian steppes.

'I believe that is true, Ma'am.' Marshal Suvorov twiddled uncomfortably with his pen.

'You *believe* that is true?'

'Yes, Ma'am.'

Her eyes turned from cold to blazing heat.

'Is it true or not, Marshal Suvorov?'

He nodded his head in silence.

'And this man—of Polish origin—is it also true that he is badly scarred across the face?'

'I have not seen the man but I believe—yes, according to all reports this is so.'

'And what does our rebel call this man of Polish origin?'

'Borodin, Your Majesty,' said Panin.

'Borodin? Just Borodin? No other name?'

'No, Ma'am.'

For a moment Catherine allowed her head to bow slightly. My God, she was tired. A week at Peterhof, away from the stink and work of Petersburg: the incessant work that woke her, sometimes two or three times a night, that never left her mind in peace. Just one week at Peterhof and part of it with Grigori alone, together, in the little house of Monplaisir built by the Great Peter within the sound of the sea; the little house from where Alexi Orlov had come to fetch her on the first stretch of road that led to the throne. She shook her head slightly and returned to the present.

'Marshal Suvorov.'

'Ma'am.'

'We do not wish another disaster like that of Kazan.'

'That will not happen again,' he said.

'Make sure it doesn't,' she said shortly. 'The eyes of Europe are on us, gentlemen. If we fail now then Russia will be seen, by her enemies, to slip back into the Dark Ages.'

No one spoke. This, thought Alexis Orlov, is a real woman, a real Empress.

'So bring them back to Moscow, Marshal Suvorov. Both of them. Pugachev *and* the man who calls himself Borodin.'

And again, to calm her, Suvorov bowed and said : 'They will be brought to Moscow.'

* * *

Pugachev had pitched his tents beyond the stench of Kazan.

The moon was full; the night was beautiful. The awful sounds of the crucified town were faint on the night breeze.

Pugachev, the Tsar, Peter the Third, was holding Court. And, opposite him, sat Henryk Barinski.

Among the others in the tent was Nazar; there was the one called Potemkin; the one called Panin; even the one called Catherine, a girl with smouldering eyes and shoulders of soft sloping grace. They had argued : Pugachev, Henryk and Nazar. Others had joined in. And while they argued they had ate and drank. As though, Henryk thought, Kazan had never existed as a city; as though all those people had not died in terrible pain and terror.

'We should go along the Volga,' said Nazar, his hair still matted with the blood of the killings.

'Yes, we agree,' said the chiefs of the Tatars. 'That's where we will get the gold and the precious jewels of the fat merchants who ply their trade from Novgorod to Astrakhan.'

'The Volga,' they echoed, 'along the banks of the Volga. That is where we will get rich.'

Pugachev lay back in his cushions. 'What do you think, Potemkin?'

'Well, Your Majesty,' said the little Cossack now called Potemkin. 'I think we should raid the Volga.'

'And you, Count Panin?' Another Cossack answered at once. 'I agree, Your Majesty. Yes, I entirely agree.'

'And you, Frol Chumakov, what do you think?'

'I think we should strike for Moscow now, while our forces are powerful and filled with victory. You have seen how the peasants are joining us. Now, I tell you, now is the moment before your army begins to dwindle.'

Pugachev looked at Chumakov reflectively. Once they had been friends: as youngsters they had raided orchards in the village; they had fought together, side by side in many battles and steppe skirmishes. Then they had fought against each other over a woman: the Polish woman who had been Pugachev's wife. Both of them had lived and were still together yet things between them were not the same although Pugachev respected the other's intelligence, and his courage. To Frol Chumakov he would listen. And to the Pole who called himself Borodin. To him also he would listen.

'Borodin, what do you think?'

'I agree with Chumakov,' Henryk answered without hesitation. 'To let this opportunity slip away would be madness.' He had not come all these blood-stained miles, sickened by many of them, to see the chances of humbling Russia thrown away by a lot of crazy argument. 'I say, go for Moscow.'

The silence was disturbed by the angry muttering of the tribesmen. Henryk thought to himself: if he says, 'the Volga', then we go home. I'm too old for war. That is a young man's game. If you could really call it a game.

'You think I did wrong to let the city of Kazan be sacked?' Pugachev emptied his glass, held it out to be refilled.

'Yes,' Henryk said.

'You don't think that our men had earned a holiday?'

'A holiday? Do you call a bloodsoaked massacre a holiday?'

'Why so squeamish, friend Borodin? I thought you knew about war.'

'I know about war,' said Henryk. The voices in the tent were silent. The girls gathered close round Pugachev gazed wide-eyed at Henryk and the scar across his face.

'But a different kind of war.'

'How is war so different?' Pugachev's voice purred.

'I think I know as much about war—' Henryk bit back his words. He was losing his temper. And if that happened then he would lose not only his temper but his life and those of the men who followed him.

As the tribesmen watched him like vultures, Pugachev said, 'People kill, people die. How is war different?'

'Again I say, we go for Moscow.'

'Very well,' said Pugachev, 'I agree.'

For the first time Henryk saw Chumakov smile. But the fury of the Tatar chiefs was growing. That he could hear.

'Silence.' Pugachev was angry. And when he was angry, Henryk thought coldly, he was crazy. That he had just seen in Kazan.

'You tell us to stay silent.' A Khirghiz chief was on his feet. 'We have followed you for many months; we have lost hundreds of our men.' He gestured to his companions. 'Are we to lose more because of this man's mad idea? To reach Moscow and become Tsar of the Russias? What are the Russias to us? We who conquered all the western world as far as . . .'

'As far as Poland.' Henryk's voice was like the rasp of steel. He had his hand on his dagger. Every eye was on him.

'And you got no further.' Pugachev lay back and roared, 'He's right. By Christ, he's right. The bloody Poles stopped you. By God, they did.'

The Tatar chiefs began to get to their feet but, before they were half-way off the soft cushions, a sudden, loud commotion broke out.

Henryk knew who it was because he suddenly recognized his brother's voice.

* * *

The brothers talked of the ride from far beyond the Dnieper to the Volga; they talked of Pugachev and the Tatars, and of why Adam had chosen to join his brother.

'How is she, Adam?' Henryk broke in.

'Missing you badly. But at least she has the horses to help occupy her mind.'

Henryk had not asked any more about her.

They talked far into the night, long after Jan Dombrowski and Sergeant Nym had fallen asleep, snoring on the earthern floor of the tent.

But before they fell asleep the four men had talked while Nyminski, Henryk's self-appointed orderly, had stirred the contents of an enormous iron cauldron, retrieved somehow from the ruins of Kazan. What exactly was in the cauldron no one asked.

'That was delicious, Nyminski. I don't know how you do it.'

'It's simple, Your Honour.' The man grinned cheerfully. 'Just light a fire, get the water hot, throw in anything you can find, some salt if you can get your hands on it, and give the whole lot about an hour—and there you are.'

Nyminski had gone to join the groups of Poles making up the two hundred who had come with Count Adam. He joined a band of some thirty riders who sat or lay round one of the many camp-fires, and listened to their stories of the long journey from Poland. Now and then he asked a question about their country. Did any of them know his village near Lwow? For he was very home-sick.

'. . . and how's your wife, Nym?' Henryk asked.

'Very well, Your—' He saw Henryk shaking his head in mock anger. 'I'm sorry, I forgot. Not Your Honour, never

Your Honour.' They laughed. The tent was pitched far from the noise and music of Pugachev's camp. 'She's with your wife—the Countess.'

'This man Pugachev,' said Jan. 'Is he mad?'

The loud music from the Tatar tents drowned the pitiful sounds of Kazan. Henryk went to the entrance to the tent and looked out over the dark glow of the ravaged city.

'Yes,' he said, 'sometimes he is. At other times he is as sane as any of us.'

'Do you think he is capable of leading an army?'

'Yes,' said Sergeant Nym, 'have we ridden all these bloody miles to follow a madman?'

Henryk said nothing. He gazed at the fire smouldering beneath the cooking-pot.

'I have followed him. I have seen what his army can do.' He poked a stick into the fading ashes. 'Do *you* know? Do you know what has happened here at Kazan?'

Dombrowski and Nym looked at each other.

'No.'

'Well, I'll tell you, gentlemen. Just listen while I tell you.'

And he told them. When he had finished no one spoke.

'I think we all know what men can do when they fight,' said Nym. 'But this.'

'Exactly,' Henryk said. 'This is something different.' After a pause he said : 'I have asked the men who have ridden with me, whether they will follow me to Moscow, or to Hell, and they have said, yes. Now I ask you the same question. Will you follow me?'

'Yes,' said Jan Dombrowski. 'We will. Anyone who would rather go back to Poland can start in the morning.'

Once again Henryk said thank you. He felt very humble, and very proud.

'So that is settled,' he added.

'Yes,' said Sergeant Nym.

* * *

The Tatars had their way. Their ancestors had conquered the Muscovite Princes; their ancestors had been waited on by naked Russian Princesses, treading on boards laid on the dead bodies of Russian Princes. They had done all those things. They did not have to prove it again.

'No,' they said with one voice, 'we do not go to Moscow. We ride along the banks of the Volga.'

Pugachev looked at Henryk.

'Well?'

'I do not agree.'

Again the angry muttering of the Tatars.

'They are many, you are one.'

'Yes, I am one. But I am also in command of close on three hundred trained horsemen.'

'How do you think you'll capture Moscow with three hundred men?' Nazar's question was supported by derisive laughter.

Henryk could see that Jan was rapidly losing his temper; he shook his head slightly.

'Very well then,' said Pugachev. 'For the next two months we will raid the Volga, recruit more men and then, when our army is twenty, thirty thousand strong, we will march on Moscow.'

* * *

Two hundred miles to the south, built on the west bank of the Volga, was the little town of Tsaritsyn.

A Russian army of thirty thousand men, under the command of General Panin, was marching towards Tsaritsyn. A veteran army of men who had fought at Kunersdorf, Zorndorf. Heavy cavalry; skilled artillerymen and steady, disciplined infantry, ably led.

Day by day the two forces drew closer to each other. But Pugachev refused to believe the reports of his Cossack scouts.

'Nonsense, there is no Russian army within miles. What have you become? A pack of old women who see an enemy under every bush?'

'Your Majesty, it is true.' If they tried to convince him they were hanged or disembowelled and left to the flies. So, soon they stopped telling him about the endless columns of Russian troops advancing on a route that must bring the two forces face to face within the next few days.

Chapter Two

SOME sixty thousand men faced each other across the glaring steppe but from where he sat on the little knoll Henryk heard only the soft sigh of the breeze in the poplars and the anxious whistling of the marmots as they called to each other in the feather grass. The leaves of the poplars showed their silvery undersides to a sun already lowering in the sky and the swallows skimmed the grass that reached to his stirrups. Beside him Adam dozed in his saddle, chin on his chest, for they had been waiting in the rustling shade of the trees for many hours. Behind him his men sat silently, with all the immense patience of experienced soldiers and their horses stood with lowered heads and lazily swishing tails while little blue butterflies settled on them or weaved among the shafts of sunlight.

At first the men had lain sleeping in the sage or whiled away the time as soldiers do before battle, in loud laughter, argument or spells of brooding silence. But since the appearance of the Imperial troops on the left of the great arena, Henryk had kept them ready in the saddle.

He looked again with practised eye and nodded grimly to himself at the skill of their dispositions. The Russian infantry stood in long ranks with their front along the broad burnt strip of grass, the cross-belts and white gaiters standing out against the blackened earth. Now and then a ripple of movement travelled along the lines of tall mitre caps but otherwise the men stood quite still, with exactly the same patience. Their left flank rested on the spur of wooded hills which curved round behind them, and on the right a regiment faced outwards to counter the encircling tactics of the Tatars.

'Those aren't raw recruits,' said Henryk, but his brother did not answer. Among their ranks he recognized the green tunics and yellow cross-belts of the Smolensk Regiment and hoped to God he would not meet Skurin.

'Let them roast in the sun,' growled Sergeant Nym. 'Then we can spit the swine and feed them to the wolves, already cooked.' Sergeant Nym had no cause to love the Russians.

'The Tatars will deal with them as they did at Troitsk,' said another voice.

'This bunch cannot be burnt out.'

'Cunning bastards!'

The talk died away as they spotted the movement at the forward edge of the trees behind the Russians. No one spoke as they watched the guns being hauled into position between the regiments. Henryk could hear the cries of the gunners and see the balls unloaded from the wagons and piled high beside the guns and, remembering Rossbach and the iron storm that swept the decks of *Huntress*, his stomach turned sick and sour. His fingers went without bidding to the scar, white across the deep brown of his face. After a few minutes of feverish activity the gunners too were still, standing by their guns.

'In the old days,' remarked Adam, 'the Tatars used to send gold ahead of them to bribe the enemy gunners.'

'Then let's hope they have sent plenty today,' said a voice from the ranks. There was some laughter at this. The wind had dropped completely; the marmots were silent; the only sounds, the quick jinkle of harness, the creak of a saddle; here and there a man coughed or spat the dust from his dry throat.

From somewhere in the wide blue dome of the sky there came the sweet song of a lark and the sound, high above that plain where men waited to hurl themselves at each others' throats, affected Henryk with a pain so exquisite that he might have lain beneath the razor knife of a torturer, and his hands gripped the reins, clenching and unclenching. His senses were filled unbearably with the scent of the sage and wormwood and the trampled summer flowers and the sound of that single bird pouring out its song of freedom and life up there, so close to the sun. But all that his eyes took in at that moment was the dull gleam of the guns.

Feeling a tickle on the back of his hand he looked down and saw an ant clambering laboriously among the hairs. Once before—how many years ago, perhaps in a previous life—he had spared another ant, kissing it from a woman's shining skin under just such a sun as this. Closing his eyes he saw her so clearly he wanted to hold out his arms and call his wife's name but instead he brushed the insect gently on to his horse's mane between the velvet ears; Rasulka shook her head, snorting at the flies buzzing round her nostrils. His eyes smarted from the brassy glare and lack of sleep, the old wound in his side stabbed sharply whenever he moved and his whole body itched uncleanly as the lice, woken by the heat, fed upon his skin.

'What I'd give for a barrel of wine and a stream of cold water,' grumbled Sergeant Nym. This time Adam answered.

'God, look at that!' Rising in his stirrups he pointed towards the wooded slope away to the flank of the Russians. Slowly the whole front of the wood turned to a long wall of flickering, shining steel.

'Cavalry! Thousands of them.' An excited muttering broke out among the Poles, infecting the horses which threw up their heads with a loud rattle of bits. The flickering ceased and the long lines of naked blades glittered steadily like the sun from the sea. But the Russian cavalry came no further: they too waited.

To his right Henryk saw the Tatars, sitting their ponies among the scrub, but without the patience of their enemies; here and there a solitary rider would dart into the open brandishing his bow, only to be called back. There was continual restless movement among them.

Further back, hidden beyond the little chalky hills to the west of Tsaritsyn, were the Cossacks.

'I hear no singing,' remarked Sergeant Nym, cocking his head on one side, pretending to listen.

'The vodka will drain out of them like wine from a pricked bladder when they see what lies ahead.' The men laughed and talked and one of them pointed suddenly and cried:

'Look, a hawk!' Their eyes followed the pointing finger, fixed on the kestrel which hovered on flashing wings, standing still in the air mid-way between the armies, searching with its sharp eyes for life in the grass, and since its coming the lark no longer sang. But tomorrow, thought Henryk dispassionately, it will sing again. He turned to look at his men ranged behind him in the murmuring shade of the blue-grey trees. A few months ago two hundred odd had ridden from the ruins of Poland to continue the struggle against Catherine, but some had fallen at Kazan, many at Samara; a few had vanished in the darkness with no word spoken and these he had not missed.

They were ragged and stained and their hair was dark with dirt. The faces, from which the blue Polish eyes stared back, bright and challenging, were burnt black by the sun and the wind of the steppes, and the colours of their coats had faded into a sort of uniform dingy brown. Many wore dirty clothes wrapped round their necks and some, instead of long boots, had bandaged their legs in rags as did the Cossacks. But they sat their horses erect; their harness was tight, the carbines clean and the sabres oiled in the battered scabbards.

Adam reading his thoughts, said quietly: 'There is still time, Henryk. Tell them. Lead them back to Poland. They can do more good there. Now, Henryk, before it is too late.'

'It *is* too late,' his face softened into a smile. 'Besides,

11

would you ask them to flee in front of other soldiers? So that the Cossacks could tell the story to their grandchildren of how the Poles ran at Tsaritsyn before a shot was fired.'

His brother sat frowning and did not answer.

'But I will try once more,' Henryk nodded towards the neighbouring knoll where Pugachev sat his white horse surrounded by his personal attendants and bodyguard. Now and then his bellowing laugh rang out and the gold tassels swung on the tall sable cap as he turned his head from side to side.

'By the time the sun goes down he'll be laughing a different tune.' Adam swore a bitter oath.

The Bashkirs made way for Henryk with their usual surly ill-grace.

'Well, my proud Pole, come to pay homage to your Tsar?' Pugachev's small eyes twinkled as he guffawed. He was in good spirits and more than a little drunk, leaning backwards and forwards in his saddle. Beside him the Cossack, Panin, held the flag of Holstein. Defeat seemed to Henryk to hang in the listless folds that clung close to the staff.

'You must order a retreat. At once, while there is still time,' he said without preamble. The good humour disappeared from Pugachev's eyes; they slowly bulged from his swarthy, sweating face and his mouth gaped open in his beard. For a full minute the two men stared at each other in a silence broken only by the pawing of a horse's hoof. Then with a great shout of scornful laughter, Nazar threw back his head.

'So the Pole wants to run. You hear that? These miserable women who call themselves soldiers!' He jerked his long lance in the direction of the Russians. 'We smashed them at Troitsk. We cut them to pieces outside Kazan. Very well, we shall do it again.'

'I have said before, if we try to fight them in the open we shall be defeated. What I see over there,' Henryk pointed at the motionless green ranks, 'does little to alter my opinion. You see those guns? They are manned by men who will not run. You see the cavalry? They are trained in the Prussian style and—'

'Prussian! What does it matter if they're led by God Himself?' Derisive laughter followed this remark. Only Pugachev did not laugh. His face set in a mask of black fury, he was hunched in the saddle staring in front of him with brooding eyes.

'So you are determined to fight?' said Henryk. But no one answered. From the restless horsemen in the scrub rose shouts and yells of impatience.

With a rasp of steel Pugachev's sabre flashed from his scabbard.

'Listen well to the words of your Tsar,' he shouted, 'for it is he who will lead you to victory today. It is he who will topple the usurper from her throne, God rot her black heart. Today, before the sun is below the Katzatchi Hills, we shall have fed their rotten flesh to the buzzards and their bones will strew the steppes between the Volga and the Don, and widows and children throughout Russia will curse the German whore who sent their men to die outside Tsaritsyn.' He was screaming now, his face dangerously flushed and tiny flecks of foam in his beard.

Thirty thousand men waited while his mad words granted them further moments in which to enjoy the warmth of the sun on their faces—and to live.

'I, Peter the Third, Tsar of All the Russias, will ride to Moscow in triumph and the people will fall on their knees in gratitude.' He lunged suddenly with his sabre towards the Imperial troops, shouting so loudly that some of the words must have faintly reached them. 'I, the Patriarch of Holy Russia, have called upon God Almighty and I tell you He is with us this day. Today, brothers, we cannot fail. We cannot fail.'

Beneath him his horse stirred and stamped uneasily and Henryk, looking on with loathing and pity, saw the man's naked soul glowing in the dark eyes.

'And those that fight beside me will go down in history

as . . .' Pugachev broke off, pointing excitedly. 'There! See them. See the army of the true Tsar. See how they have come in their thousands to die for their Emperor.'

From a hidden *balka* beyond the Tatars, came pouring like ants from a crack in the earth, a stream of dark humanity: the motley tattered multitude of Pugachev's infantry, the sunlight striking from the weapons of a peasant army. Scythe blades, sickles, axes and pitchforks waved above the yellow dust that rolled from under the trampling, shuffling feet, and with them came the rebels' few pathetic cannon, hauled by half-naked men. They wound in a dusty serpent from the ground, spreading into some sort of ragged formation where they stood, a dark mass, seething but silent as they gazed through the haze at their enemies, not going forward, not going back; just waiting with the incredible patience of the Russian peasant for what might be coming to him.

Henryk watched as the guns were manhandled into position then, without a word, he wheeled the mare and rode back to his men.

'You heard what was said?'

Adam nodded, his mouth tight. Those of the Poles who knew Russian were growling angrily among themselves. Henryk held up his hand for silence.

'Any man among you who wants to leave is free to go.'

No one moved, though one or two glanced at each other questioningly.

'If you stay then it will be to fight.'

'We shall fight,' said Sergeant Nym.

'God bless His Imperial Majesty for giving us this last chance, that's what I say.' A burst of laughter died away into a silence where nothing stirred, and the only movement was that of the hawk's swiftly beating wings. Then the bird dropped and, as it rose with a wriggling mouse in its talons so the first rebel gun fired. Henryk saw the strike of the shot some fifty yards short and heard the faint hum of the ball as it passed over the Russian infantry.

'What's the use of that then?'

'Might as well throw stones at them . . .'

'Wheel them up to twenty yards and they'd not hit a bloody herd of cows.'

Far away the sky filled with a swarm of crows, startled by the gun-shot. They heard Pugachev's voice.

'Let the Tatars attack!'

One of the Bashkirs sounded a long note on the great war-horn. Before the echoes had faded among the little hills the Tatars were riding at full gallop out of the scrub, dividing into the twin encircling claws as they headed for the Russians, with a loud *'Oura!'* Nazar led the Bashkirs down to join the Tatars, his blond hair streaming in the wind, and as they swept down the slope, the war-horn's challenge boomed across the steppe. A flash of blinding light ran along the Russian ranks as the men brought their bayonets to the ready. The rebel guns were firing without cohesion and none of the shots reached their target, raising feathers of black dust from the burnt grass.

The Poles were calling out excitedly.

'This is what they did at Troitsk . . . Mother of God, but those devils can ride . . . Creatures from Hell . . . And eager enough to get back there, by the looks of them . . . They'll not get round the flanks this time.'

The Tatars wheeled and circled, each rider enclosed in his own plume of dust, trying to find the way to the Russian rear; short, fierce yells mingled with the hiss of the arrows and the drumming of the hooves as the little ponies darted in and out of the dust. But the infantry, veterans of Kirsova and Shumla, battles in the Turkish war, commanded by officers who had fought the Prussians at Kunersdorf and Zorndorf, stood firm under the scattered storm of arrows and did not break as had their brothers at Troitsk. Here and there a soldier fell transfixed and at once a man stepped forward to take his place. They did not fire unless a horseman rode in too close and then half a dozen muskets fired in a sputter of white smoke to bring the man and pony to the ground.

'They've met their match today,' said Adam.

'Did we expect anything else?' Henryk watched gloomily as the Tatars, dismayed by this unexpected reaction, drew back and rode up and down just out of musket shot waving their lances in empty defiance or galloped about the plain uttering their harsh war-cries and taunting the Russians to come forward and fight like men. But the infantry did not move, not even when Nazar led his men close in a tight bunch to fire a deadly clutch of arrows that cut a sudden gap in the ranks, then, with amazing speed wheeling out of range. The horn sounded and they went back to repeat the attack but this time a gun fired and the grape tore the little band to shreds.

A pony came out of the dust, galloping wildly back, and as it passed below the Poles they could see the headless body of Nazar swaying in the saddle, spouting great founts of blood. Blinded and terrified the pony swerved this way and that, trying to rid itself of the terrible burden, but the dead Nazar fell forward on the animal's neck with his arms trailing almost to the ground and as the maddened pony rushed his rider from the field, so a new sound filled the air, a deep chanting song from thousands of throats, swelling to a mighty roar as the air above the peasant army twinkled with the waving blades. It was as if a fierce squall had struck the dark sea, flinging it into sudden desperate agitation; those in front were waving their arms, pointing towards the Russians. Some were on their knees praying to the hot blue sky. The mass surged forward, then back, then forward again, and this time it did not stop, but moved across the steppe gathering speed as it entered the arena.

'No!' Henryk heard himself shout. 'In the name of Heaven, no. This is madness!'

'It's bloody murder,' said Sergeant Nym, again without expression. Let the swine kill each other, what did it matter to him?

'The Cossacks! Break them with the Cossacks. Not this.' Henryk was cursing, with words he had not used since *Huntress*. But Pugachev did not answer. He sat with head thrown back, his beard jutting forward, his eyes half-closed.

'Now you will see,' he was repeating, 'now you will see how they die for their Tsar.'

They were running, streaming in a tattered horde towards the waiting hedge of bayonets, the hungry mouths of the guns. The Tatars rode out to the flanks where they sat and watched, like Sergeant Nym, not greatly caring. The chanting had turned to a formless bellow of sound; the howling of beasts on the scent. All the hopeless misery of their lives came welling and raging from six thousand throats; all the longing for revenge. Already little groups were out in front, a solitary figure with an axe leaping ahead.

'God help them,' breathed Adam. Henryk saw the muskets come up and in his mind he heard the clear orders.

'Muskets at the ready! . . . Raise cocks! . . .'

'Poor stupid bastards,' said little Kinski.

'For what they are about to receive,' thought Henryk as the leading peasants hurled themselves forward to death.

'Fire! . . .'

A long roll of white smoke rose from the crash of the volley and the peasants were swept away like grass in that shrivelling blast of fire. But the man with the axe staggered on through the black haze of smoke and dust.

'Christ!' exclaimed Sergeant Nym. 'Jesus Christ, just look at that.'

The Russians did not fire but let him fall forward on the bayonets. Those who had followed him vanished in the next volley. The main mass recoiled, hesitated and stood still like sheep faced by a wolf-pack. Fear rose into the air, ugly as swamp mist. Many of those in front, hearing the harsh orders of the Imperial officers, turned and fought their way back through the mob, crying in animal terror and throwing away their pitchforks and sickles.

'They're running!'

'And who can blame them?'

Leaving the steppe strewn with their pathetic weapons, the peasant army of Pugachev fled, vanishing back into the *balka*, reappearing the other side; and as they ran with flailing arms the cries of fear floated across the sunlit plain.

'That's not the way to Moscow,' said a voice, but no one laughed.

'Nothing will stop them now, not till they reach the Volga.' The dust settled, the smoke drifted away, thinning on a sudden puff of wind, and the screams of the wounded crawling and squirming like cut worms in the ashes came to Henryk on the breeze that stirred the leaves of the poplars and made the little blue butterflies dance. He could feel Rasulka trembling and patted the quivering satin of her neck.

'We could have been on the other side of the river by now,' said Adam in a low voice. 'And not forced to watch our strength being thrown away bit by bit.' He scratched at the sores on his hand.

'In a moment the Cossacks will come out from behind those hills; they will ride round them, between them, perhaps over them and then they will charge. The gunners will wait, and wait, and then they'll fire, and the grape will—' Henryk struck his fist hard against the pommel of his saddle. 'And for what? Answer me that, Adam? For what? Those guns will make widows of a thousand Cossack women. A few hundred Russians will never go home and you and I—'

He was interrupted by Pugachev's strident voice demanding to know why the Cossacks had not moved.

'Are they also cowards? Like those miserable scum who ran at the first sound of a musket ball? Let them attack at once and make an end to this business. Have they not received our orders, Marshal Potemkin? Is there no one here today except myself who knows how to wage war?'

'Your Excellency, the messenger can barely have reached them,' answered the Cossack Potemkin.

'Messenger! What do they need with messengers? We did not wait, you whining fools. When we found an enemy we attacked, we did not lie skulking under cover hoping the orders wouldn't reach us.' He turned to face the Poles.

'Isn't that right, Borodin? You have seen the Cossacks fight.'

'Yes, and today I shall see them die,' Henryk called back in answer. Pugachev glowered but made no answer.

The wounded peasants were still screaming in their fear and pain, and crows came drifting lazily on the summer wind. The battle could have stopped then, petered out into stalemate with both sides watching each other, but the Cossacks came round and between the little white shining hills so like a woman's breasts, and the crows gathered hopefully, perching in clouds on the distant trees. The horsemen shook themselves out into formation, squadron after squadron appearing until Pugachev's cavalry was ready. It seemed to Henryk so leisurely, so lacking in urgency that he found it hard to believe that these men were going to attack.

'Taking their time, aren't they?' Sergeant Nym asked scornfully.

'It's too fine a day to go to heaven,' piped up little Kinski.

With a harsh sound three thousand sabres sprang from the scabbards, drawing glinting arcs of light through the haze. Henryk heard the hiss of indrawn breath behind him. The horses stamped and whickered : they knew what was coming.

'Show them the flag,' ordered Pugachev. 'Give them the signal.'

The Cossack Panin held aloft the flag of Holstein, fluttering in the warm wind, stained and torn. Below, the blades dipped in salute then rose again as the horsemen began to move forward at a trot. At first the dust was so deep that they moved with no sound, rank upon rank, Cossacks of the Don, of the Dnieper, of the Kuban, floating through a yellow sea.

Then they were out of the soft dust and galloping on the hard drum of the earth, faster, faster, until the ground shook to the thunder of the pounding hooves and the terrible battle-cry of the Cossacks burst from three thousand throats.

'*Netchai*! *Netchai*! Cut! Cut!'

There was movement in the Russian ranks as the infantry braced themselves to meet the shock while the great mass of horsemen swept towards them, and the gunners crouched by their guns.

The Polish horses were tossing their heads and pulling hard at their bits, prancing and pawing, the riders calling out to Henryk to lead them into the battle.

'Have patience, your turn will come.' But they continued to urge him, shouting wildly above the mighty rumble of the hooves. Henryk saw Pugachev's mouth gaping black in his beard but heard no sound; the man was beside himself, jerking and twisting as though in a fit. It was as Henryk had said: the gunners waited, and waited, as the guns trembled beneath their hands as though alive and the leading ranks of Cossacks came tearing at them like the rising, curling lip of a great dark wave.

'They must fire! Now, or it will be too late. Now!' Henryk's nails dug into the wet palms of his hands. 'Now!' He saw the arms go up. And as the Cossacks reached the strip of ash so the arms came down and twenty guns went off as one. Men and horses were thrown in the air by the monstrous blast of grape, hurled back among each other, mangled and shredded by the whirring metal so that the leading ranks had become in a second a writhing rampart of dead and wounded. The ash, dust and smoke was lit by the flames of the guns. Line upon line of horsemen vanished into that black fog. Out of it came riderless horses, men stumbling and falling with hands pressed to their faces; the broken cries of men, the awful screaming of wounded horses.

'*Netchai! Netchai!*'

The guns were firing singly and they could hear the

crackle of the muskets. Then little Kinski, his voice breaking shrilly, 'Holy Mother, they're through! Look, boys, look! The bloody Cossacks have done it, they've broken them, they're through!'

'Go on, go on!'

'Don't keep us here.'

'That's right. Why should we sit and watch? Lead us!' The Poles were waving their carbines, gesticulating and pointing impatiently at the fleeing green figures and the Cossacks who rode among them cutting and slashing.

'Victory, victory!' Pugachev seized the flag from the Cossack Panin and waved it high above his head.

'To Moscow! To the Holy city! Death to the murderess. Death to ...'

At this moment the Russian dragoons smashed into the flank of the Cossacks and the shock of the impact was heard above the din of battle, for these were big men on heavy horses who had charged in the Prussian manner, at full tilt. The leading squadrons struck the main body of the Cossacks obliquely and sent them reeling back so that they came tumbling helter-skelter from the billowing dust, crying, 'Save yourselves, brothers!'

Many did not flee but fought with a desperate courage, hurling themselves from their horses on to the dragoons; many who were unhorsed slashed with their long daggers at the bellies of the Russian horses before being crushed and broken by the hooves.

But the Poles could see little of what went on within the black cloud. All they saw was the defeat of the Cossacks on the open steppe and the irresistible advance of the heavy cavalry. They saw dark clusters of Cossacks surrounded in a sea of blue; they saw the Russian infantry re-forming and they smelt the stink of powder and ash carried on the gentle little wind.

'If we could hit them before they've re-formed.' Henryk glanced quickly at his brother.

'Ninety men?' Adam sounded incredulous.

'Take them through that dust, whilst the cavalry's engaged. We could still turn the day.' His eyes were shining, all his fear and gloom forgotten. Then doubt clouded his face. 'Have I the right?' Adam shrugged and smiled slightly; leaning across, he touched Henryk's arm.

'I'll follow you,' he said.

Henryk turned swiftly to Sergeant Nym.

'We're going to attack.' Though he had not fear for himself, Henryk could not bear to look at them as they checked their weapons for the last time, calling out jokes to each other, patting their restless horses.

It was hopeless. They both knew that. They knew it was the finish; that within the next few minutes the horsemen of Poland would cease to exist.

'God be with you, Adam,' he said.

'And with you, Henryk.'

'Ready, Sergeant Nym?' Henryk asked.

'Ready.'

Dombrowski reached up to unfurl the tattered folds of the standard. Raising his voice Henryk called out, 'Follow it well and may God go with you.'

Most of the men crossed themselves; some, like Gurowski and Sergeant Nym, settled themselves more firmly in the saddle.

Rasulka tossed her head and snorted softly with pleasure at being on the move again as she trotted from the shelter of the trees and into the first thin wisps of smoke.

And Pugachev, slumped on his white horse as he watched his Cossacks being relentlessly rolled back, did not even see the Poles riding out to battle. A desperate little army riding at the trot with parade ground precision; three ranks, each of thirty men. Led by the man who had helped him gamble for a throne and who now, impelled by some strange, quixotic loyalty, was going out to die for him. But the sham Tsar, sunk in defeat, did not notice. He stared with the blank and vacant gaze of a man shocked beyond reason, his broken mind filled with visions of fresh armies that could never come. Round him his few remaining attendants muttered uneasily among themselves, already looking over their shoulders. Almost all the Bashkirs had gone, vanishing swiftly into the steppe as is the way of the Tatars. Of the Cossacks only Potemkin, Panin and Chumakov remained, their eyes fixed on the Poles, exclaiming in grudging admiration.

'The crazy fools! What good do they think they can do?'

'Ox-heads!'

'They're throwing away their carbines. What use is that now?'

'Would you use a musket if you had a sabre at your side?'

'Ten thousand men are scattered like corn-chaff on the wind and our Polish brothers think they can do the job themselves.' The Cossack Potemkin spat disgustedly.

'See, they're going to charge.'

To Henryk the clear, sharp note of the bugle sounding the charge was as unbearable as the lark's song. With the fierce excitement rising to choke him he slackened the pressure on the reins.

'Go, little mare, you are free!'

Rasulka took the bit between her teeth and stretched out at speed, and as Henryk felt the wind rising against his face he heard the loud vibrant voice of Gurowski. *'Long live Poland!'*

For a short moment Adam kept level, then slowly the big chestnut dropped back and Henryk was riding alone. The mare flew over the ground, faster she went, and faster, with ears laid back and all her smooth power surging between his legs. No horse born could catch her now, no rider stop her.

Away to his right a confused mass of horsemen milled and struggled in the dusty haze; the wind on his face was hot and stinging and the smell of battle took him by the throat. Behind the thud of hooves was fainter. Over his shoulder he saw his brother and Jan Dombrowski riding side by side; above them the white eagle streamed defiantly. Gurowski shouting something; little Kinski, who had lost his precious fur cap, and the imperturbable Sergeant Nym, riding as though on manoeuvres. The rest were blotted out by dust.

Now Rasulka began to swerve and jink, avoiding the bodies that lay in her path; without slackening speed she threaded her way with wonderful skill between the dead and wounded. The day was dark with smoking dust; shadowy figures loomed, seemed to rush at him, then he was past. Somewhere in this black fog the infantry waited, thinking the battle was over. He strained ahead with eyes half blinded by the reeking, swirling clouds; a riderless horse galloped beside them, its white fur saddle cloth streaked with blood, its eyes rolling in terror. Another horse, and yet another, all with empty saddles, running aimlessly; a wounded man waving feebly from the ashes, a second one spinning in slow motion trying to keep the blood inside his shattered face with red hands, staggering in front of Henryk. The mare swerved so violently that Henryk was almost thrown.

'Don't fall, Rasulka! Don't stumble!'

There were sudden patches in the fog partially cleared by the wind, filled with dim figures, running, standing, crawling; the flash of muskets, sabres rising and falling, bewildered horses sinking to their knees. Then in front a low hedge of bodies. She did not hesitate but leapt high and true, picking up her stride just before they reached the waiting ranks of infantry.

Officers waving swords, shouting wildly; men half turning to face this apparition rushing at them . . . muskets raised, a sword in the air, mouths gaping and yelling . . . Henryk, bent low on her neck, saw the white smoke of the volley as the air trembled from the wicked hum of the balls. Badly shaken by the Cossacks, hemmed-in by the blackness all round, their aim had been hurried, and he was into them. Men went down shrieking beneath her deadly hooves . . . tall mitre caps spun in the air ... arms grabbing, filthy oaths cut off as his sword came down ... the explosion of a musket almost in his face. A bayonet ripped his boot, another the skin of Rasulka's flank. She was still galloping and the soldiers ran from her path as Henryk slashed from side to side ... slicing the top from a skull, neat as an egg ... opening a startled face in a wide red slit ... *'A-a-aaah!'* ... A very young officer ran at him bravely with toy sword raised, and was left gazing stupidly at the hand and the sword lying at his feet ... a bearded head jumped from a severed neck as cleanly as a thistle parts from the stalk ... Musket balls sang past him as Henryk vanished into the rolling smoke.

A blast of flame tore apart the black cloud and he swerved Rasulka sharply, setting her at the gunners. He was among them before they knew it, cursing, panting, the breath sobbing in his throat as he hacked savagely at the arms flung up to protect their heads. He left them dead and dying by their gun and rode on blindly. Faces came and went as he searched for his men.

He was laughing insanely now as the smoke-tears streamed from his eyes, and his voice when he tried to shout was a harsh croak.

'Adam! Jan!'

Rasulka had slowed to a walk. He reined her in and she stood with heaving flanks near two fallen Cossacks and an infantryman with a Tatar arrow through the throat.

'The trumpeter of Krakow,' he thought stupidly. 'Why's he so far from home? Why's everyone so far from home?' There were voices everywhere, calling for water and for God. Guns fired somewhere and he heard the howl of the shot.

'Sergeant Nym!'

He spat the black muck from his mouth. His arm hung slack and blood gathered at the point of his sword. In a moment they would go on searching, but now, just for a minute he and his horse must rest.

The commanding officer of the Smolensk Regiment was

also lost and searching for his men. He rode out of the smoke and came face to face with Henryk. And now it was not armies nor squadrons, but just two men watched by the dead.

The Russian came at Henryk who, as the man drew closer, recognized him to be Colonel Skurin.

They drew up their horses. In the hell crashing and howling about them, they sat looking at each other.

'Colonel Skurin,' Henryk gasped.

'I'm sorry,' said Skurin, 'I'm very sorry.' The blood dripped slowly from Henryk's sabre.

'I am sorry, too.'

'What do we do now?' Skurin asked. They were alone in a little oasis of the battle.

'We say farewell,' said Henryk. 'We say farewell and go our own ways. Or do we have to fight?'

'There's been enough fighting today.'

Colonel Skurin raised his sabre in salute. 'We have not seen each other, Count Barinski.'

Henryk raised his broken sword.

'When I get back to Lipno, I shall tell my wife of this meeting, Colonel Skurin. And now, if I were you, I'd get out of this shambles as quickly as you can. That's what I intend to do.'

Both men smiled.

'So we part as friends?' Colonel Skurin sheathed his sword as he rode closer, holding out his hand.

Henryk took it.

'Goodbye, Colonel Skurin. Never forget you will always be welcome at Lipno.' The Colonel raised his tricorne hat in farewell as he rode away into the darkness of the dust and smoke.

* * *

When they found him, Henryk had fallen forward, his

face against Rasulka's mane, utterly spent.

'Thank God, Your Honour,' gasped Sergeant Nym. Dark blood ran down from a wound in his shoulder and trickled between his fingers. Beside him Jan Dombrowski held aloft what remained of the white eagle, torn in ribbons.

'You have carried it well, Jan,' said Henryk, raising himself to face them.

'There's nothing left,' said Dombrowski. His bloodshot eyes stared from a grey-black mask; his voice was a hoarse croak.

'We broke the infantry all right but the smoke cleared suddenly and we rode into the guns. Then the dragoons came. It was no one's fault.' He spoke quickly and jerkily and tears drew wet furrows in the mask.

'They fought well,' said Sergeant Nym. 'As you would have wished.' He was breathing hard, now and then touching the wound, but he sat his lathered horse very straight.

'My brother?'

'I don't know. I didn't see. We got split up. I don't know.' Henryk knew that Jan was hiding the truth.

'Little Kinski got a ball in the head. Gurowski went down fighting like a madman—at least six of them. Yes, it must have been at least six.' He was swaying slightly and slurring his words.

'And my brother? He's dead, isn't he?'

'Yes,' answered Sergeant Nym. Beyond a quick blinking of his eyes, Henryk gave no sign of having heard.

'We cannot stay here,' he said.

The noise had receded leaving them in a little backwater. There was no more regular firing, only scattered shots, the distant drumming of hooves and the hopeless chorus of the wounded.

'There is nothing,' repeated Dombrowski. 'Nothing but this.' He lowered the standard and tore the remnants from the staff, shoving them inside his shirt. 'Only this,' he kept saying.

'Some of them got away,' said Nym. 'And these Russian carthorses will never catch our boys, not if they had red-hot bayonets up their tails. Come, Your Honour,' he added more gently, 'we can do no more good here.'

'You're sure he was dead?' The two men nodded. But Henryk still did not move. He could hear horsemen approaching, but it did not seem to matter.

'Come on! Hurry!' Sergeant Nym seized Henryk's bridle. 'Your Honour, please!' The ground trembled beneath them; the horsemen were very close, the leading riders dimly visible through the fading smoke.

'Back the way we came then!' Henryk wheeled the mare sharply and they followed him into the clean evening air.

'Can you hold on, Jan?'

'I'm all right.'

'Very well, we'll make for the river, south of the town.' They urged on the tired horses and their long shadows raced beside them across the steppe as the sun lowered into the dark rain-clouds and a great fan of golden rays spread across the western sky.

* * *

At sunset the skies opened and the rain came down as long, glinting threads joining heaven to the black earth where men raised their faces thankfully to the water. It washed away the stains of battle and splashed un-noticed into the open mouths of the dead. Cool and cleansing, the rain poured in a wonderful flood down the flanks of the horses; the wind blew it in their faces and they whickered with pleasure.

Soon the living huddled in their cloaks by the drowned fires cursing the day they had ever become soldiers; the horses shivered and huddled close while the thunder rolled across the sky and lightning played impishly among the clouds. But Adam Barinski and the countless dead lying out on the steppe, they did not care any more.

And on the small knoll among the dancing poplar trees, the little flag of Holstein lay crumpled and forgotten as a sodden autumn leaf.

Chapter Three

AND as the dead lay not caring about the rain that poured down, little groups of fugitives made their way in different directions trying to find their way in the rain-lashed darkness; their bodies, suffering from wounds and the shock of battle, shook uncontrollably.

'This way!' Henryk could hear the river above the sound of the rain. Three other riders were with him: Pugachev, his head bowed low in defeat; Frol Chumakov and the Cossack called by the name of Potemkin.

But the leader was undoubtedly Henryk Barinski.

They had skirted round Tsaritsyn well to the south and reached the river at a point where it ran slowly round the edges of a small bay, before rejoining the main flood stream.

'How do we cross?'

'Yes,' echoed Potemkin, 'how can we cross? Must be over eight hundred yards wide.'

'If we cannot find a boat we'll have to find a raft. If we can't find a raft then we'll have to swim,' Henryk shouted into the wind and rain. 'We must be across before daybreak. The dragoons will be searching all along the banks.'

'I cannot swim.' Chumakov shrugged, wiping the blood from his eyes.

'Very well then, we'll look for a boat. It's the sort of sheltered place where the fishermen might keep them.'

They found a boat: half water-logged and without oars, but a boat.

'Find branches, sticks, anything,' Henryk ordered. They scoured the bank, all except for Pugachev who still sat hunched forward in his saddle totally oblivious of everything going on around him. A man completely and utterly buried in the disaster of the last few hours.

They found birch branches which they bound together into bunches like broomheads, under Henryk's directions they hauled the boat clear of the water, turned her over, emptied her.

'What about the horses?' Chumakov asked.

'Let them go,' said the Cossack Potemkin. 'They won't starve.'

Henryk knew the moment had come; he felt sick in the pit of his stomach as he looked at Rasulka. Her ears were pricked as always; she nuzzled his hand affectionately as he felt for the pistol under his coat.

He thought of the first Rasulka; he thought of this animal that trusted him, that was more of a friend than anyone in the world except for Kasia. He bent his head against her neck as he had done so often before. This horse, this brave, beautiful horse who had carried him so faithfully through so many battles, never swerving from the bellowing guns.

'Goodbye, Rasulka. I am sorry,' he whispered, and she whickered softly as she always did when he spoke to her.

Then he shot her behind the ear. The pelting rain washed the tears from his face and he went down to the boat without looking back.

* * *

How they got across the Volga Henryk never knew. But somehow, baling frantically with their hats, their hands; paddling equally frantically with the birchwood paddles they reached the other side with an inch of freeboard to spare.

Soaked and shivering they waded ashore into a wilderness

of tall wet reeds. Until dawn came to bring a grey, drizzling day they remained huddled together for warmth, then they set about looking for somewhere to make a temporary camp.

They had no food, no tools, scanty weapons between them; everything was wet and deep in mud—and they were beaten men.

Pugachev lay down in the morass and still said nothing. Since the moment he was hustled from the battlefield of Tsaritsyn, he had not uttered one single word. Except for the fact that he blinked his eyes and that his chest rose and fell to his breathing he might just as well have been dead.

So, instinctively, the others turned to Henryk—even Chumakov. They were Cossacks, trained to war, to living off what they could find, under every kind of conditions, and yet they turned to him. Not to Pugachev, the Tsar, Peter the Third, who was to lead them to St Petersburg and glory, but to the Pole who called himself Borodin.

* * *

On the west bank of the Volga another little group of men made their way from the disaster of Tsaritsyn.

Jan Dombrowski, carrying the tattered flag of Poland beneath the remnants of his old tunic, ripped in a dozen places by splinters, musket-balls and bayonets. Sergeant Nym, the wound in his shoulder partially staunched by a bundle of cloth, and half a dozen Poles who had escaped the holocaust of the Russian cavalry.

Their leader, Jan Dombrowski, after consultation with Sergeant Nym, decided to head westwards towards their homes.

'Count Barinski,' he too had to shout against the wind and rain, 'has disappeared. We've no idea where he has gone. Perhaps—' Here he stopped. Perhaps we shall meet him waiting for us on the road back to Poland? Was that what he had been going to say? Oh God, Jan, pull yourself together. These men are looking for leadership, not miracles.

'Before dawn we must put as many miles between us and the Russians as we can. However tired your horses are they must keep going until they drop or we'll find ourselves hanging at the end of Russian ropes.'

They set off towards the west, heartbroken that they were leaving behind them Count Henryk Barinski.

* * *

There were the other four who reached a spot where they decided to make camp. Henryk, Pugachev, Frol Chumakov and the Cossack called Potemkin.

'This is the place,' Henryk said. 'This is where we must stop.' No one argued.

It was a little island surrounded by swamp water; an island of dry land head-high in reeds, big enough for at least eight men.

For two days and nights they had blundered about in the marshes, sometimes finding tracks, sometimes wading up to their waists in muddy water. Already their faces and hands were swollen from the insect bites, their feet deadened by the water.

They saw no human being. All around them they heard the call of the waterfowl, the continuous croaking of the frogs, the sigh of the wind in the reeds, but no human sound.

'This is where we'll stay,' said Henryk. 'At least we'll be out of the water.' With their rusting sabres they cut open spaces in the reeds; they made shelters and scooped drains to let the water escape from the camp.

Soon they had plaited the damp pliant reeds and made rough nets in which they trapped birds. They cooked them over small fires, carefully concealed so that the smoke did not drift above the reeds.

They built a little raft of tightly bound rushes on which

they took it in turns to paddle slowly and cautiously among the maze of little swamp streams and stretches of open water. But they still saw no signs of other humans, heard no human voices.

It was now early October and the nights were becoming bitterly cold; nearly every day there was rain or a thick, drenching mist. They were never dry and at all times one or other of them had marsh-fever; they all developed coughs; their legs and feet became soft and white, pitted with ulcers. Their eyes were sunk deep in their skulls.

All their weapons were rusted now. Henryk threw his pistol away; it was useless and besides, he had no powder. The continual diet of water-birds and frogs spitted on sticks over the damp fire sickened their stomachs.

Another week passed, and then another. The Cossack Potemkin had the fever so badly that he could not speak between his chattering teeth and his skin had turned a horrible shade of greyish blue.

'He'll be dead within two days,' said Chumakov. He tore angrily at the half-cooked carcass of a waterhen, spitting out charred feathers. 'We'll all be dead within a week.' The rain dripped through the sodden roof and the mist moved across the water like writhing grey snakes.

That night Potemkin gurgled an incomprehensible noise through his clacking teeth and died.

They put him on the raft and Henryk paddled the body some way from their terrible resting place and tipped it into the water.

'He's lucky,' said Chumakov bitterly. 'By Christ above, he's lucky.'

Pugachev said nothing. Since they had reached their little island he had hardly uttered more than half a dozen words. He ate what they gave him listlessly; he never seemed to sleep but just sat huddled, gazing at nothing with dead eyes.

'He's mad,' said Chumakov. 'He's always been a bit crazy

ever since we were boys but now,' he touched his forehead and shrugged, 'now he's finished. He never thought he could be beaten.' Chumakov rubbed his leg grimacing with pain.

'This bloody wet.'

'I know,' said Henryk.

'How long can we go on?' Chumakov asked.

'Not more than another week,' said Henryk calmly. But what a place in which to die. No banners or trumpets or musket salutes here. Just pain, loneliness and the stink of the marshes. And, of course, death. Kasia would never know where or how he had died. He prayed to God that she never discovered the truth.

For about half an hour a cold sun broke through the mists and brought a tiny feel of warmth to their soaking bodies.

'One of us should go for help,' Chumakov said suddenly. Steam rose from his rotting clothes; he kept his eyes averted from Henryk.

'Help? And where in Hell d'you think you're going to find help in this filthy wilderness?' Henryk laughed. 'Are the frogs going to help us?' He glanced at Pugachev; he was sunk in his usual torpor, so deep that it was almost a coma. He never did more than nod slowly or grunt; his face showed absolutely no expression whatsoever; it resembled that of a dirty, bearded dummy.

'He won't help us any more.' Chumakov spat contemptuously.

'I thought you were his friend.'

Chumakov did not answer. Then, 'I'll go for help,' he said suddenly. In the night he had heard faint sounds with his lynx-like ears that even Henryk had missed: a small splash that was not caused by a bird or fish; a slight rustle among the reeds not made by the wind, for there was no wind; one tiny whisper that could have been a human voice.

Somewhere, beyond the forest of reeds there were people—of that he was sure.

'But—' Henryk began.

'I shall go,' Chumakov repeated. 'You stay and take care of our friend here.' Pugachev gave no sign of having heard the interchange.

'What makes you so sure you will find help?' Henryk asked. 'We've seen no signs that anything lives within miles of here. We don't even know where we are.'

They once knew that they had been heading north. And they now knew—or Henryk knew—that they were hopelessly lost in the great swamplands stretching from the northern fringe of Khazakstan to Samara.

'Very well then, you go,' said Henryk.

'Thank you, Your Honour.' Chumakov's tone was sarcastic. No one was leader anymore, he thought, not here, not under these conditions. He'll take the raft, he may never come back, Henryk thought, quite dispassionately: either deliberately or because he is lost and starving. What did it matter any more what any of them did?

Then he saw Kasia in his mind, so clearly she could have been standing close beside them on this little morass which kept them alive. Once she had hovered for days on the very edge of death and, by her courage and love, had hung on to life. Could he not do the same?

'The raft will only hold one,' he said. 'Whilst you are away I'll make myself a new one—something to carry two.'

'In case I don't come back?'

'Yes,' said Henryk. 'In case you don't come back.'

* * *

A Russian cavalry patrol reached the edge of the marshlands as dusk was falling.

Thirty men under a lieutenant.

'What the hell do I do now?' he thought desperately for he was not very old.

As he was trying to make up his mind something stirred among the reeds.

'What the—?' said his sergeant who was a veteran of ten battles.

'I'm a friend. A friend,' shouted a voice.

The sergeant nodded.

'All right then, come over here.' The Russians waited, their carbines ready, peering into the icy mist.

A vague shape appeared on the black water. They saw it was a single man up to his thighs in water.

'Well,' said the lieutenant, much encouraged by the sight of one man. 'Well, what do you want?'

At last, he thought, at last, after weeks of fruitless searching, of abominable discomfort, at last they might be getting somewhere.

The man paddled slowly towards them on his waterlogged raft.

'Who are you,' he asked in a weak, wheezy voice.

'Her Majesty's Dragoon Guards.'

'What Majesty?' Chumakov's voice was, as usual, contemptuous.

The lieutenant spluttered.

'Her Imperial Majesty, Empress Catherine—'

'Oh, her,' said Chumakov. As usual, he spat. A dozen carbines were aimed at him, and he knew it.

'All right,' he shouted. 'I give up.' He paddled slowly towards the men on the shore.

'Supposing,' he asked in bad Russian, 'I could take you to where the Cossack, Pugachev, is hiding?'

The lieutenant drew in a quick breath, if this was true then—then he had no more worries.

'You could be leading us into a trap.'

After a short pause Chumakov answered: 'Yes, that is

true.' He, in his turn, was silent for a moment. 'But,' he said, 'why should I risk my life for a rebel who has fought against the Empress of Russia?'

'I agree,' said the young officer, feeling tremendous power in his words.

Frol Chumakov paddled his sinking raft towards the bank.

'Yes,' he said, in answer to the questions thrown at him. 'Yes. I can take you there.'

* * *

Henryk heard the gentle swirl of the boats as they approached the little island. There was nothing he could do : he knew that.

They appeared on a stretch of open water : six boats, in a way like Indian canoes, bark and canvas and paddled by dark-skinned men in hairy coats and tall fur hats. So these were the people of the marshes who must have been watching them for days.

In each canoe there were four apprehensive looking soldiers, gazing at the water far more keenly than at their other surroundings.

But when he saw Chumakov in the leading boat, Henryk knew that the revolt he had helped to lead was finished.

'There,' said Chumakov, pointing at the little island. 'They are there.'

Well, thought Henryk, so you have got your revenge over the man who defeated you in a fight over *my* wife. Ironical.

'Be ready, men,' shouted the officer.

Henryk looked at the young lieutenant. You miserable little pipsqueak. Once, long ago he had been like this young man. 'There is nothing to be ready for,' he said, coming down to the edge of the water. Two men : one a half-dead vegetable, the other a verminous, frozen creature who would give his soul for a decent meal and hours of sleep in a dry warm bed. The rewards one asks, he thought, are really very small.

With much loud shouting and splashing the soldiers struggled ashore.

'Who are you?' The Russian officer pointed a pistol at Henryk.

'Who am I?' Henryk looked at the young man. 'Well, who are you?'

'I am myself. That's who I am.' And now he'll start to bluster decided Henryk and he was right.

Frustrated, the lieutenant asked: 'And who is this?' He pointed at the crumpled figure of Pugachev.

'This is Emylyan Pugachev, Cossack of the Don, leader of the unlawful rebellion against our rightful Empress, Catherine.' Chumakov's words rang out across the empty marshes.

'So you have betrayed him,' Henryk said. Chumakov did not answer. 'I hope that, when the time comes, you will die in the same agony as all of us.'

Henryk thought: never in my life have I ever said anything like that. But, as he watched Pugachev, the wreck of what had once been a man, being dragged down to the boat, the thought was still in his mind. He had seen horrors; he had endured the wild screams of those tortured beyond human endurance. He knew about human suffering, and he wished it on no man. But now it had reached out, this octopus of pain, and was going to entwine them all.

'And who are you?'

'Borodin,' said Henryk. 'My name is Borodin.'

'Right then, you will come with us.'

'Of course, *Your Honour*,' said Henryk, imagining the long dagger between the shoulder-blades.

In this way they went, as prisoners, to the camp of Colonel Michelson, the officer in charge of the capture of Emylyan Pugachev.

* * *

Colonel Michelson was a humane man. He admired brave opponents.

'So you are Emylyan Pugachev and you are the man called Borodin?' They sat in a peasant's hut, a hundred miles to the west of the marshes.

'Yes,' said Henryk. 'I am the man called Borodin.'

'Ah.' The officer wrote something with his squeaky pen. 'But you are not Pugachev?'

'No.'

'Well then, who are you? What is your real name?'

'That is up to you, isn't it? I have told you : Borodin.'

After a long pause Michelson said : 'Very well. But, I warn you; somewhere someone will find out the truth. That is fortunately not my job.' The Colonel was a soldier, not a torturer.

'You will remain here under guard for the night and tomorrow you will be taken to the headquarters of Marshal Suvorov. After that . . .' He shrugged.

'And Chumakov?'

'The man who betrayed you? He will go with you of course. What they will do to him God knows. He expects a pardon for his treachery. Personally, if it was my decision I'd make him swing from the nearest tree.' He nodded at the two sentries.

'Goodbye, Borodin.'

'Goodbye, Colonel. May I wish you luck in your profession.' As he reached the doorway Henryk said over his shoulder : 'If some day we meet in Heaven you must let me give you a vodka.'

Michelson smiled, then bent his head over the papers strewn across the rough table. Henryk was taken back to the hut where Pugachev lay on a bed of straw. Two sentries stood, one on each side of the door, while two others patrolled round the building.

Henryk lay down on his own patch of straw pulling much of it on top of himself. Above Pugachev's grunting snores

Henryk heard the hard patter of hail on the roof and the heavy stamping as the sentries tried to keep warm. Of Chumakov there was no sign.

After his nightly prayer to God asking Him to look after Kasia and their child, Henryk fell into an exhausted, feverish sleep.

* * *

Marshal Suvorov regarded them coldly with his pale blue eyes, deep-set in his thin, pale monk's face.

'So you are the two men who have caused such trouble to Her Imperial Majesty's armies—to myself.' He had the same sort of face as Skurin, Henryk decided. But this man had no humour in him, not one scrap.

'Do we have to be tied like common criminals?' All Henryk's latent hatred of the Russians welled up into his question.

'What else are you?' Suvorov's answer was harder than ice.

'We are soldiers, just as you are.'

The Field-Marshal leant back in his chair, his fingers joined together in a slender pyramid.

'There I cannot agree,' he said. 'You are rebels against your Empress and, as such . . .'

'She is not my Empress.'

'That I understand,' Suvorov agreed. 'You are not Russian. You are, God knows what you are. Half Pole, half Cossack. It does not matter to me what you are. You will go to Moscow with your friend.' Here he paused to scribble some notes. 'Or is he not your friend?'

Henryk did not answer.

'I see.' Suvorov looked up again with his pale eyes. Like a fish we caught in the West Indies, Henryk thought, remembering the cruise in the Caribbean when Captain Primrose had allowed them a week off : to bathe, to laze in the sun, and to fish.

He smiled quietly to himself. If only I had known. We could have called that fish Marshal Suvorov.

'There is something amusing in what I say?'

'No,' said Henryk truthfully. 'No, nothing at all.'

'Take them away.' Soldiers pushed them out of the small manor-house occupied by the Field-Marshal and his staff.

The men who threw them into the darkness of a small hut were not gentle.

For three days, or so Henryk calculated by the changing of day to night, they were kept in that hole. And all the time he could hear the clang of hammers on iron. Though he dug a small hole in the timber walls he could see nothing but falling snow and, occasionally, the sentries as they plodded up and down.

Then, on the fourth day, the door was flung open and once again they were taken before Suvorov.

'Tomorrow, we start for Moscow.' So at last it has begun, thought Henryk : the final road to Calvary.

'My men have something they would like to show you.' Suvorov nodded his dismissal. Outside stood an iron cage on snow-runners; the sort of cage usually occupied by some unfortunate performing bear where he could be pelted with mud by the street urchins, or prodded by long sticks thrust through the bars.

'That's for you, Cossack,' shouted the soldiers. 'In that you can ride in style to Moscow. In a style befitting our late lamented Tsar, Peter the Third.'

'And you who call yourself Borodin, will ride behind. You are no longer a fit companion for an Emperor.' Again the guffaws of merciless laughter. 'But,' said a sergeant with a thin, drawn face, 'so that you can perhaps think about the error of your ways and look back on your crimes you will ride facing the way you have come.'

This evoked gales of mirth. But the Russians got little

satisfaction from their taunts and laughter for neither Henryk nor Pugachev showed the slightest reaction. Annoyed, the sergeant shouted : 'Throw the swine back into their pig-sty. In a day or two they'll be singing a different tune.'

* * *

The sky was blue when the procession set out for Moscow.

In front rode a detachment of the Cavalry of the Imperial Guard, sending up a fine spray of snow from their polished hooves.

Then came the iron cage, drawn by ten horses. In it crouched a figure in a mass of rags and cloths, a few pieces of moth-eaten fur. 'We don't want him to die before Red Square.'

On each side of the cage were lancers with sharpened lances. If they wanted him to cry out it was simple for them to prod his body with pointed steel. Not that it gave them any satisfaction for Pugachev never uttered a whimper. Soon they got bored and turned to the man bound, facing the horse's tail : the classic indignity.

They taunted Henryk; they cursed him with every obscenity in the Russian language, but, having felt the knout of the Secret Chancery and the lash of the bos'ns' mates in the British Navy, he was able to close his mind to the present and let it wander free, to where it would always arrive—Kasia.

Give me a sabre, he often thought, and I'd cut these cattle to small pieces. Since I have no sabre, then ignore them.

* * *

At nights everything was the same.

Pugachev remained in his cage, gnawing at the scraps of food thrown to him. When the cold increased they gave him blankets. 'We don't want you to die before Red Square.' That was the extent of their mercy.

Henryk they put into any shelter they could find not occupied by the Imperial Guards.

And next morning the whole ghastly charade began again. He was put on to the Cossack pony: his ankles were tied beneath the animal's belly; his wrists held together, very tightly, and he faced towards the way they had ridden the day before.

In the villages the soldiers shouted to the inhabitants to come out and see the rebels who had caused such fire and slaughter; to throw muck at them; to enjoy themselves. But no one came to spit, nor to throw anything at these two men.

And the commander of the Imperial Cavalry grew more and more angry.

'Are these peasant serfs not grateful for what we have done?'

'Burn them out,' urged his second-in-command. 'That's all they're good for.'

In one village there had been heard the muffled cries of: 'God bless the Cossack,' and 'He's not the one who should die.'

When the dawn broke the snow melted in the heat of the flames which had burnt the little village to ashes.

'Perhaps,' said the commander, 'they will now understand.'

As they came closer to Moscow the picture changed. In every village the people came out to jeer and, not only to jeer, but to hurl clods of frozen earth at the creature in the cage. The fact that some had been paid to do this was not spoken about.

Pugachev hid himself under his mass of rags as they came to spit on him and revile him as 'The Anti-Christ'.

Henryk, bound to his horse, could not hide. His face was bruised and cut from the lumps of earth and dung which flew at him from the hands of these mindless brutes. He had endured worse on battlefields, at sea—at least these were not made of iron. But he wished he could have had Jan, Nym, and many others, including his gun-crew from *Huntress*, beside him now. Between them they could have shown these fancy soldiers of the Imperial Guard a trick or two.

The snow grew heavier as they approached Moscow; the cold harder. Was it colder than Catherine's heart? For Kasia he would beg, entreat, implore. To save her life he would grovel. But his wife would not be like that; she would rather die.

Henryk endured another shrieking torment of abuse and the hard blows of objects hurled at him from the anonymity of snowflakes. He faced backwards, like a tortured clown, lowering his head to avoid the frozen filth.

Moscow came closer and closer. The next day they saw the spires of the Kremlin and the little timber houses of the outskirts.

'There you are, Cossack. Take a look at your last resting place.' The cavalrymen poked at Pugachev with their lances and the blood froze as it oozed from the small, sharp wounds. But still he did not speak.

'Have you nothing to say to us? Have you no gratitude to us for escorting Your Imperial Majesty over these long and weary miles?'

In answer Pugachev spat through the bars, and huddled back into his nest of verminous rags.

'And you, my proud Pole, the great Borodin, have you nothing to say?' Henryk winced from the pain of the lance point in his back.

'If you're half as brave against a real armed enemy as you are against two helpless men, then Russia has nothing to fear.' For that he got a blow across his head that knocked him unconscious, held to the horse only by his bonds.

They reached the end of that nightmare as dusk was falling over the city.

The escort turned them over to the Kremlin guards and rode off to find food, drink and a warm night in the arms of big-breasted Muscovite girls.

For them the long, agonizing ride was over. For the two men left shivering in the snow while their gaolers took as long as they could over finding keys and writing down details they already knew by heart, it was the beginning of a new, apparently endless nightmare.

Chapter Four

PULAWY, the magnificent country palace of the Czartoryskis, was situated in the small part of the country still able to call itself the Kingdom of Poland; the part ruled nominally by Stanislas Poniatowski but in reality by Catherine's ambassador to Warsaw. Set in the middle of a vast estate Adam Czartoryski ruled as he and his forebears had done for centuries, their home more of a Court than a nobleman's house. A Lord Chamberlain, major domos, butlers and footmen by the score; servants by the hundred and anything up to twenty thousand serfs living and working in the villages of Pulawy.

Politically the family had been, if not exactly pro-Russia, at least they believed in working for peace with their mighty neighbour instead of ceaseless, useless war. For that they were labelled contemptuously 'Catherine's Court Jesters', and bitter jokes were told among the Confederates and all those who hated the Russian Empress and despised King Poniatowski.

'But, Aunt Constantia, how *can* you say that the Confederates were wrong to take up arms? You mean that Henryk was wrong, is that it?'

The two women were in a small sheltered arbour in a corner of one of the vast gardens. As they sat for a moment without speaking, Kasia heard voices, children's laughter; somewhere far off a girl sang a gay Polish song. It was always like that here, she had to admit; always laughter and song and children playing, for the place teemed with Czartoryski relations who always seemed to be changing; as soon as one lot departed another batch would arrive and the endless round of pleasure and luxury would continue unbroken.

'Was all that bloodshed essential, my dear? In the end, what did it achieve?'

'At least it is better to fight even if you lose,' said Kasia hotly.

'And all those people who had to die, were their deaths necessary?' Her aunt spoke very gently. She loved her niece and knew what it must be like for her to sit and smile and be continuously polite when her heart was hundreds of miles away with Henryk who rode the savage eastern steppes of Russia, still fighting his stubborn forlorn battle among a gang of murderous cut-throat Cossacks and Tatars. Secretly she thought his action to be selfish; after all, did he not have a son as well as this ravishing wife. Kasia, of course, defended his decision with the hot loyalty Constantia would have expected from her sister's daughter. She laid her embroidery in the lap of her very wide, slightly old-fashioned skirt and lay back in the garden chair, shutting her eyes.

Kasia was very like her mother, both in looks and character. More forceful perhaps, more defiant, a little more arrogant in argument; but who could blame her after what she had been through. Her Mother, Marie Radienska, had after all led a sheltered life at Volochisk somewhere in the wilds of the Ukraine. Sometimes the sisters met in Warsaw when Jan Radienski went to make one of his hot-tempered speeches at the Diet, but gradually, through the years, they had drifted apart. Marie had become ill, always tired and listless and—Kasia saw an expression of pain twist her aunt's face. But not physical pain, rather that of some unbearable mental pang.

And then the unspeakable tragedy of Volochisk. Her hands tightened on the arms of the chair as she prayed, as she had prayed so often, that her sister had died quickly.

There had been a son, Jacek. But no one knew what had become of him. And now another smaller Jacek played with the other children in the garden. She prayed for him too.

Aunt Constantia opened her eyes and, sitting up briskly, began deftly to ply her needle with speed. What was done was done and it did nobody any good to succumb to memories. No good at all. Enjoy, Constantia, the sounds of children at play. She had never married. There had been a young man, a lancer of the Royal Guard, but he had to ride to war, proud and confident—and did not return. Now, Constantia, pull yourself together.

'Jacek is enjoying being here,' she said. 'Among children of his own kind.'

'He is happy at Lipno.'

Her aunt shot her a swift glance from under hooded eyelids. So she too was remembering.

'Oh, I know he's happy. Very happy. He's told me so. But a change from the village boys will do him no harm.' The flash of her needle paused. 'In the basket, Kasia. A thread to match this tulip.' The flowers coming to glowing, lustrous life on the canvas, were the work of a superb artist.

'Yes,' said her aunt firmly. 'The change will do him good.'

'It's sad you never came here before, my dear. But I can understand. I think we all do. It would not have been easy for you. Henryk would never have come?' She asked almost wistfully.

'No Aunt. I'm afraid he wouldn't.'

After a long silence Constantia said, 'I've asked you before, Kasia. I ask you again. Why must you always call me "Aunt"? It makes me feel older than Noah, or Noah's wife. I've no idea what she was called. Have you?'

'None at all. Something like Bathsheba or Shalah. I don't know.' They both laughed.

'That's one of the things I like about you,' said Constantia. 'You laugh, you don't simper or giggle, you really laugh.' She looked at the wide mouth and the little crooked tooth that was somehow so much an added attraction. There must have been many men mad with love for this woman, she thought.

'Thank you, Aunt—'

'Ah-ah.' Constantia wagged her finger.

'Thank you, C-constantia.'

'Tell me, Kasia. This impediment of yours, does it bother you badly?'

'No, not really. I've got used to it. Besides it only comes on if I'm ill or tired.'

Or worried, thought her aunt, finishing off the small, crimson tulip. She sat back, her head on one side, her round red face shining with pleasure.

'Yes,' she said in a satisfied tone. 'Yes, that is not too bad, not too bad at all.' She must have been attractive in her youth, Kasia suddenly decided. She had lovely eyes, a sort of mauvy-blue and a wry, humorous twist of her lips. Unlike most of the grand ladies of her age and upbringing, she wore no rouge, no colouring on her lips, just a touch of powder on her cheeks which, unfortunately, had caked in the heat.

Her body was stout, her tall white wig always slightly crooked, but she no longer cared about such petty trifles. She was fun to talk to, and wise as well. And a great one for suddenly springing surprise questions. But Kasia was totally unprepared for the one that followed.

'By the way, does the King know Henryk?'

'The King? Henryk? I d-don't know. They may perhaps have met—perhaps when—' When they were both in St Petersburg, she thought. But Aunt Constantia knew nothing of that affair between the three of them. No, the four of them, including herself. Henryk, Stanislas Poniatowski, Catherine and Kasia.

Then she remembered. Of course they had met. At Volochisk. When they were all very young, and Catherine was still little Sophia von Anhalt-Zerbst; 'Figgy', to them. She told all this to her aunt.

'I remember Stanislas, that is, His Majesty.' Constantia detected the scorn in her voice. 'I remember he would never come out in the snow with us or ride or climb trees and things. He was always cooped-up in his room poring over French books.'

'He knows about Henryk's part in the Confederacy?'

'I have no idea,' said Kasia coldly. 'I imagine so.'

'Then you will have your answers ready, my dear, should His Majesty—' Kasia saw a quick glint of a smile in the mauvy-blue eyes, caught the inflection of her voice.

'—enquire about your husband.'

'Why should he enquire about my husband?'

'Because, Kasia, the King is coming to stay at Pulawy at the beginning of next month.' After a long pause she said.

'You can always make your excuses and go back to Lipno.' She saw the answering flash in the blue eyes; the flash she used to see in Marie's eyes.

'No.' Kasia thumped the arm of her chair. 'No. Why should I run away from—from—'

'Don't say any more. There is no need. I think I understand. Now, before we are interrupted, for I hear the loud and melodious voice of your son rapidly approaching, let us get one thing settled once and for all. Only you, your brother-in-law, Adam, and I, know the whereabouts and the present activities of your husband. Is that correct?'

'Yes.' Well, almost. Kasia did not mention Dmitri.

And now Adam had gone to join his brother, to prove himself a soldier and with him had ridden Jan Dombrowski and Sergeant Nym.

'We have fought beside him so often,' Jan had said to her with his wide grin.

'Yes,' added Nym, 'Count Henryk needs us to look after him. Why without us he's like a babe in arms.'

But this she did not tell her aunt.

'Very well then, that is how it shall be.' She picked up the needle. 'A strand of yellow, the deep yellow.' She threaded the needle. 'You do trust me, Kasia?'

'Of course I do, you know that.' Kasia got up and kissed her aunt on both cheeks.

'There, that'll do.' With a sharp exclamation she jabbed the needle into her finger.

'Now look what you've made me do.' But beneath her lowered lashes her eyes were moist.

With a loud burst of shrill sound Jacek burst in upon them.

'Mama, Mama, look.'

'I can see,' said Kasia. His velvet suit, so unlike what he wore daily at home, was dirty and torn across the knees; his face was streaked with dust and sweat.

'We climbed the pear trees on the wall. I fell off and—'

'I can see that,' said Kasia. How Henryk would have loved this.

'But it's been fun,' said Constantia. She looked at the dark curls, the small eager face, tanned by the suns and winds of four years; the deep blue eyes and what promised to be the same wide mouth as that of his mother.

'Oh, yes, Aunt Constantia.' He was not always altogether successful with her name.

'It would seem', she said to Kasia, 'that you have greater problems on your mind at the moment than the arrival of His Majesty. That dirt seems to have stuck fast.'

As Kasia took her son by the hand and stood up to escort him for yet another cleaning, she said, 'Thank you, Constantia. With all my heart, I thank you.'

Her aunt simply nodded, bent low over her work. But to herself she whispered, 'God, take care of them, these three. Take care of them and allow them some happiness together.'

* * *

The King of Poland came to Pulawy. He came to be entertained. In the hunting-field; in the drawing-rooms; in the ballroom. He was Stanislas Poniatowski, by the Grace of God—and Catherine of Russia—King of Poland. His entourage stretched all the way back to Warsaw, Kasia thought as she watched the Royal arrival through the thick cover of shrubbery.

'Ooh, Mama, who's that man getting out of the coach?'

'That's the King, darling.'

'Why is everyone bowing and curtseying?'

'Because he's the King, Jacek.'

'Ooh.'

She watched the curtseying and the bowing, and caught only a quick glimpse of the figure that vanished into the depths of Pulawy.

'What's a King, Mama?'

'A King?' She pretended to search for a different thread. 'Well, a King is someone who can make everyone do what he says.' For a while Jacek was silent. Kasia thought of her husband: the father of their son. The man who was this King's enemy.

'Could he tell me why Mayflies only last such a short time?'

'I'm sure he could,' she said with all the assurance she could muster.

'Ooh, he must be a nice man.'

To this she did not answer.

* * *

That night there was a ball. There was also a thunder-storm. In the ballroom the heat was almost intolerable.

'Do you remember the ball in the Winter Palace?' the King asked Kasia. He was dressed in immaculate finery: a coat of dark blue watered silk; a milk-white wig—everything gleaming, shining: all the stars, the sashes, the jewels on his podgy white fingers.

So this is the King of Poland, Kasia thought. This is Stanislas Poniatowski. But not the same person as I used to know; not the studious youth who used to stay in his room reading while the others: Catherine—little 'Figgy'—Henryk, Adam and herself rode or climbed trees or played in the snow at Volochisk. This surely could not be the man to whom Catherine had lost her heart?

His good looks had almost vanished beneath a heavy coating of fat; his face had a blotchy, dissipated appearance and his once luminous blue eyes were faded and slightly bloodshot.

She had noticed that he had his glass refilled very often and that he was never entirely still. As he talked his head turned this way and that as if he was continually on the watch for something.

'Yes, sir,' she said, remembering well how he had obliquely offered her love.

'It was hot that night.'

There had been a thousand candles lighting the ballroom of the Winter Palace. Tonight there must be double that number. She could see the sweat caking the powder on the women's faces and feel it trickling from her armpits. The King mopped cautiously at his face.

'If the night had been fine we could have walked in the gardens, cousin.'

Even his smile had lost its charm. A smile that Catherine had once described as the most radiant in the world.

The music had stopped and above the loud monkey-chatter of the huge gilded room she heard the rumble of thunder.

Outside, the horses twisted and jumped nervously in the shafts of the great coaches as the lightning struck from the blackness down into the ground and the rain fell as a solid wall of water.

The King motioned with his glass and at once a footman in gorgeous livery was there to refill it with *tokay*, the rich, golden drink of Hungary.

'You do not drink, cousin?' In his eyes she could see the look she had seen in the Winter Palace all those years ago.

'Only on special occasions,' she said.

'And is this not a special occasion?' His voice had sharpened.

'Of course, sir.' She glanced down to hide the contempt in her eyes. In the old days this man, this King, had been slim and handsome and very desirable to women but now they came to him because he wore a crown.

He summoned the footman. 'A glass for Countess Radienska.'

The man bowed. 'At once, Your Majesty.'

'Barinska, sir,' said Kasia. 'My name is Barinska.'

For a moment the King looked puzzled then he laughed, showing yellow teeth with three gaps. 'Of course. How stupid of me. And how is . . . ?' He paused, at a loss.

'Henryk,' she said gently. 'I think you may remember him from the old days at Volochisk.'

'Yes. Henryk. Dark, curly hair. A young devil with the girls even in those days. How is he? Where is he?' He looked round the huge, crowded room, taking in the blaze of colour; the magnificent dresses of silk and brocade; the velvet suits and white stockings; the dazzling sparkle of the jewels; the swift movement of the pictured fans and the tall feathers in the women's white-powdered hair.

The flames of the candles fluttered in the breeze of many hundreds of fans.

'A small toast, cousin.' She raised her glass to his, watched curiously by dozens of eyes.

'To us,' he said wistfully. 'Before we all became Empresses and Kings.' At that moment, as she sipped the sweet, thick wine, she felt sorry for this man who had been forced into kingship.

Behind the fans many questions were being asked. 'Who is she?' ... 'I've never seen her before' ... 'How much longer is she going to spend in his company?'

And the men too wondered. 'By God, it's worth being a King' ... 'and those shoulders' ... 'And everything else.' There was muffled laughter. They watched as a courtier approached the King and was waved away. 'He's not going to give her up ...' 'And do you blame him?'

'Kasia?'

'Sir.' She was trying to stifle her revulsion at the sickly Hungarian wine; even raw Cossack vodka was preferable to this stuff.

'I have been looking very carefully and so far—' he smiled, and, for the first time she saw traces of the old charm—'I have seen no woman in this vast, great room who even begins to rival you.'

'That is a great compliment, sir.'

'It is not a compliment. I mean it.'

She smiled with her wide mouth.

'You and I are roughly the same age.' He waved away another courtier.

'Sir,' she said, 'ought you not to ...'

'No, cousin. I ought not. That's one advantage to being a King; people have to obey you.' He emptied his glass and signalled for more. 'But you, you would obey no one unless you wanted to. That I do remember. Except perhaps your husband.'

He sighed. 'If there's a man I really envy, it is Henryk Barinski.'

She looked superb, he thought. Her hair shining like black ice in the moonlight, bright as the diamonds round her smooth white neck, white satin dipping down into the curving slope of her shoulders and the little dark shadow between her breasts.

Her dark blue eyes regarded him steadily. This woman

did not frighten easily. He had never seen such splendid eyes.

'They match your dress,' he said.

'Sir?'

'Your eyes, Kasia, your eyes.'

'You are paying compliments again.' She said the words without any trace of coquetry.

For a little while he was silent. The music had started again and he watched the colourful sweep of the *mazurka*, tapping his foot to the tune.

Kasia watched too, thinking of Henryk. While she sat, the King's cousin, the King's favourite, in the comfortable splendour of this palace, how was Henryk spending this night of rain and thunder? Where was he? How was he? Oh God, how was he?

'Is there anything wrong?' She heard the King's voice from miles away.

'You look—well, strange.'

'No, there's nothing wrong. Just the heat, I think. That's all.'

The dance came to an end. Everyone bowed to everyone else and the fans broke into renewed activity.

'I don't think I heard your answer about Henryk.'

The King's sudden remark startled her but she gave no sign. 'He's in England.'

'England?' The King put his glass on the marble table. 'And what, may I ask, is he doing there?'

'Trying to interest the English in Polish horses.'

He smoothed his smooth blue breeches. 'Ah yes, I had heard something of this. You have started to build a stud farm at your home. Is that correct?'

She nodded.

'A very praiseworthy idea. And do you manage to sell many horses to the English?'

For the first time she noticed a shrewd look in his eyes.

'This is our first attempt,' she said.

She sensed the growing agitation among the courtiers and ladies-in-waiting grouped behind them; she saw the worried looks between her Czartoryski cousins, and she smiled to herself. It meant nothing to her and, for a brief moment, the country cousin was basking in glory.

The crash of thunder was directly overhead. Many painted faces glanced up at the painted ceiling as though expecting another Pompeii.

'A nasty storm.'

'Yes,' Kasia's thoughts were miles away. Somewhere Henryk was lying out in this, perhaps wounded, perhaps . . .

'And when does he return to Poland?'

Kasia pulled her wits together. 'In a month, two months. It all depends on the English.'

'I see.' Again he held out his glass.

'He must know the English well,' he said thickly. 'Five years, or was it seven, in the British Navy must have taught him a lot about those strange people.' He stared at her over his glass. 'You look surprised. My dear, a King is like a spider. He collects information as the spider collects flies. I know a lot about your husband. He also served in the French army, fighting against the Prussians at Rossbach. Am I right?'

'Yes.' Once again his glass was refilled.

'This husband of yours, he's led an adventurous life.' He glanced briefly at the gay, coloured movements of the dancers and she remembered how short-sighted he was. Probably he saw nothing. 'Would you not rather he was with you and not in England?'

In the ranks behind them a stampede was almost building up.

'Of course.'

After a silence he said: 'I said I envy him. I envy you both. I would have liked to be that sort of man.' His face seemed to crumple as she watched it. 'Rather than a King.'

Kasia did not answer.

'You know what's happening in Russia?'

'No.' His question startled her. Her heart began to thump and she had to draw deep breaths.

'Well, you know there has been this trouble?'

'What trouble, sir?' Her eyes were innocent as those of a baby.

He stared fixedly into the *tokay* in his glass.

'It seems,' he said, 'that some damned Cossack rebel started a revolt against Catherine—against the Empress. It spread among the common people and has become a peasant war.' Kasia thought of the common people of Zimoveskaya: some good, some bad. She looked round the unbelievable richness of the room and remembered the small hut where she had lain with Pugachev and borne their son.

Soon, very soon, she would have to leave.

'There is a man with this rebel who calls himself by a Russian name.' His eyes roamed across the dancers, seeing little but a blur of colour.

'A Russian name.' He circled his fingers round the edge of the glass. 'Now I remember it. Borodin. He is the man who has advised this—bandit, who has helped this Cossack to reach almost as far as Moscow.'

Kasia was far away, with Borodin, with her husband, not caring on whose side he was, only that he came home to her.

'And what do you think, pretty cousin?'

The lightning must have been directly overhead for the candle-flames shook wildly and the crash of the thunder was louder than a ship's broadside.

'I don't know,' she said. 'I have never heard of this—what do you call it—this revolt?'

'Well, this is happening, in Russia. There is bloodshed, fire, murder—anything you like to think of—it is all going on.'

'How awful.'

'Yes,' he said. 'We are lucky here in Poland that the war is over. And, if rumour is to be believed, this petty revolt has not lasted long.' She felt a sudden stab of fear.

'You mean that the C-Cossack has b-been defeated?' The King looked at her with surprise. It was the first time she had stammered throughout their conversation; peering more closely still he saw how pale she had gone.

'We have no reliable news yet, nothing official from Petersburg but it seems there was a battle on the Volga near some place called—called—oh, it doesn't matter. What matters is that the rebels appear to have been soundly beaten by Suvorov, or General Panin, one of them anyway.'

She had to cling to the arms of her chair to prevent herself from swaying. She felt violently sick and thought she was going to faint.

'Yes,' he repeated. 'Soundly beaten and the leaders on their way to Moscow, or so we have heard. To Moscow and a most unpleasant death, for Catherine cannot afford to pardon men who have taken up arms against her. No Sovereign can afford—why, Kasia, what's the matter? You're not well. Quickly someone, she's ill.'

Her cousin Natalie hurried forward.

'Kasia, my dear, what is it?'

'It's n-nothing, the heat—' Everything was spinning. Desperately she clung to the chair, willing herself not to faint.

'Water, a glass of water. Quickly!' She drank the water and the dizziness calmed, but her heart was beating so hard and fast that she almost expected it to leap from her body.

'Your Majesty,' said Natalie 'may she be excused? I think she should go to bed.'

'Of course, of course.' The King sounded really concerned. 'She did complain about the heat but I never thought—oh dear, the poor creature. I am very sorry.'

'Elizabeth. Teresa. Help Kasia to her room and see that she is put straight to bed.' Natalie's two sisters helped her from the chair. Though swaying on her feet she insisted on curtseying to the King who patted her hand. 'Never mind, my dear. A good night's sleep and you'll be fine. Won't she, Natalie?'

'Yes, sire.'

The King watched until Kasia's blue and silver dress faded to the usual blur which was all he could see beyond a certain distance.

'Most distressing,' he kept muttering, half to himself. 'Was it something I said, d'you suppose?'

'I am sure it wasn't,' said Natalie soothingly.

'Very sad. A lovely woman, our cousin. Very lovely.'

It was not the heat, Aunt Constantia decided. It *was* something the King had said; of that she was certain. She was ensconced in her favourite chair contentedly watching the dancing just close enough to the King to have heard the name Borodin and something about death in Moscow.

She slowly swished her fan. Aunt Constantia was not nearly so deaf as she was inclined to make out, nor so blind either.

Poor child. She would go and visit her in the morning and they would talk. Perhaps she could be of some comfort.

But if anything had happened to Henryk no one in the world could be of any comfort. That she did know.

She looked over her fan at the woman who had taken Kasia's place. Another pretty lady, she thought, but compared to Kasia no more than a painted doll.

But the King seemed pleased enough.

* * *

Upstairs, in her huge four-poster bed, Kasia lay staring into the darkness. Faintly, through the curtains, she saw the fading flashes of the lightning and the distant grumble of the thunder. The rain still dripped monotonously from the roof. Down below, the dull drone of the music rang through her brain.

She tried to close her eyes but they would not stay shut.

They opened and, in the blackness, she saw strange and terrible visions.

Ever since her escape from Zimoveskaya and her journey through the rain and snow of the early autumn, she had suffered from these recurrent fevers that sent her temperature soaring and filled her mind with strange, mad shapes. Fatigue, worry, ordinary sickness—any of these could bring on these attacks.

She could feel the heat building up inside her body; a dry burning heat like that which comes with the 'spotted fever'.

Soon she was flinging herself about and crying out wildly. Taking it in turns, the two sisters came in to sponge her forehead with vinegar and water and try to soothe her, for they loved her as if she was their own mother.

In the sound of the receding storm she heard the thunder of guns; she called out Henryk's name over and over again. At one moment in the middle of the night they had to hold her down.

Aunt Constantia came to help, shuffling in her old-fashioned night gown. 'How is she?'

They shook their heads. 'She's not going to die?'

They looked at her dumbly.

'No,' she said firmly. 'She's not going to die. Not Kasia.'

She insisted on sitting by the bed, very frightened for all her brave words, until her niece dropped off to sleep. However good her intentions she was an old woman and it was four o'clock in the morning.

And, above the palace of Pulawy, the thunderstorm drifted slowly away into a distant flicker of light deep down on the horizon. Soon the dawn rose, waking Jacek to his usual high spirits. But on this particular morning he was not allowed to go tearing into his mother's room.

'She's not feeling very well, Jacek dear. She wants to sleep. Come and play with the others.' All right, he thought, Mama wants to sleep. I'll go out and play in the sunshine and then, when she wakes up, I'll go and play on her bed.

The morning went by, and the afternoon and still he was not allowed to go and play on her bed. For two days he was not allowed to see her.

At the peak of the fever she knew no one, had no idea where she was. Her mind was filled with fantasies, but somewhere in the middle of every fantasy were visions of Henryk, so clear that she would call his name and stretch out her hand to touch him.

Aunt Constantia slept during the day but insisted on sitting up with her at night, wiping her forehead with damp cloths, trying to soothe her wild outbursts.

During the second night they thought she was going to die.

All through the night Kasia called for her husband.

'Henryk! Henryk! Oh, my God, please let him come to me. Please.'

'My poor child,' whispered her aunt. 'Oh, my poor child.'

Then, on the third day Jacek was allowed to see his mother.

'Hello, Mama,' he said shyly, clambering on to the bed and taking her hand. She kissed him.

'Why wouldn't they let me see you?'

'I wasn't very well. But I'm all right now. Tell me, what have you been doing?'

'I helped to finish the tree-house and then we had to catch Katya's pet rabbit and . . .' She listened happily as he chattered away. Unless he completely changed he was going to be the image of his father: the same dark, curly hair and blue eyes.

But through his excited descriptions of life at Pulawy, she kept remembering the words of the King: '. . . to Moscow . . . an unpleasant death . . .'

Later that evening she said to her aunt: 'We must go back to Lipno. You do understand, don't you?'

'Of course I understand.' Aunt Constantia took her hand. 'But not until you are strong enough.'

'But—'

'No buts, Kasia.'

'He may come home. Don't you see, he may come home.'

'And when he comes home you must be there. That I understand. I have spoken to Natalie.'

* * *

Five days later Kasia and her son arrived home after an exhausting journey, changing horse teams time after time; a few hours of snatched sleep. At first Jacek was excited and enthralled by everything he saw from the coach windows, but now he lay, curled up in a corner, out to the world. Every delay or pause drove her almost crazy.

At one time they were held up by a column of Austrian infantry. They drove with the windows closed against the dust raised by the marching boots.

For a while Jacek was fascinated by the tap of the drums and the colourful uniforms and the sun glinting from the bayonets, but soon he began to complain about the heat building up inside the coach.

It was not until the infantry turned off down a side road that the coach could pick up speed again and they could open the windows.

'What were those soldiers doing, Mama?'

'I expect they were just having a march. I don't know.'

'The Polish soldiers are the best, aren't they?' She nodded. The coach lurched heavily into a bad pothole. 'They were very smart,' he said proudly. 'Yes, darling.'

How long would it be before Polish soldiers would once again march along their own roads?

* * *

The coach rumbled into the cobbled yard of Lipno.

And then the crying, the welcome home, the warm sympathy and comfort for Jacek.

'Let me take him, Kasia.' Old Katushka came forward to the coach and took the sleeping child from her arms.

Stepan hobbled about to the best of his ability, getting in the way and talking too much.

'No one is here?'

Maryshka Nym shook her head. Dmitri shook his head.

'Not yet,' he said. 'But do not worry. He will come back. Borodin will always come back.'

But the days passed and no one came back. Even Dmitri was beginning to doubt.

Kasia tried desperately to concentrate on the stud-farm. Dmitri, who understood her problem more than anyone, tried his best to help and comfort her.

'Look at this stallion ... And these mares, how well they are doing ... Now, what d'you think should be done here? A new fence? Or a larger paddock?'

Looking at her, he thought: she's miles away. Many, many miles away. Looking for her husband to appear. He was a Cossack; she was a Pole: an aristocratic Pole but they were friends. Suddenly an entirely new thought entered his head: why should they not all be friends?

'Could I ask you something?' he asked.

'Of course, Dmitri.'

They were riding back from the paddocks and the stables.

'Do we always have to be enemies?'

'Enemies, Dmitri? What do you mean by that?'

For a while they rode in silence.

'Well, do we always have to be on opposite sides?'

He rode in silence.

'No, we don't,' she said. 'Why should we?'

'That's what I hoped.'

Then she said, 'Thank you for all you have done for this place. That new fencing is a wonderful idea.' The horses cantered along the fence, keeping pace with them, puffs of snow flying from their hooves; soon, when the sun began to go down, they would be taken into their warm stables; their bran and their hay. For the moment they were enjoying their freedom.

'I hope you will stay with us. Dmitri.'

'Yes,' he said, 'I shall stay.' He shouted at a mare which ran too close to the fence, threatening to cut herself on the rough woodwork. 'Go on, you stupid animal, get out of it. Go on!' He waved his whip and the horse shied away, snorting.

'You love them, don't you?'

'Love them?' He thought for a moment. 'Well yes, I suppose I do. I've always loved horses.' He laughed. 'I don't know what we'd do without the stupid creatures,' he added fondly.

'Dmitri?'

'Yes.' He was always respectful but had never overburdened himself with 'Your Honours or Excellencies'.

'They are not the only thing you love at Lipno.' He reddened. 'Am I not right?'

He nodded, for once quite speechless.

'She's a lovely girl,' said Kasia. 'And she'll make you a wonderful wife. I'm glad for you both.'

'So you know?'

'Yes, I know. There's not much that goes on in Lipno that doesn't reach my ears sooner or later.' Fat snow-clouds were slowly rising above the eastern horizon, tinged flamingo-pink by the lowering sun.

'You've chosen well, Dmitri. I have known Sonya since she was about fourteen. And I've known her parents.'

'I thought there might be trouble, me being a Cossack but . . .'

'They've taken you to their hearts.'

'And me a Cossack. Not that I'm not proud of it,' he said challengingly. 'But, well, you know how it is. I'm not a Catholic like all of you. How are we going to get married? That's what worries me. How are we going to get married?'

Kasia did not answer. She remembered a conversation

from years ago, within the sound of the Don . . . 'we must be married. Under the willow tree, in the Cossack way . . .'

And now the man who had said that was defeated and the man she loved with all her being was . . .

From far away she heard Dmitri's voice.

'Tell me, please,' he asked very humbly. 'You're a grand lady, very educated. Does it matter how you are married? Provided God approves.'

'No,' Kasia said without hesitation. 'No, I don't think it does.' The first snow-flake touched her face. 'It is time to get them in.'

For a moment they forgot their private worries.

'Yes,' he agreed, glancing at the sky. 'It's going to be heavy. I'll get those idle grooms out of their snug stables.'

'It'll do them good,' she said. They both laughed and she rode slowly towards the house.

* * *

Through the thickening snow Kasia saw two riders and behind them more, hunched in the saddles.

'Dmitri!' But he had reached the stables and did not answer.

'Who are you?' She gripped the whip more tightly, wondering how to warn the village.

'Kasia!' Vaguely she recognized the voice. 'Kasia!'

The snow was very thick now, blotting out the sunset.

And then, through the white curtain there appeared the leading riders. Both were slumped forward in their saddles; the horses could hardly stand. Round the head of the second rider she could see the red circlet of bloody cloth.

'Maryshka,' she called as loud as she could. 'Maryshka!' For she recognized the larger man as Sergeant Nym, his face caked with frozen blood. Behind him rode Jan Dombrowski. A trail of horsemen followed them, half visible through the drifting snow.

But, however hard she stared through the snow she could not see the man she was praying for. 'Please', she begged, 'please'. But nothing came from Heaven but the snow.

Maryshka Nym came running from the house, crying out her husband's name.

He fell from his horse, frozen and weak.

'Dmitri! Send for Dmitri!' Even in her bitter sorrow, Kasia remembered the horses, horses, she learned later, that had carried them for ten terrible days and nights.

The other Poles who had ridden to safety with these two, climbed slowly off their beasts. Some slumped to the ground; others hung on to the stirrups.

'Bring them into the house, Maryshka. Stepan! Stepan, where are you? Katushka, hot food, drink, blankets. Fetch the girls, tell them to prepare beds! Hurry!' And all the time her heart was frozen as hard as the ground beneath her feet.

He was not there. Henryk had not come home.

* * *

They put up long trestle tables in the barn: the barn where the guests had eaten and danced after her marriage to Henryk. But this time there was no dancing or singing. Thirty men, all that had come back from Russia out of three hundred, ate ravenously and drank till their heads fell forward on to the table, but they ate and drank in almost total silence, too exhausted for speech, let alone laughter.

Their horses munched slowly at the sweet-smelling hay and fell asleep.

Kasia's servant girls were appalled by the men's appearance. Haggard, grey, with sunken eyes outlined by heavy black shadows: eyes that showed hardly a spark of life.

The girls had never seen anything so sad. They did their best to help the men to the warm comfort of the hay, bringing blankets. Some of the survivors mumbled their thanks but most of them just collapsed into snoring comas.

'My God,' said one of the girls, 'what they must have been through.'

'At least they are alive and safe,' said one of the others.

'Not like—' she stopped.

'Not like Count Adam and Count Henryk, you mean?'

'Yes.'

* * *

Kasia sat in silence at the head of her table, her face a pale, hard mask.

'But how do you *know* this? Did you see it happen, with your own eyes? Was he captured alone, or with Pugachev? Well?'

She knew it was not their fault that they were sitting at her table and Henryk was helpless in the hands of the Russians.

'No,' said Jan. 'We did not see it. But one of our men saw it happen. He was hiding in the marshes beyond the Volga; he had been hiding for days. Russian soldiers, guided by a treacherous Cossack, found where they were hiding—he and Pugachev. This Pole followed and watched.' Jan paused, glancing quickly at Nym; the latter nodded slightly.

'They were taken to the headquarters of Marshal Suvorov.'

'And then?' Kasia sat entirely motionless.

'Knowing the language, the Pole pretended to be a Russian peasant and got among the soldiers. He asked what would happen to the rebels—' Again Jan paused.

'Go on,' she said. 'Don't stop now.'

'They will be taken to Moscow and then it is up to the Empress.'

'Oh, my God.' Jan jumped to his feet, thinking she might faint.

'No, I'm all right.'

'This man,' she said, after a moment's pause, 'I should like to speak to him.'

'I'm afraid that's not possible. He's dead. He was shot and wounded by a Russian dragoon. He just managed to ride after us and find us—then he died.'

'But this—this p-p-poor man definitely told you what he had seen?'

'Yes,' Jan said.

'How was—were they to be t-taken to Moscow?'

'That he did not find out.'

'I see.' Jan and Nym watched her. Still the mask did not, would not crack.

Maryshka came back into the room.

'Jacek's asleep. So are the men in the stables.'

'Thank you, Maryshka.' Kasia got to her feet.

'And thank you all.' She inclined her head towards Jan and Nym, and his wife.

'Now, if you'll excuse me, I think I'll go to bed. Goodnight, my friends—my very dear friends.' The door closed behind her. The silence was broken by Sergeant Nym.

'A wonderful woman.' He blew his nose loudly.

'Yes,' said Jan, looking down into his glass.

Outside the door they heard Kasia break.

PART FIVE

Chapter One

MARYSHKA ran from the room. 'Come,' she said to Kasia, 'come, my dear—my poor dear.' It was no longer a question of rank and position : it was two women who were fond of each other, respected each other. And one wanted to comfort the other.

'What can we do,' asked Jan. 'What, in Hell's name, can we *do*?'

'Nothing,' said Sergeant Nym. 'We can't do a damned thing. And we know it.'

* * *

In the morning, after a sleepless night, Kasia had made up her mind. When Jacek came tearing into her room, she knew what she had to do.

'Mama, Mama, it's snowing again. Can I go sledging with the others?' The others were his friends in the village.

'Of course.' She stopped for a moment, wondering how to tell him. 'But only for today. Tomorrow we are going on a journey.'

'Oh, but Mama, why do we have to go away, just when the snow is getting right for the sledges and the sliding?'

'We're going to see Papa, darling.'

His eyes began to brim.

'There'll be lots and lots of sledging,' she tried to comfort him.

'Where,' he interrupted urgently. 'Where, Mama?'

'The place where we're going,' she said diplomatically. With that he seemed satisfied.

'What time are we starting? Is Maryshka coming? Is old Stepan coming? And Katushka?' She shook her head.

'No, Jacek. Just us two.'

'Is it a long way?' he asked. 'And what about Dmitri?'

'Yes, darling, it is. No, I'm afraid he'll have to stay here.'

She thought of all the snow-bound miles that stretched between Lipno and St Petersburg. The bug-ridden inns; the blizzards which could easily kill them; the Cossacks who could find them, stuck fast in the snow. But her courage never faltered.

They, she and her son, were going to St Petersburg, to demand audience with Her Imperial Majesty, Catherine, the Empress of Russia. 'Little Figgy', she thought sadly.

Because that was the only chance to save her husband's life—that was, if he were still alive.

She, Kasia Radienska, who had fought, who had killed, was prepared to go on her knees before 'little Figgy' to save Henryk's life. Her pride meant nothing; her courage meant nothing. She would crawl to anyone if it would save his life.

And so tomorrow they would leave.

There had been arguments. Jan and Nym had wanted to come with her.

'No, you have done enough. Stay here. Help Dmitri keep this place alive. Trust a Cossack this time, I beg of you. He won't let us down. Please.' They nodded. Sergeant Nym even smiled.

'Yes, we'll trust him—for your sake we'll trust him.'

'Soon we will be back—all three of us.' The men had not dared to look at each other.

In the morning she and her son got into the sledge and tucked themselves into the bearskin rugs.

'Take care of them,' said Jan to the driver. 'If you don't, then never come back to Lipno.'

'I understand.' The driver showed the musket and the

pistol and the dagger at his belt. 'I'll do my best.'

They drove away into a light flurry of snow, leaving many people weeping unashamedly.

'Oh, God in Heaven,' moaned Katushka. 'Oh, God in Heaven.'

'They will be all right. Don't you worry, they will be all right.' Maryshka tried to comfort the distracted old woman.

'But who will look after them?'

'They will be looked after,' said Sergeant Nym.

'Of course they will.' Jan Dombrowski saw the sun break through the snow-clouds. In the distance the sleigh was a black dot on a great white field of snow which was blinding in the sun.

* * *

They stopped at many uncomfortable inns. The snow got deeper, the winds more piercing. Sometimes Kasia took over the driving-seat. And, at these times, she began to understand how past experiences helped.

Then they came to Russia itself, and a Russian cavalry patrol. They were civil, correct but very firm.

Thank God she had brought Catherine's 'laissez-passer' of many years ago. On it was the signature of the Empress. The officer-in-charge was sufficiently impressed to let them through. He even saluted.

'They were nice men,' Jacek said sleepily.

'Yes, darling, weren't they?'

The snow got deeper, the cold more intense as they approached closer and closer to St Petersburg. And the pass, signed with the magic name of Catherine of Russia, allowed them through. Sometimes they were regarded with suspicion; sometimes, as Poles, with dislike, but, with that piece of paper in her hands, Kasia was never stopped.

And one morning when the sun was free of snow-clouds they saw the tall pinnacle of the Admiralty shining like a golden needle against the pale blue sky, and then the crooked spire of the St Peter and Paul fortress beyond the Neva.

She had many memories of this city; in some strange way it was like coming home. But, on this occasion, three lives depended on the journey, and, as the sledge bumped along the rutted streets, Kasia prayed for the wisdom, and the strength, to carry out her task.

'Where are we going, Mama? This is a huge place, isn't it? Where are we going?' Jacek's eyes were round with the wonder of it all. He had never seen so many people, nor heard so many different sounds: the street-vendors, the sledge-drivers cursing at each other; the bells of the great churches, but chiefly the masses of people.

'Ooh, Mama, look!' A great disturbance was going on round a charcoal stove at the corner of a street, where people were shouting and yelling; two men were rolling in the brown snow, fighting and struggling.

They passed grand sledges with occupants wrapped in furs of sable and mink; they passed an endless procession of people muffled in un-tanned leather and rags; they passed children hurling snowballs and sliding along strips of ice.

'Can't we stop,' he entreated. 'Please, can't we stop? It looks such fun.'

'Yes, darling, soon we'll stop.'

Her head was splitting, her feet were blocks of ice. In ten minutes or so they would turn into the great square overlooked by the Winter Palace; she would tell the sentries who she was, show her crumpled piece of paper—and wait. Would Catherine even see her? After all these years; after everything which had happened.

'Mama, there's a ship. Look, a ship with sails.' She saw the red sails beyond the embankment of the Neva as the sledge turned into the Winter Palace square.

There it stood, just the same; green and white, with the black iron railings round the roof and the black iron statues standing out against the green tiles. And there, beside the great doors stood the sentries of the Imperial Guard, enormous in their tall mitre hats.

The sleigh drew up at the doors.

The soldiers did not move but one called out something from the corner of his mouth. Nothing happened. After a pause he tried again, slightly louder. A sergeant appeared, pulling on his tunic. Nothing had changed, Kasia thought; the pomp, the grandeur—the slovenliness; the inefficiency, the courage. Nothing will ever change with these people.

'Yes?' The sergeant thrust his face inside the sleigh.

She held out the paper. 'I am Countess Radienska. I wish to see Her Imperial Majesty, the Empress of Russia.'

And this, she thought, is the only approach. Don't ask them; order them.

He looked at her with suspicion. She answered with a haughty smile.

'Please,' she said, softening the smile slightly. The man saw her face framed in the fur hood and heard the little squeaks of excitement from the small boy. He both appreciated a beautiful face and was a father.

'Very well,' he said. 'Wait here.' He vanished into the palace.

'Who lives here, Mama?'

'Someone called Catherine.'

'But does she need all this, just for herself? It's—it's—oh, it must be ten, a hundred times as big as Lipno. What a huge moustache that soldier had, didn't he, Mama?'

'Yes, darling, he did.' She tried desperately to sound calm and normal as she waited for the answer on which might depend the fate of Henryk, her husband, the father of this little wide-eyed boy. After an eternity another figure came slowly down the marble steps. This time it was an officer. He opened the door of the sleigh and said courteously.

'Please,' indicating the great doorway. Once they were inside, in the comparative warmth of the outer hallway he said. 'Forgive me, Madame, but—you claim acquaintanceship with Her Imperial Majesty?'

'If you count being her Lady-in-Waiting for five years then, yes, I am an acquaintance.' She smiled: her most radiant smile. The young man blushed.

'Of course, I had no idea.' But she knew that her name had reached Catherine. This was all part of a very necessary routine.

A man was walking very slowly down the broad staircase. She felt Jacek's small hand clutching very tightly and returned the pressure reassuringly.

'Kasia?'

For all her outward calm and poise the voice shocked her. He entered the circle of light thrown by the hallway candles.

'Lev!'

'Yes, Lev Bubin. The man who brought you to Petersburg all those years ago.' He stepped closer.

'My God, you have not changed.' He tried to take her hand but she kept it out of reach.

Jacek clutched even tighter. He did not like this man; she knew that.

'And what brings you back to our fair city?'

He was more poised, she thought, more assured of himself than when he had brought her from his home in the Province of Voronesh. As they slowly ascended the tiers of marble stairs Kasia remembered her time with this man in his shining brocade and silken embroidery, his smooth talk. The man, Count Lev Bubin, who had found her almost dead in the snow during her attempted escape from the Don back to Poland. The man who had made her his mistress and brought her to the Court of the Empress Elizabeth; the Grand Ducal Court of Catherine and Peter and, finally, to the side of the new Empress, Catherine. She owed a lot to this man, and yet she hated him, despised him. And he knew it.

They went along the great corridors she knew so well,

past the ramrod sentries. They reached a small door. The two huge soldiers crossed their bayonets across the entrance.

Lev said something in a low voice and the long steel blades snapped apart at once.

'Are you ready?'

'Yes,' she said. Turning aside to Jacek she said: 'Now, remember to bow to the lady.' He nodded, for once speechless, tears forming in his eyes.

'It's all right, darling, it's all right. She won't eat you.' But as the door opened her own heart was beating fast for she knew why they had come and what depended on the whim of one woman.

Then they were in the room and there was Catherine, 'little Figgy', coming towards her with hands held out.

'Kasia. My dear. After all this time.' They embraced fondly. She turned to Lev Bubin.

'Very well, Count Bubin, you may go, and thank you.' Bubin bowed himself out. Still the same charm, thought Kasia. Still the dismissal with the smile.

'Ma'am,' she went down in a deep curtsey.

'What a wonderful surprise! Let me look at you. No, the years have not changed you, not one bit. And so this is your son.'

Catherine held out her hand to Jacek. But he would not leave his mother's side.

'He's got your eyes, Kasia but—' She did not go on. The thought of Henryk came between them: a spectre that could not be hidden.

'Now we'll have some tea. You always enjoyed Russian tea, didn't you, my dear? But first let us show your little man where you and he shall sleep.' This was Catherine at her best, not showing off for the benefit of her public, but genuine and warm.

The Empress prattled away like a young girl as she led them personally, waving away ladies-in-waiting and courtiers with small, imperious gestures.

Jacek was left in charge of a kindly woman of ample proportions and half a dozen maids. At first he cried for his mother but then, soothed by the nurse and the strange, enormous size of the rooms, he began to cheer up and ask questions.

* * *

'I am so very glad to see you again, Kasia,' said Catherine as they sipped the lemon-flavoured tea.

'Yes, Ma'am.'

'Please, not "Ma'am". When we are alone I like to be called Figgy, as it was long ago. Now, tell me, what is it that has brought you to Petersburg after all this time? Is it to tell me that, even after all this unpleasantness between our two countries, you are still fond of an old friend? Or is it—?' Catherine paused.

And now it is coming, Kasia thought with a tremor of fear. Now she is going to ask.

'To show your little Jacek the sights of the city where you lived for so long?' She laughed. Then after a pause she said:

'You had a brother called Jacek, didn't you?'

Kasia nodded.

'If it is painful for you then please—I am sorry. But what happened to him?' Catherine asked gently.

'With me he was t-taken by the Turks on the night when Volochisk was burnt. At the frontier—at the frontier they—' Kasia could not go on. Even after all these years she remembered the filthy things they did to him. 'I'm s-sorry—'

'No, my dear, it is I who should be sorry for bringing back a sad subject. Please forgive me.'

'I believe they took him to Constantinople—I don't know—'

Catherine leaned forward and patted her hand.

'But now you have another Jacek.'

'Yes.'

Catherine got up and went to the fire: a sure sign she was either agitated or going to ask questions.

'You have left your husband in Poland so as to visit me?'

Kasia was nonplussed. Was Catherine playing 'cat-and-mouse' with her? She knew the Empress and her character, probably as well as anyone.

'Oh, of course I know that he fought against my soldiers in the Confederate Wars, Kasia. But that is over. Let's have no bitterness between us. You and I have been through so much together. I owe you a debt almost impossible to repay for the part you played in placing me on the throne of Russia.' Catherine did what she always did if she was not certain of her next words: she began to pace the room. 'All I can say once again is, thank you.' She resumed her seat. 'And now, tell me, how is your husband?'

Has everything that has happened in these last few years so turned 'Figgy' to such hatred that she can use torture such as this hidden behind a smile?

Kasia did not answer for a moment.

'You mean Henryk, don't you, Ma'am?'

'Naturally, as he is your husband. What a strange question.' She looked closely at Kasia and her eyes were filled with concern. 'He's not? I am truly sorry if I said . . . Please believe me, Kasia, I—'

'I believe you.'

Kasia knew now that Catherine did not recognize Borodin and Henryk Barinski as the same man. So her problem—and anguish—were twice as awful.

There was a long silence.

'No,' Kasia said at last. 'No, he's not dead.' In her heart she prayed as never before that she had told the truth. 'He did not want to come with me.'

'That I understand . . . But what I cannot understand, Kasia, is why you came back to see me.'

'Perhaps I just wanted to see someone I admired, Ma'am; someone who had been good to me—someone I could call my friend, a real friend. To show her my son.'

'That you can always do.'

Unless she's a better actress than I have always thought her, then Catherine is either performing the best part of her life, or else she is speaking every calculated cruel word for a purpose.

'He stayed to look after Lipno. You remember Lipno, M-Figgy? Bordering on Volochisk.'

'Yes, I remember Volochisk. The home of the Barinskis.'

Catherine poured more tea from the big, golden samovar.

'No, my home. The home of the Radienskis.'

'Still the same proud Pole.' Catherine smiled. 'For various reasons I have a great admiration for your countrymen.' Kasia remembered the love between the Empress and Stanislas Poniatowski, now Poland's despised King. She said nothing.

'They have always fought against Russia. They are great fighters.'

'Yes,' said Kasia. 'And they always will be.'

'They don't count their losses.'

'No.'

'While there is one Pole alive then their country is not dead. Isn't that correct?'

'Yes.'

Catherine sighed. 'What a waste of lives, young and old,' she said sadly. Then, suddenly changing the subject, she said, 'At the end of the week I leave for Moscow.' Catherine filled another glass of tea.

'You have never seen Moscow, have you?'

'No.'

'Something is upsetting you, Kasia. Tell me, don't you want to see Moscow?'

'Yes. I've always w-wanted to see M-Moscow?'

Catherine put down her glass. 'Good. Now we will talk of happy days: when you were here at the Court. First, I will tell you something. Count Bubin is shortly going to

Stockholm as Ambassador. Can you imagine it? But he has become something of a diplomat—would you ever have thought it? Strange to think it was through him that we first met, except of course as children.' She sipped at her tea.

'Fate,' she said. 'Very banal, I know, but one can't help wondering. If Count Bubin had not brought you here many years ago well—well, we would not be sitting drinking tea. So I hope you have something to thank him for.'

Some good, some bad, Kasia thought, and now something on which her whole future and, more important, the life of her husband depended.

'I had never thought of Lev Bubin as a diplomat,' she said.

Catherine laughed. 'Nor had I. But his behaviour at Court; ladies-in-waiting, that sort of thing, You understand?'

'Yes,' said Kasia with feeling. 'I understand.' She remembered the contempt she had felt for him, mingled with a little pity.

'And yet,' Catherine went on, 'through the years he has, in his own devious way, learnt to be a statesman. He has served me well.'

'What diplomat is not devious, Ma'am?'

'So the years have taught you that also.'

'Among other things, yes.'

Catherine nodded slowly. 'That I can understand. After all, time is a waste if we don't learn something from it. This tea is too sweet. I keep telling them but, always too much sugar. As Empress I am supposed to have all Russia at my feet and yet—the tea is too sweet.'

They laughed and the restraint between them fell away. They talked and remembered the happy days, the sad days, the exciting days. And then, as the marble clock struck two, Catherine said, 'Now Kasia, it is time for bed.' Kasia rose to her feet. Catherine picked up a poker and prodded the dying fire.

'Within a few days, as I said, I shall be leaving for Moscow.' Kasia felt her heart pounding in her ears. 'But you and your son are welcome to stay here as long as you like. You know that, don't you?'

'Yes.'

'You, of all people, can truly call this your other home.'

'Thank you, Figgy.' She calmed herself. 'Ma'am?'

'Yes.' Catherine did not turn from the fire. 'What is it?'

'I would like to come with you, if I may.'

The poker stirred the fire into a shower of sparks.

'There's nothing to see in Moscow. No river. No ships. Nothing but the walls of the Kremlin. Shut in. Cut off from the sky. You wouldn't like it, Kasia.'

'Still I ask if I may come with you.'

For a long time the room was silent but for a faint sputter from the embers.

'Very well, if that is what you wish, of course. I shall be glad of company on the journey.'

Just for a minute Kasia wondered about Potemkin. Would he not be company enough? As though seeing into Kasia's mind Catherine said, 'Marshal Potemkin is already in Moscow.' She smiled slightly.

'And now, to bed.'

Chapter Two

AT the end of the week they set out for Moscow, using the same little painted house on sledge-runners that had been built for the Empress Elizabeth : Catherine, Kasia and a retinue of courtiers and ladies-in-waiting.

During the journey Catherine remained silent for hours at a time, huddling deep in her nest of Imperial sables.

They entered Moscow in the midst of a snowstorm, practically unnoticed by the people of the city.

'Typical !' Catherine was angry. She disliked Moscow : she always had.

They passed through the Kremlin gates and the massive walls vanished into the grey, twilight world of driving snow.

But, Kasia thought, she does not like what she has come here for. Yet she has nothing to complain of. She is not going to lose the man she loves.

The massive gates thudded shut behind them.

As they mounted the icy steps she felt the snow gripping her like some white demon; engulfing her whole body, especially her heart. She shuddered, not only from the cold but from the awful premonition of what the next few days might bring.

* * *

The dungeons of the Kremlin were very deep and were filled with the squeaking of the rats and the drip of water from the leaking ceilings. The only light that penetrated into the small, stinking cells, came from tiny iron gratings high up in the walls.

Every cell had chains and shackles bolted to the mouldering stones. Every shackle was fastened round the wrist and ankle of a man, or woman. Some of these were still normal; some were screaming, some were groaning, gasping for air, food, light—and some were dead. In many cells skeletons hung from the walls, stripped to the bone by the hungry rats, long forgotten by their gaolers.

Each day that passed for the inmates of these awful places was exactly like the one before. One piece of bread, a bowl of thin soup and a cup of stale water.

Otherwise nothing—*absolutely nothing*. No conversation, no reading; nothing to see except the dark outlines of the cell walls; the only movement, the scurry of the rats. Even they became friends after weeks, months in that hell-hole.

Then, one day, the key would turn and a voice would shout: 'Come on! Your turn!'

And possibly they would welcome the rope or the axe.

They had gone. Another came to fill their place. The rats would squeak and devour; the water would drip. Nothing would have changed in the dungeons of the Kremlin, except the prisoners clamped to the walls.

* * *

Some of the cells were tiny, no more than glorified cupboards in which a man could not lie down on the rotting straw without drawing-up his knees; but there were others large enough to hold three, even four prisoners.

In this one, Cell Number Ninety Five, three men were chained to the wet, green stones. Emylyan Pugachev, Frol Chumakov and Henryk Barinski.

They did not speak. Pugachev had barely uttered one single word since their capture; he never moved except to eat the revolting muck brought to them as food; he just lay, at the limit of his chain, staring up at the dripping roof; sometimes his eyes were open, but more often shut. He might just as well have been dead, Henryk thought. Well, poor devil, he soon would be. He knew enough about politics and power to see that Catherine could never grant a pardon.

And Chumakov? The man who had betrayed, either through hatred or in the hope of mercy? Instead of his pieces of silver he had received sodden straw; instead of freedom and a pardon he had got shackles, and a fever which was rapidly killing him. All the time, day and night, he muttered and shouted, twisting and turning in his chains, burning up with fever. Henryk had seen the symptoms of this fever in *Huntress* and during the campaign outside Orenburg : the 'spotted fever', that killed men by literally turning them black as though they had been roasted alive, with breath so foul it made others retch. He had watched as Chumakov sucked black water from the bundle of straw beneath him, opened his gaping mouth to catch the drops from the roof.

Out of pity, not revenge, Henryk hoped the man would die soon. He may have betrayed them, but no man deserved to die like this.

And then he would think of himself. He supposed he would join Pugachev on the scaffold. For a short while, as they walked across Red Square, he would see the sky, perhaps even the sun. Well, he had faced death many times, had felt the skeleton hand reach out for him but at least he had had an even chance. Now the skeleton would claim him and the odds were heavily stacked on the side of Death. In these conditions it was not difficult to imagine such spectres. There was a rustling near his head.

'Get out, get away, you filthy vermin !' He struck out with his chained wrist. For always, throughout his life, Henryk had loathed and feared rats with their vicious little squeaks and obscene, naked tails. Catherine was punishing him enough by putting him at the mercy of rats without having him strapped to the wheel or the rack.

Yes, he thought again, trying to shut his ears to Chumakov's ravings, Christ in Heaven, give me a moment's freedom and a sharp knife and I could at least put him out of his misery. Yes, I shall see the sky on this last walk of my life but I won't see Kasia; never again will I see the woman who has shared my life, who has fought and waited and loved. Nor my son.

He felt a rat run over his legs.

Then, suddenly, he noticed something. Chumakov was silent. Henryk listened hard. He knew Pugachev's snoring; the rattle of his chains; the squelching sound of his straw. In a place like this you got to know these small things.

Chumakov had gone. Frol Chumakov, the childhood friend of Pugachev, was dead. So that left the two of them.

* * *

'And so, gentlemen, what do we do?'

Catherine sat at the head of her table of State. Before her were the three men upon whom she depended : Count Panin, Count Alexei Orlov and Field-Marshal Suvorov, the man who had crushed the rebellion of Pugachev, the Cossack of the Don. Privately she thought that Suvorov had done about as much as a mouse capturing a lion.

He was a wonderful general, that she agreed, but dealing with men like these he was perhaps slightly out of his depth. Besides it had been Panin's brother who had beaten Pugachev; and it was this thin, monk-like man who was claiming the credit.

The credit for bringing the rebels to Moscow as clowns. The Paper Tsar and his last remaining courtier.

'He should suffer the sentence laid down for treason,' said

Panin in his prim voice.

'Yes,' agreed Suvorov, 'he took up arms against his Sovereign and therefore deserves nothing less.'

Catherine had read the ghastly death prescribed for treason and the cold words had sickened her. The paper was before her on the table.

> '... he or she shall be taken to the place of execution and there have inflicted upon him or her the just rewards of his or her crimes ... the flesh of his or her body shall be ripped with red-hot hooks and into the wounds shall be poured molten sulphur ... the executioners shall break the limbs of the accused with heavy hammers ... pull the arms from the body with the aid of pulleys ... the body to be slit open and the bowels to be displayed to the public ... and then, and only then, shall his head, or hers, be severed from the body and stuck upon a pike for all to see ...'

In many countries of Europe she was known as the Enlightened Empress but, if she put her signature to this—this barbaric horror—what would they call her then? And yet it was only some twenty years ago that a man named Damiens had suffered this unbelievable fate for trying to stab Louis the Fifteenth of France with a pen-knife.

Though the windows were covered with thick ferns of frost her forehead felt damp with a cold sweat and her blood ran hot with a sudden fever.

'And you, Count Orlov? You have said nothing.'

'I think you would be wise, Ma'am, to commute this sentence to a quicker death, either by rope or axe. In the end he will be just as dead.'

'In Red Square?' The relief sounded in her voice.

'Yes, Ma'am. Pugachev's death must be public, and swift. He must not be given time to address the people.'

'Thank you, Count Orlov.'

Panin was pale with anger. He did not like Orlov, he never had; in fact he had always been deadly jealous of the influence of the Orlov brothers on the Empress.

Suvorov did not mind one way or the other how the rebel died as long as he was seen to die, and by as many people as possible.

Panin was on his feet.

'Your Imperial Majesty, I feel I must ...'

'Must what, Count Panin?'

She felt cooler now that she had reached her decision. Or had Alexei reached it for her? It did not matter. Ever since the day of Pugachev's capture she had thought of little else; seeing the blood-soaked scaffold and trying to shut her ears to the screams of a man undergoing pain that could hardly be imagined.

'Very well,' she said quietly. 'I have decided. He shall die by the axe.'

'And the man Borodin?' asked Panin acidly. 'How shall he die?'

Catherine did not answer at once. 'That we shall have to consider. And now, gentlemen, if you'll excuse me. I have a slight headache.'

They withdrew, bowing as they went.

'Alexei.'

'Ma'am?'

'Thank you.'

Though Grigori Potemkin, the love of her life, had been half blinded by the Orlov brothers, she still held Alexei, the giant of the five, in especial esteem. For she was realistic enough to know that, without him, she would not be Empress and Autocrat of Russia. Which, she thought with wry humour, would have spared her the decision with which she had just been faced. Well, you can't have it both ways. With power goes responsibility, duty, decisions and never-ending hard work. She sighed.

'You don't like Grigori Potemkin, do you,' she asked a little sadly.

'No,' he answered firmly. 'I don't.'

Catherine smiled. 'You have always answered a straight question with a very straight answer, both you and your elder brother.' She paused, staring down at the papers littered on the table. 'Again, Alexei, I thank you—and your brother—for your help and loyal support.'

And my brother's love, he wondered as he stood, towering above the small seated figure.

'I hope that one day Russia will recognize what the Orlov family has done for her.' She paused again, buried deep in memories then, brusquely, as was her way, she looked up, smiling again. 'As I said, a headache. I shall lie down for a short while.'

Alexei Orlov nodded, expressionless. 'May I say something, Ma'am?'

'Of course.'

'I have known you for many years and would just like to tell you how much . . .' For the first time since they had known each other Catherine saw that he was lost for words.

'Yes?' She asked gently.

'How very much I admire and respect you.' He drew a deep breath. 'Both as an Empress, and a woman.'

She felt the tears gathering behind her eyes.

'Thank you again, Alexei.' He bowed, turned sharply in a military manner and left the room.

For a long time Catherine sat at her table deep in thought. The door opened and two men entered carrying trays of documents.

'Papers, Your Majesty. From Warsaw and Paris.'

'Important,' she asked wearily.

'I fear so, Your Majesty.'

'Very well, I'll look through them.'

'As Your Majesty wishes.' The bulging trays were placed in front of her.

'As a matter of fact Her Majesty does not wish.' But her smile took the sting from her words.

And that was why, in one way at least, Catherine was called Great.

Chapter Three

'SIT down, Kasia.'

Kasia knew from the old days how worried Catherine was. She paced the room, stopped to look out of the window, then more pacing. And she knew what was worrying her.

'You do see, Kasia, that I cannot afford to pardon this Cossack.' Kasia thought back to the days when 'this Cossack' had been her so-called husband, married beneath the willow tree; the moment when she had borne him a son.

'Yes, Ma'am, that I understand.'

'So. Then what do I do? I cannot afford to pardon a man who has led a revolt against the throne. Do you agree?'

Kasia nodded slowly.

'An example must be made.'

'Supposing—?'

'Yes, go on.'

'Supposing you were to invite them, the Cossacks, not order them or they will fight you all the more bitterly, but ask them to join the Russian Empire, would they not make magnificent allies?'

Catherine paced the floor six times before she answered.

'I think they would, if they could be disciplined.'

And who has ever disciplined a Cossack, thought Kasia, except their own leaders.

'There could be no alternative, Ma'am? Siberia?'

'No, Kasia, my dear. He would still be alive. A magnet for revolutionaries. No, it is not possible. He must die.' Kasia heard the steel in Catherine's voice and knew there was no use in arguing.

'Like Ivan in Schlüsselburg?' Kasia knew she had thrown down her last card.

Catherine stopped in the middle of the room. Kasia prepared to meet the onslaught.

'I think you take too much for granted, Countess, on account of our friendship.'

'Yes, Ma'am, perhaps I do, but I am willing to take the risk.'

Catherine stared at her with cold eyes, devoid of any sort of pity. Kasia returned the look without even blinking.

'You have not altered, Kasia. You still have the same courage as you always had.' Catherine glanced away, unnerved by Kasia's steady look.

Kasia dared not mention the name Borodin. Let Catherine think that Henryk was safely in Poland.

'You show a great concern for the Cossack, Kasia. But then, of course, I remember. You spent some years with them in one of their Don villages. You once told me you had a son by one; a little boy who died, wasn't that it?'

'Yes.'

Catherine frowned. 'You *must* see, once and for all, that this man Pugachev cannot be allowed to go free to return to his village. To be hailed as a hero from the Dnieper to the Volga.'

Kasia nodded, thinking of the tiny body of Mikhail being laid in his miniature coffin while his father, Emylyan Pugachev lay stretched above the stove so drunk he could not speak.

Hearing Catherine's voice from many miles away she pulled herself together.

'... I shall go to the dungeons tomorrow. I wish to see this rebel, I ...' She stopped, not certain how to go on, knowing full well the reason : curiosity. An insatiable curiosity to see with her own eyes the man who had dared to rouse the country against her.

'I would like to come with you, Ma'am—if I may.'

'Why?'

'I—I d-don't know quite. But I w-would. Please.'

Catherine thought for a while.

'Very well, if that is what you want. But I warn you, it will not be very pleasant.'

'I know that,' Kasia said quietly. 'But I have seen and experienced many terrible things in my life.'

Catherine looked out over Red Square, scene of so many blood-stained horrors, and was blinded by the beauty of the sunlight reflected from glittering snow unspotted by anything but the shadows of small clouds passing across the sun.

'Very well,' she repeated in a dull voice. 'You may come with me.'

* * *

Jacek she left behind. At first he had made a scene and clung to her skirts.

'Please, Mama, why can't I come too,' he asked between sobs. 'Please.'

She took him on her knee. 'You'd be bored, darling. It is all grown-up nonsense.' Kasia thought of Henryk. Biting back her own tears, she smiled as she stroked the curly black hair.

'It will be all talk and there'll be nothing for you to do.'

'I hate Moscow.' He clenched his small fists. 'I *hate* it.'

She hugged him to her. 'So do I,' she thought bitterly. 'By God, so do I.'

His tears had dried after watching his mother drive away with the Grand Lady, and he soon cheered up under the kindness of the elderly, red-cheeked woman, former nurse to the Grand Duke Paul, and the fun and laughter of the younger ladies-in-waiting who took the little boy to their hearts.

* * *

The Governor of the prison, grovelling and scraping; the iron clang and slam of heavy doors; the echo of their footsteps in the long stone corridors; the sudden shout or scream from behind some locked door. That was what Kasia registered in her brain as they followed the lanterns of the guardians of this terrible place. And the grand hat worn by the Governor; the smell of his *pomander*, not able to vie with the foul stenches of this living graveyard.

'My apologies, Your Imperial Majesty,' he kept repeating as they went lower and lower into the foetid bowels of his prison. Catherine must have been reminded, all too vividly, of her visit to Schlüsselburg to see the wreck that was Ivan the Sixth. And that had been curiosity too. If I had a knife, Kasia thought with a sudden vicious spurt of hatred, I know exactly where I would stick it.

In the light of the lanterns she could see water: on the walls, the roof—everywhere, water and green mould thick as seaweed.

'My Christ,' exploded Potemkin suddenly. 'Surely it is better to kill the poor bastards than to keep them in a place like this?'

Catherine did not answer so no one else spoke.

'My apologies—' began the Governor.

'Get on with it, man!' When Potemkin was angry he sounded angry.

And, at last, they reached Cell Number Ninety-Five. By now Kasia was shivering violently: from the dank cold and from what she might see.

The key turned; the massive bolts were withdrawn. The door was open.

'Your Imperial Majesty—' The Governor bowed, his gilt,

feathered hat sweeping the floor.

'The smell,' he began, 'I can only say, Your Imperial—'

'We understand,' said Catherine. 'Please let me pass.' Kasia, in a daze of horror, followed her into the cell.

'God in Hell,' exclaimed Potemkin behind her.

'They are here, Your Majesty,' said the Governor in an unctuous tone. 'These rebels, these criminals are here awaiting your justice, your—'

'That I can see for myself,' said Catherine tartly.

Behind her Kasia caught her breath. In the corner, sitting up, straining against his shackles, was the man she had expected to see: her husband.

In the other corner was crouched another figure, face turned to the wall. Yet Kasia saw nothing but Henryk's dirty, bearded face, the scar a grey line across the top of his nose and between the eyes which brightened in the lantern-light as they saw her. The two women were cloaked and heavily hooded; the light was unsteady and poor and yet Henryk knew the taller of the two was his wife. That was all that mattered. But he gave no sign of recognition.

Catherine stepped closer to him.

'Hold up the lantern,' she ordered.

'My God,' she whispered. 'It's you, Henri de Bonville. So you are . . .' Henryk nodded, his eyes fixed on his wife, standing behind the Empress.

'That is not the rebel Pugachev.'

'No, no, Your Majesty. Pugachev is over here. Guards, kick the animal into life!'

'Leave him!'

She continued to stand close to Henryk. Now it all began to make some kind of crazy sense. For a moment Catherine was far away from the vileness of the moment. The wheel had turned full circle with a vengeance.

'You are also—?' Henryk nodded again. She glanced sideways at Kasia, and Kasia realized that now at last the

Empress knew the truth—Barinski and De Bonville were one and the same.

'Marshal Potemkin!' called out the Empress.

Potemkin went forward.

'Do you recognize this man?'

Potemkin smiled at Henryk, his one eye gleaming in the half-light.

'Yes, I remember you. The man at Chocim.'

Henryk tried to smile back. But he could not speak. He nodded. He remembered the black patch.

Kasia watched it all with her senses fading, then, by intense will-power, she pulled herself back to the present. This could not be happening, God, this could not be happening.

But it was. In this place of dark horror, for a few short moments they were together again. Three were here. Three—Adam, Stanislas Poniatowski and her brother—were missing. The guards were kicking Pugachev so that at last he roused himself and slowly rolled over towards the light.

His face, under the thick beard, was ashen. Every time he moved, he coughed—a rough, hollow cough that stirred the wet straw packed underneath his body. It would be kinder, Henryk thought, to put a musket-ball into his head. He had done the most appalling cruelties but—well, for God's sake, put him out of his misery.

'Your Imperial Majesty—' The Governor hesitated, sensing her mood. He cleared his throat. 'Over here the rebel, Pugachev.'

Catherine went slowly across to Pugachev. She looked at him and said nothing. He looked back at her and then spoke his first words for weeks.

'So you are Catherine of Russia?'

'Yes, I am.'

'I am Emylyan Pugachev, Cossack of the Don.' His voice, though weak, was proud. 'I am not asking for mercy. But what I say is this, if the Tsars would accept the Cossacks as allies instead of enemies, then Russia could become really great.' He coughed harshly.

'But your people have always been enemies of Russia.' Catherine was sickened to see a man reduced to this.

Pugachev did not answer, except to cough and turn his head away from her.

'You are the man they called Borodin?' Kasia heard Potemkin's question from afar.

'Yes.' Henryk's voice was stronger than Pugachev's but hoarser.

'You're a Pole, aren't you?'

'Yes.' Henryk tried to hold up his head.

'Why did you take up arms against Her Imperial Majesty?'

'Because I wanted, like many other Poles, to keep our country free.'

'And to do that you are willing to die?'

'Yes.'

How his wife had got here or why he could not think; half-starved, exhausted, boiling with fever at one moment then shivering in icy-cold spasms, his thoughts were muddled, confused.

'You're a brave man,' said Potemkin.

'And what has happened to the other man? The one who betrayed them.' The Empress turned to the Governor.

'A million apologies, Your Majesty, but the miserable cur died. We did all we could but he cheated the scaffold—'

'It does not matter.' She cut him off coldly.

Kasia felt herself swaying. She longed to clutch on to some support, to grab at Catherine's shoulder or steady herself against a wall, faced as she was by the spectacle of the two men who had fathered her sons chained like beasts in a pit.

'Very well,' said Catherine in a dull voice. 'That is enough. We will leave.'

'Yes, Your Imperial Majesty, of course—of course.' The

Governor bowed and swept his hat in a wide semi-circle. 'This is no fit place for—'

'If I had not wished to visit these men I would not have come.' Her voice was cold but Kasia detected a note of agitation—distress even.

She followed her out and, as she reached the doorway, Kasia looked back. Henryk sat at the very length of his chain. He raised a hand in greeting—or was it farewell? And she saw his smile, trying to give her courage for what lay ahead.

The rasping clang of the door was the end of the world to both of them. As the darkness closed round them Henryk knew the reality of the words : 'The utter loneliness of Hell.'

And he had not even been able to take in her face because of that great clown Potemkin and his ridiculous questions.

A sad way in which to take final leave of the woman you loved. And Catherine had recognized him; certainly, he realized, as the man who had slept with her but whether only as a Frenchman or as Henryk Barinski he could not tell. Pugachev's hacking cough disturbed his thoughts.

He felt the fever taking hold, insidious as a drug. He drifted away into a nightmare world peopled by shapes, some who spoke, some who crouched on his throat so that he tore himself awake with a huge effort, gasping, into the real nightmare.

* * *

During the short journey in the sleigh from the filth of a prison to the splendour of a palace, they were very silent. Catherine sat huddled deep within her furs. Kasia was in a state of shock, trying to remember what she had seen and yet on the other hand, trying to forget.

It was Potemkin who spoke.

'I don't care a damn, about Pugachev. But the other one, Borodin. He should be removed to better quarters.'

The snow hissed beneath the runners. Bells were echoing in the brittle, night air. Catherine did not answer. Kasia used up all the prayers she knew.

'Until Your Majesty has decided on the punishment for the Pole then I think he deserves better treatment.' He sat back in silence. 'I speak as a soldier,' he said.

They drew up at the entrance to the Palace. The sound of the bells was deafening.

'Yes,' answered Catherine, and she had to pitch her voice high against the brazen clangour.

'And what do you think, Countess?' Kasia knew she had to answer. But she took refuge by nodding.

They went into the hot luxury of the Palace rooms, with liveried servants at every corner to answer their slightest beck and call.

Potemkin was his usual boisterous, roaring self, shouting for drink. But Catherine was tight-lipped and frowning.

'Tomorrow, Countess Barinska, we will have a talk.' It was a long time until next morning.

Between the strokes of her *grande sonnerie* carriage clock she lay awake. He's alive. At least, he's alive. I have seen him, in dirt, squalor and degradation but he is alive.

And, throughout the long night, hearing the bells of the Kremlin churches and the distant chanting of the monks who did so much for the ordinary human beings simply trying to hold on to their faith, she heard the rattle of Henryk's chains, and wondered if these monks prayed for such as him.

* * *

The drums rolled in Red Square.

People were packed like bugs in a mattress to watch the spectacle offered for their entertainment.

In the centre of the Square was a scaffold, or a sort of scaffold. A square of timber, raised above the cobbles, round it a wooden railing and, in the middle, a simple block. Some of the crowd were disappointed. They had hoped for tackles, hooks, branding-irons and a red hot brazier. They had come a long way: all the miles from the huts of the steppes and the mountains, to watch the death of a man who had dared to challenge the authority of their Tsar.

They came for Pugachev at noon.

Henryk listened to the sound of his shackles being severed from the wall.

'Well, friend Borodin, it does not seem as if you and I will meet again. I thank you for what you did for me.' He spoke calmly. 'You were right, I was wrong: I should not have used those methods. I should not . . .' By then, he was too far away and Henryk could not hear.

But they made him watch and listen.

'Get up there!' His gaolers forced him on to a stool. 'You will want to see your friend going on his last journey.'

Having been chained for so long, Pugachev stumbled every now and then; twice he fell and was hauled to his feet by the escort taking him to the red-draped scaffold where the solitary executioner stood, leaning on his axe.

Over the last few yards Pugachev never hesitated; somehow he pulled himself to his full height and mounted the steps proudly as though mounting his horse to lead his Cossacks on another campaign or raid.

The crowds fell silent as the priest stepped forward and raised the Cross before Pugachev's face. The Cossack bowed his head. Then turning he shouted: 'Goodbye, friends. My thanks to you for coming all this way to see how a Cossack can die.'

His voice, though hoarse, was strong.

Waving aside the black bandage, he knelt and placed his neck on the block. Henryk saw the flash of the morning sun on the great blade and closed his eyes.

Emylyan Pugachev may have been cruel; he may have been half-mad but, by God, he was a brave man.

The silence in Red Square was so intense that he heard the thud which meant it was all over. A sound filled the Square, half a sigh, half a prayer.

'Well, he's gone,' said one of the gaolers. 'And good riddance. Russia can do without scum like that.'

'Tomorrow it'll be his turn.' Henryk heard them laugh as the door slammed and the key turned in the lock.

He sat down on the stool at the rough table. At least Catherine had been gracious enough to free him from his chains for his last few hours of life. Oh, my God, he thought, what have I brought on Kasia and our son? What have I done? And all in the name of our country, in the name of Polish pride. And what were they worth compared to the happiness of the woman I've loved for so long. At last something deep inside him broke. Laying his head on his folded arms Henryk wept; unashamedly he allowed the grief to escape.

'Poor devil,' said the gaoler with a softer heart.

'Why's he here then?' asked his friend. 'He's asked for it. Why waste your pity on a dog of a Pole who took up arms against our Tsarina?'

'I know but—' The other man turned from the sight of Henryk's heaving shoulders.

'The trouble with you is, you shouldn't be in this job. Anyway, by this time tomorrow he'll be out of it all.'

They left the iron inspection grill.

And still Henryk Barinski wept his heart out. Not at the thought of his own death but for what he so soon was to be leaving.

Chapter Four

'SO Emylyan Pugachev is dead.' Potemkin sprawled on a gilded *chaise-longue*; clad in a stained dressing-gown open to reveal the thick tangle of black hair covering his massive chest, he held a vast mug of his favourite *tokay* in a large, grubby hand. His hair was long and greasy, his eye blood-shot from drink as it watched his Empress and mistress prepare herself for bed.

Her personal maid was brushing her hair with long, slow strokes. One hundred times she did this every night—exactly one hundred sweeps of the brush; not one less, not one more.

Still luxuriant, hardly touched with grey, it hung down to her waist, shining like a golden-brown waterfall in the light of the candles and the fire.

'Yes,' said Catherine to her image in the huge ornate looking-glass on her dressing-table laden with the golden pots and jars that held her powders and creams and rouges. 'Yes, he is dead.'

'You were too kind to the—' Potemkin used a foul word. He spoke like that even in front of her servants, her ladies-in-waiting. Ever since he had become her lover—and it was hinted throughout the houses and palaces of the great in Petersburg and Moscow, but only behind closed doors, that there had been a secret marriage. Potemkin was a law unto himself. You did not cross him, not if you were wise.

And she loved him with so deep and desperate a passion that she blinded herself to his language, his dirt, his treatment of her body, his insults to her mind. Because, when he was sober and rational she had, at last, found a man with whom she could talk as an equal; a man who gave her good advice, who argued if he thought she was wrong, with whom she discussed affairs of state.

'Really, Grigori darling, have you not drunk enough?' She said it fondly. The girl continued her brushing impassively. She had heard worse. Ninety-six ... ninety-seven. Her arm was aching, as it always did. But for Catherine she would have brushed until she dropped. Ninety-nine ... One hundred.

'There, Your Majesty.' She stepped back.

'How does it look, Natasha?'

'Beautiful, Your Majesty.'

'Lucky Pugachev didn't have hair like that,' said Potemkin with a great bellow of raucous laughter. 'The axe wouldn't have got through it.'

When Natasha had gone and they were alone, Catherine still remained sitting before her glass. Over her shoulder she could see him lying there, the dressing-gown falling open. Her body began to stir but she tried to calm herself for she had something to discuss and tomorrow might be too late.

'Grigori, my angel.'

'Yes, woman.' He always called her that before making love to her.

'Pugachev is dead but— but, what about the other one?'

'Well, what about him? He's alive. For the moment anyway.'

'Exactly.' She paused and then turned to face him. 'But should he stay alive?' She thought back over the long years of her friendship with Kasia. And now—a decision such as this! Could she sign Henryk's death warrant?

'Come here,' ordered Potemkin curtly. Catherine averted her eyes from his body, feeling herself beginning to tremble.

'In a moment, my sweetheart.' She longed to fling herself upon him and rouse him to the peak of a frenzy that drove them both close to madness, but first she had to have his advice.

Controlling herself with a superhuman effort, she asked again, 'Should he stay alive?'

'What, the Pole with the scar? The man I faced at Chocim?' For a moment Potemkin became totally sober. After a long pause, during which he stared into the mug and scratched reflectively at his dirty black hair, he spoke.

'Yes,' he said, 'he's a brave man. Yes, he should. For one thing, I owe my life to him. He could have killed me at Chocim.'

'For that, my golden cockerel, my great tiger, for that I would spare the life of Satan himself. But on one condition and that—'

'I don't care what that is. Can't you see how much I want you, woman?'

'Yes—I can see.'

She flung off her robe and came to him.

* * *

The sound of the sleigh bells drowned their words so that the driver and the outriders standing on the broad sledge-runners behind them could not overhear what was said.

They talked, the Empress and Kasia, as they drove across the shining white country outside Moscow; through pine woods where the branches bowed to the ground under the weight of a fresh snowfall; out on to the snowfields, sparkling with a million diamonds, broken here and there by the little timber houses buried up to their eaves behind high walls of snow.

'It is very beautiful, the winter in Russia,' Catherine said from deep within her sable hood.

'And cruel,' said Kasia.

'Yes, my dear—and cruel.' The two women were snug and

warm, buried within many layers of furs; their feet deep in dry hay.

They drove slowly between banks of smooth, newly cut snow where men were toiling with long-handled shovels to open the road.

'A hard country inhabited by a brave people. As brave in their slow, dogged way as your own, Kasia.' Catherine watched the men in their rough fur jackets and the ragged cloths wound round their legs, as they swung the snow high over their shoulders in throwing it in clouds from the shovels.

'Give them the discipline of the Prussians and they could be moulded into the conquerors of the world.' She gazed at a giant of a man in a rabbit-skin hat swinging his arms across his chest.

'If they would only let themselves be led and not always driven.'

The sleigh moved slowly forwards, until clear of the drift, then picked up speed until the runners sang beneath them.

'You're very quiet, Kasia? Is something the matter?' The moment had come. The moment on which Henryk's life depended. On her words, extra loud to overcome the hiss of the snow, the gay jingle of the bells and the crack of the long whip, hung the life of her husband.

'May I speak frankly, Ma'am?'

'When haven't you?' Catherine laughed for the first time.

'And could I ask that you listen until I have told everything, Ma'am—Figgy?'

'Yes.'

It was a long time before Kasia spoke, groping for the right words, the absolute right words.

'Well, Kasia, what is it? You can surely tell me.' They were out of the sunshine, travelling slowly among tall, shadowy trees.

'Ma'am, Borodin—the man we saw in the dungeon is—' She could not go on. Is the Frenchman De Bonville, Catherine thought bleakly, who had once made love to her. Through diplomatic necessity, she thought, but no longer bitterly.

'The person you saw chained to the wall like an animal—Borodin—is . . .' She gave up the word.

'That was Henryk Barinski? Am I not correct? Your husband.' She touched Kasia gently on the arm. 'I knew. The picture came clear in the dungeon.'

'You kn-knew?'

'Yes, Kasia. I knew by the way he looked at you—the scar. Suddenly I knew.'

After a long, brooding silence Catherine suddenly stirred herself. Leaning forward she called out sharply, 'Stop!'

Thankfully the driver reined-in the horses, for his face was almost flayed by the cold.

'We will get out,' said Catherine, and the tone of her voice told Kasia nothing.

'Wait here.'

'Yes, Your Imperial Majesty.'

The driver and the outriders watched the two women, voluminous in their furs and thick felt boots.

'God above, how long are they going to keep us here freezing into bloody blocks of ice?' The outrider held gloved hands to his scarlet nose.

'Oh, it doesn't matter to the grand ones,' said his companion, sneezing loudly. 'Nothing matters to them except which dress to wear at the next ball, or how many serfs to have branded.'

'Or which man to take to bed with them.'

They both swore loudly. The horses' breath steamed. The driver wondered whether to put on their blankets. The figures grew smaller against the snow. Yes, he would.

'Heh,' he shouted angrily, 'stop your damned whining and help me with the horses.'

* * *

'So that is understood then?'

'Yes,' said Kasia. 'And—and—there are no ways in which I can thank you. No w-words in the world.' Her voice choked.

'Well then, don't try.' Catherine picked up a handful of snow and threw it away. Kasia heard the catch in her voice. She reached out for Catherine's hand.

'Thank you,' she said. 'With all my heart I th-thank you,' she hesitated for an instant, 'Figgy.'

Catherine pretended a great interest in the snow: picking it up, kicking it and generally behaving like a child let out from school.

'Neither your husband,' she drew a deep breath, 'nor you, nor your son nor any other children of your marriage may ever return to Russia during any or all of your lifetimes. If you do then I will not be able,'—she paused—'or willing, to save you.'

They were making their slow way back to the sleigh.

'As I have said, I do not wish to see your husband, Kasia. Arrangements will be made for your journey to the Russian frontier. From then on you will have to manage for yourselves. No doubt the Austrians will help you to reach Lipno in safety. You have done a great deal for me during your life, Kasia, and for that I will always be grateful. Always. And now it is getting cold. We will go back.'

'Thank the Lord,' said the outrider with the red nose. 'Another half an hour and we'd have been frozen meat.'

'Shut your bloody mouth,' snarled the driver, removing the blankets. 'She thinks more of us lot than any of the Tsars before her.'

The two other men snorted contemptuously. Catherine and Kasia settled themselves warmly into the bearskins.

'Now we'll go back to Moscow, Pawel.'

You see, thought the driver, she even knows my name.

Chapter Five

THEY were ready to leave. Kasia dressed in her travelling clothes of blue velvet trimmed with thick brown ermine. Beside her stood Jacek in his small fur coat.

The door opened and Catherine came in.

'Kasia, my dear. And Jacek.' This time the child did not draw back but allowed himself to be kissed by the Grand Lady.

'All is arranged,' said Catherine. Almost too briskly, Kasia thought. The Empress was trying to disguise her true feelings. She fussed about, never still.

'The men of the escort who go with you are to be trusted implicitly—as long as H—your husband's name is never mentioned.'

Kasia nodded.

'Obey the instructions of the officer in command and all will go well.'

'Yes, Ma'am.'

Catherine turned away. 'This last time, could it not be Figgy?' Her voice was muffled.

Kasia felt the lump forming in her throat. 'Yes—Figgy.' The room was blurred. She felt the grip of her son's hand tighten.

'What is it, Mama?'

Catherine came towards her with outstretched hands. She grasped Kasia's hands in her own.

'May God protect you—and your family—wherever you are, wherever you go.' Gently she patted Jacek's head. 'If this little man takes care of you as I'm sure his father will, then you are a very fortunate woman, Kasia.'

'I know. And I also know that, without your—'

Catherine held up an imperious hand. 'That will do. Now go. Quickly!'

'Thank you, Figgy. Once again, thank you.' Kasia curtseyed.

'Come, Jacek.' They left the room.

'But, Mama, what's wrong? Is the Grand Lady angry?'

'No, darling, of course not. It's just—well, she's very busy and—oh, do come on, Jacek.'

On the way down the great marble stairs, for the last time, he began to cry.

'Jacek?' she said as they were tucked into the rugs in the sleigh.

'Yes, Mama.'

'We're soon going to see Papa.'

'Papa?'

The sleigh began to move across the hard snow, watched from a window by Catherine, Empress of All the Russias, unashamedly weeping.

'Yes, Papa. After all this long time, we'll soon see him again.'

In front and behind the sleigh the cavalrymen of the Imperial Guard broke into a trot as they rode out of the Kremlin.

And Kasia did not look back.

* * *

It was dark when they reached the inn somewhere south-west of Moscow. Kasia woke from a half-sleep, filled with nightmares and phantoms.

'We are here, Madam.' But where? Lipno? Volochisk and the horror of the flames and Henryk's bloodied face? Kerch and Diran Bey? Pugachev and the black wind of the steppes?

'We are here.' Slowly she roused herself, forcing her body to obey the commands of her mind as she stepped out of the sleigh.

The officer of the escort lowered his sword to her. 'Madam.'

She and her son entered the shabby inn, covered in snow. Icicles shone in the lantern light of the innkeeper who was jumping about like a demented grasshopper.

'Your Honour—Your Excellency—My gracious lady—' The poor man was beside himself with excitement. Great ladies dressed in sables; magnificent soldiers of the Imperial Guard. What could it all mean? Never had such things happened to him before. Perhaps now his inn would become famous; perhaps the great people would come here from Moscow and St Petersburg, those sort of places. He would be rich.

Kasia carried Jacek into the inn, fast asleep in her arms. And, as she entered the dimly lit room with its smoke-stained timbers, she saw, coming towards her, Henryk Barinski, her husband.

* * *

They did not speak much as they ate the simple food provided by the innkeeper's wife.

'Who are they, Piotr?' she kept asking.

'I don't *know*. All I do know is this. If we do not look after them as well as we can then—' He stopped, glancing across at the cavalrymen, enjoying themselves with their pots of ale.

'Poor souls,' said the wife who had a soft heart. 'They look worn out. And the child, he ought to be in bed.'

'Leave them,' said her husband. 'They are happy.'

Kasia and Henryk sat at the rough table, her hand in his.

'At least you have shaved,' she smiled at him across the table. 'I don't like beards,' she added. 'Which you have always known. Unless absolutely essential. In fact you are looking very tidy—considering.'

'Considering what?' Henryk smiled.

'Considering the fact that you might not have had a head to shave.' Her voice broke slightly.

He took her hand.

'Come,' she said, 'We'll go to bed. And quietly, Jacek's asleep.'

'One more drink, landlord. And have one yourself.' Henryk's voice was slurred. Kasia sat back against the wall, not daring to believe that Henryk was sitting opposite her, half asleep, his head slipping from side to side.

He was dressed in clean, fustian grey. He no longer smelt of the foul black straw. He was thin and pale, his hand was shaking, but he was still Henryk.

'We will go to bed,' said Kasia. 'Now, at once, before you fall asleep against the wall.' With the help of the inn-keeper she got him up the rickety stairs, his feet dragging against the steps.

'He has been ill,' she said. 'He's been very ill.'

'You needn't bother to tell us that, m'lady,' said the inn-keeper. 'I've been a soldier. I've been wounded and seen men so exhausted they wouldn't have known their wives or mothers.'

'You're a good kind man,' Kasia said.

'Well, m'lady, it wouldn't be much of a world if some didn't try to help would it now?' She shook her head.

Behind them followed the innkeeper's wife, Jacek sound asleep in her arms. A few good-natured ribaldries were shouted by the soldiers.

They laid Henryk upon one of the narrow little beds and covered him with a pile of blankets.

Jacek would sleep on the floor snuggled in furs from the sleigh.

The inn-keeper and his wife stood in the doorway.

'We hope—my wife and I—that you will be comfortable,

and we'll try to keep them quiet.' He gestured downwards with his thumb. 'But you know what we soldiers are.'

'Yes,' said Kasia. 'I do.'

They backed from the room and the Barinskis were alone: Kasia, Jacek and a miracle.

She looked across at her husband in the faint light of the smelly tallow candle. He lay on his back, dead to the world, but alive. He was *alive*! She did not want to snuff out the candle but just to lie and watch him.

His face was hollow, dark and deep with shadows. On the floor their son suddenly laughed in his sleep and then made noises as if he was eating.

Kasia was smiling as she put out the candle. She had them both with her. But she would not laugh or even show her happiness until they reached Lipno and could safely say they were home. She knew Fate, and did not dare.

It was not until shortly before dawn that she finally fell asleep, but she had not minded the snores and mutterings of Henryk as he tossed and turned in the creaking bed. She had not minded the scuttling of the rats in the walls.

On a day that produces a miracle you do not notice such things.

* * *

They took three days to reach the frontier between Russia and what was now Austrian Poland. During that time it was Jacek who did all the talking, asking about this, asking about that, always asking.

'Papa is tired, darling,' Kasia kept saying. 'Let him sleep.'

Henryk woke now and then for short periods as they slowly crossed the vast white steppes of Russia. For the last time, she thought, but with no sense of loss. Catherine had shown herself to be a true friend; she had given back to her what she wanted more than life itself. And Henryk would have to accept that, or he'd get a large piece of her mind.

You accept charity if it gives you back the person you love.

He lay back in his corner of the bumping sleigh, looking drawn and still utterly exhausted. God only knows what he has been through, she thought. But she could imagine. One day he might tell her—small bits and pieces: those that made her laugh. The rest she would never hear. Like his years in the British Navy.

Once he is home—her thoughts were sharply interrupted by the cries of the sleigh-driver and the orders of the officer commanding the Imperial Guard.

'What's happening? What's going on? Where's Kasia? Kasia!'

'I'm here, my darling. I'm here.' Slowly she watched the opaque look fade from his eyes.

She held his hands very tightly. 'I'm here. I'll always be here.' But she still could not be absolutely certain that he recognized her.

'Your papers, please.' A small, fat officer in Austrian uniform stood by the sleigh.

'Who's this man,' Henryk demanded angrily. 'Why does he want our papers? What the hell—'

'Please forgive my husband,' said Kasia, summoning-up her most charming smile. 'He has not been well. I am taking him home so that he can get better.'

The little fat Austrian looked at her, at the papers and then at the Russian cavalry, menacing with drawn sabres.

'You have grand friends, Madame,' he said, bowing slightly. 'Very grand.' He peered more closely into the depths of the sleigh.

'And who is that?'

'That is my husband.' And are we going to be stopped at the last minute by a pompous, bumbling ass of an Austrian officer, she thought. No, by God, we are not.

'What is the meaning of this?' asked the Imperial Guard commander. 'Why is there this barrier across the road? And these men—?' He glanced down with contempt from the saddle of his big bay horse at the Austrian soldiers lounging, leaning on their muskets, laughing and talking among themselves in a strange soft kind of German.

'Do not worry, Captain,' Kasia smiled up at the young officer. 'You have brought us safely back to Poland—*Austrian* Poland, and for that we thank you. Now your job is done and you can return to Petersburg.'

'We shall not leave until we see that you are provided with a decent sleigh for the rest of your journey, and that you are safe with these—' He could not think of any words to describe adequately what he thought about the slovenly, grinning soldiers of the Empress Maria Theresa.

But the pompous little officer proved to be kind and obliging. He ushered them into the house taken over as his headquarters. A greasy stew was provided and some rather sour wine.

'At least it's better than the Kremlin food.'

'I like it,' said Jacek and was promptly sick.

The little officer appeared and explained in a curious mixture of German, French and Polish that the sleigh was waiting and that they could continue on their way.

They said goodbye to the officer of the escort, and even Henryk shook his hand. For the last time the Captain raised and lowered his sword in salute.

'I shall report personally to Her Imperial Majesty that you reached Poland safely.'

'Thank you,' said Kasia. Henryk tried to smile. And Jacek, quite recovered, called out, 'I shall miss you, and your horse,' in very bad Russian.

The young officer smiled, wheeled his horse to the east, shouted a command and, for the last time in her life, Kasia watched Russian soldiers ride away in a light cloud of powdered snow.

'And now,' she said to her husband and son, 'now we will go home.'

* * *

A few miles short of Lipno the sun broke through the grey overcast and Kasia felt herself trembling as the well-known landscape shone in the bright, crystal air.

Henryk was still asleep. She pulled up the fur rug to cover his face from the biting cold; very softly and with infinite tenderness, she shielded him from the freezing air, from the world itself, she thought. For he had been through enough. If she had to crack him on the head with a club—well, at least he would never leave her again. She smiled to herself: she'd have to hit him very hard.

Beside the driver, Jacek was jumping up and down with excitement.

'We're nearly home, aren't we, Mama?'

'Yes, darling. Not long now.' Henryk mumbled something.

'We're there, my love. We're almost there.' He held on tightly to her hand.

'Lipno?'

'Yes, Henryk. Lipno.'

There was something of his old strength in his grip. His eyes were open, and clearer than they had been since Moscow. But she recognized in his flushed face and bright eyes another of the fevers he had suffered periodically since his time in the English ship.

'Faster,' she urged the driver. 'Please go faster.'

He whipped up the horses and the runners of the sleigh almost screamed over the hard snow.

If he can be got to bed, she thought.

'Mama, look; It's Dmitri. I'm sure it's Dmitri.' Jacek's excited voice broke her thoughts.

Three horsemen cantered towards them. 'Dmitri!'

'Stop the sleigh,' Kasia ordered sharply.

The Cossack smiled at her as he doffed his lambskin cap, topped with the bright scarlet of the Don Cossacks.

'Welcome home, Madam.' He had never learned, nor really wanted to learn, what to call her.

But Jacek he swept up into his lap. 'So you've come back

to us after all these weeks, you young devil.'

Dmitri peered down into the corner where Henryk lay, beginning to shiver under the rugs. 'Is that—?'

'Yes, Dmitri, that is the man you knew as Borodin.'

'Borodin? And he got out of Russia alive?'

'Yes. And here he is. Not well, but very much alive.' He shifted in his saddle.

'May I say, Madam, how fortunate you are to have such a man as this to be your husband—and'—he patted Jacek on the shoulder and said, 'you have got a father to be very proud of. Never forget that.' Turning aside he told one of the grooms, 'Ride to the village and the house and tell them.' The man grinned. He understood.

'Where's he going,' Jacek asked.

'Oh, just to bring in the horses from exercise.'

'Ah,' said Jacek wisely.

Chapter Six

THEY entered the village to the sounds of cheering, laughter, gaiety. '. . . The Countess . . . our Kasia . . . you're home, you're safe . . .' The villagers of Lipno crowded round the slowly moving sleigh, until it was forced to a halt.

'And Jacek . . .'

'*Silence*! All of you, silence!'

Dmitri rode into the midst of the crowd. 'Do you want me to show you the sharp edge of a Cossack sabre?'

'Oh no, Dmitri,' they answered in mock submission.

So they get on with each other, Kasia thought with real pleasure.

'Very well then, listen to me. Your master, *our* master,' they shouted delightedly at this alteration, 'has come home.' Kasia smiled and nodded her gratitude, praying that Katushka had arranged for the stoves and the warming-pans to be heated so that Henryk could be put to bed with one of her sleeping draughts to keep him asleep for at least fifteen hours.

'And we welcome him from the bottom of our hearts.' Dmitri's sabre flashed from its sheath as he rose in his stirrups, calling out: 'Let us escort them to their home in proper fashion, as due to two very brave people.'

And of all the throng that ran beside the sleigh none was prouder of the young Cossack than Sonya, the dark-haired daughter of Simeon, the venerable, and venerated Village Elder.

'You'll find the horses well,' said Dmitri, leaning from his saddle.

'I'm sure I shall,' Kasia smiled up at the dark young face. The faint black line above his upper lip was now a full-blooded Cossack moustache, a thick, black crescent.

'Tomorrow we'll talk about them.'

With the children still running, hanging on to the sleigh, crying and singing : 'Our Kasia is back !', they rode the last yards to Lipno. They had always loved her, ever since the days she had given them poppy-seed cakes and sugar-coated buns.

'Our Kasia !'

'And our Count Barinski—the man called Borodin—' Called out an unknown voice.

The sleigh drew up before the door of Lipno.

In the golden light of the interior, Katushka and Stepan, were softly silhouetted.

'Where are we, Mama?' Jacek had half woken.

'Home, darling. Home.'

Dmitri got off his horse. 'Please?'

'Yes, Dmitri, and thank you.'

The Cossack carried Jacek into the house. Henryk, still only half-conscious, was helped up the steps by the villagers.

And from below, in the driveway that led to the village, came the continuous cry : 'He's come home. He's come back. Count Henryk has come back !'

Upstairs, Kasia was trying to get her husband to bed, helped by many willing hands.

'Please, Katushka, Stepan, Dmitri, get them out. Thank them—thank you,' she called out. 'Thank you—all of you. When the Count is stronger we will celebrate. Such a celebration.'

'Go on with you. Out, out, all of you ! Can't you see, the Master's sick. Go on, I say !' The old woman shooed them out of the room, out of the house, as if they were a lot of wayward hens. She slammed shut the heavy door.

'Cheeky village vermin,' she muttered as she struggled slowly up the stairs, puffing and panting. 'I'll teach 'em to come in here. I'll—' But secretly she was delighted at the way they had received him home.

'And now, where's that old fool, Stepan? Never about when he's wanted.' But he was, standing by the bed.

'Now, Master Henryk, you just calm yourself and do what the Countess says. You're not fighting your Russians now. You're safe at home, and in your own bed. Master Henryk, I warned you; I'll have to turn nasty unless you obey the Countess.'

The sleeping draught was taking its time, but gradually Henryk was settling, just moving restlessly and turning his head from side to side, and always calling for his wife.

'I'm here, my darling. It's me, Kasia. I'm here.' She wiped his face with a damp cloth. 'I'll always be here.' He gripped her hand very tightly. Grimacing slightly she thought, 'Well, at least he hasn't lost any of his strength.'

Then the grip relaxed. For a moment she was terrified, but his face was peaceful, the deep shadowy lines less dark. His breathing was calm and steady. He slept.

'Go,' she whispered to the old man and woman. 'And thank you both. From my heart I thank you.'

It was Katushka who had to nudge Stepan sharply in the ribs.

'Come on,' she whispered loudly. 'Come on. Can't you see she wants to be alone with him?'

* * *

Kasia lay awake on the small bed brought in to be beside their four poster. She watched the little, darting streaks of light moving on the ceiling as the stove slowly died down. From the village she heard the sounds of song and music, and drunken laughter.

And she smiled. For now she knew how much they loved

him. Love? She smiled again. Admired him; respected him; liked him. But love? Oh no, that was for her alone.

Throughout the night she woke in terror, thinking that his breathing had stopped. Then, at last, worn out she fell into a black sleep to be woken, with the bright beams of the morning sun, to a voice that said: 'Kasia? Are you there? What's for breakfast? I'm as hungry as a wolf in Hell.'

For the first time in nearly two years Kasia laughed aloud: 'Anything you want—Polish Cossack!'

* * *

'Such a celebration', Kasia had said. And she was right. Such a celebration!

The big barn was used. The same barn used for the festivities which had brought their wedding-day to such a wonderful climax.

The same long trestle tables, bent under the weight of food: sucking-pig turning slowly above the slow heat; the same thick odours of excited bodies, wine and spilled beer; the rich scent of the hay calling to the young girls and boys who sat beside them.

Mountains of food; gallons of drink: vodka, mead, beer. Trout from the Dniester; salted ham; cucumbers and cream; shiny, golden loaves of bread, maize in every form.

'D'you remember, darling,' Kasia asked. 'The boys throwing water on the walls to cool the heat of the fire?'

'Yes, I remember.' Henryk was enjoying himself. He was home among his own people. He sat beside his wife.

'Yes,' he reached for her hand. 'I remember. How could I forget the most wonderful night of my life?'

'Our lives,' she said firmly.

He nodded and kissed her. 'And do you remember, there were gipsies who played, who played for you, darling?'

'Yes. They played. They played the *banduras*. And who can not dance to the sound of the *banduras*?'

'Well, I can't, for one.' He laughed. 'I can't even get through a *mazurka* without tripping over something, or someone.'

A certain amount of confusion arose among the gathering. 'Is the Countess going to dance the *gopak* for us as she did?'

'No,' said Henryk, now on his feet. 'She is not.'

'Why?'

'Because she has had enough. She is going to sit quietly and enjoy the evening,' Henryk's voice was very loud. For a moment there was silence. Then a voice shouted, 'God bless the Countess!'

'Dmitri!' Henryk called.

The Cossack got to his feet. 'Yes, Your Honour.'

'Can you leave Sonya alone for a moment?' The barn was shaken by uproarious laughter. Dmitri went red. 'You remember when you danced the *gopak* in the monastery?' The young man nodded.

'Will you dance it again for us now?'

'Yes.'

'Go on, Dmitri! Dance for us.' The barn echoed to their cries and the banging of mugs on the tables.

'Very well. For you, Countess—and for you *dunya*.' He bent and kissed the top of Sonya's thick plaited hair. Although she blushed as she looked up into his smiling eyes her heart was almost bursting with pride and the thought that, within the week, she would be his wife.

More huge logs were piled on the great open fire; the flagons of vodka, beer and mead were passed up and down the tables.

Henryk stood and called for silence.

'Who will play?' There was a buzz of talk and argument. 'Pawel.' No, not Pawel, he plays like a tortured lynx.

'Yes, yes, Pawel.'

'No, for God's sake, no!'

After a time of argument and good-natured shouting they decided for Pawel and Stas—a fiddle and a *bandura*.

A space was cleared. Dmitri took off his sabre and handed it to Henryk.

'Now I don't fight. I dance.' Henryk accepted it with a smile. The barn almost lost the roof in the tumult of cheering and singing.

The space was cleared. Dmitri bowed to all the people gathered in the barn. Slowly the two instruments began the dance; slowly the pace increased. To Henryk the fiddle sounded like a tormented cat but the plucking notes of the *bandura* were exciting.

Dmitri span on the earthern floor, leaping and crouching, his legs kicking out to the sound of the music. His hands beat at the floor. He cried out the words of the dance: *'Ahi, dou, dou, dou!'*

Kasia felt her hand covered by the soft strength of Henryk's fingers. Throughout the barn arms slid round trembling waists; hands felt for breasts or round, warm thighs.

With a spectacular spin, three times round and never a mistake, Dmitri finished his dance. On his feet he raised his arms and bowed to his audience.

Henryk was also on his feet. 'Thank you, Dmitri.'

A roar of applause shook the barn.

'And thank you, Pawel and Stas.'

Dmitri sat down beside his Sonya. A Cossack and a Pole? He answered the question swiftly: by a long; deep kiss on her lips.

Suddenly Simeon, the father of Sonya, the Elder of Lipno, got slowly to his feet.

'Count Henryk, Countess Kasia.' He paused. 'I am an old man. May I claim this privilege in order to say what I would like?'

The barn was silent as a graveyard. All eyes were turned towards the old man.

'Of course,' said Henryk. 'And my wife agrees.'

'That I know.' Simeon bowed towards Kasia. 'She is a very great lady.'

For a moment there was not a sound except the flames of the fire, and the rising wind outside.

'So, go on,' said Henryk.

'I will. My daughter is going to be married to a Cossack.' No one said a word.

'Yes,' Henryk said.

'Well—I mean—is there anything wrong in that?'

Henryk regarded him quietly, looked at Dmitri, and said: 'No. There is nothing wrong in that.'

There was applause from all round the barn.

Henryk was on his feet. 'So. We are all agreed that Sonya should become the wife of Dmitri, Cossack of the Don?'

'*Yes.*' The answer nearly lifted the roof into the sky.

Henryk sat down, taking Kasia's hand in his own.

'And may God bless them both,' Kasia called out.

'God bless them both,' echoed many voices. One or two of the young men of Lipno felt twinges of jealousy, for Sonya was a very pretty girl with a figure to turn the head of any male between the ages of sixteen and eighty. Among the elders there was a bit of head-shaking among the thick clouds of pipe-smoke.

'. . . Who would have thought to see the day,' went on the old man, 'when one of our girls married a Cossack . . . Oh, he's a good lad . . . One of the best riders I've ever seen . . . They're all born on a saddle, the wild devils . . .' The other old men cackled into their mugs and puffed at their long, clay pipes, nodding wisely and criticizing the dancing of the young men and women.

The wail of the *banduras* grew louder and the fiddles sang to the next *mazurka*. Henryk danced it with his wife, still not believing it was Kasia, dressed again in the clothes she had worn on the evening of their marriage; the clothes she had worn when she came to meet him on the ridge in the first days of their love: the gay clothes of the Ukraine. The

18

wide, swirling red skirt, the embroidered blouse and soft calf-skin boots of red leather.

But this time she had not plaited her hair.

'We are perhaps just a little too—well, mature for that now, darling.'

'If you say so, wife.' Henryk grinned at her through the smoke. But this was not the smoke of battle. This was the smoke of happiness, of utter joy, although it stank.

'You're twice as beautiful,' he said as he held her close, much closer than was customary in the *mazurka*.

'Only twice?'

'All right. Three times then ... A hundred times. I won't argue.'

The old ones watching, nudged each other ... 'They make a fine pair' ... 'How the old Count would have enjoyed this ... Ah.'

At last Henryk whispered to his wife. 'And now it is time, for us anyway, to creep away to bed.' He felt her body pressing closely against his. 'But before we go I must say a few words.'

She nodded.

Seizing the opportunity of a brief moment of comparative quiet, Henryk got up and this time he climbed on to the table.

'Look out, Your Honour!'

'Careful, sir, you'll have us all over.' The roars of tipsy laughter rocked the barn. While the cheering continued, Kasia looked up at his face and saw tears in his eyes.

He held up his hand. 'My friends,' he paused. 'My very good friends. Thank you. I cannot say anything more than that. Thank you.' He was silent.

'Have another mug of vodka, Your Honour. That'll get you going!'

'I'll ask you a question, friend,' Henryk said. 'Have you ever drunk the rum provided by the British Navy?'

There was a stupefied silence.

'No.'

'Well, friend, I can tell you this: it would certainly get *you* going.'

When the laughter had died away, he said: 'Before my wife and I leave this scene of entertainment—' There were groans and shouts. 'Stay. Please stay!'

'You are very kind but our advancing age—'

'Speak for yourself,' said Kasia very clearly. They loved that and cheered her until they were hoarse.

'And now, before I—we—leave, there are a few things I would like to say.' They stared up at him. Some saw him clearly as Count Henryk Barinski; some saw a vague, shadowy figure above them, slightly blurred; some saw nothing at all, for their faces were flat on the tables.

'Firstly I would like to thank those who—' here he hesitated. 'Who fought with us and did not return,' again he paused. 'Including my brother.' Kasia reached up to touch his hand.

'Count Adam,' mumbled many voices. Henryk blinked rapidly and went on.

'And now to those with us here tonight. Pan Dombrowski —Jan Dombrowski to many of us—for what he has done over these last years—for our country.' Henryk stopped abruptly.

'Jan Dombrowski!' Jan stumbled to his feet.

'If you can disentangle yourself from—'

And, at that moment Kasia thought: 'Yes, Henryk has the gift of leadership. He knows when to shout and when to encourage.'

But she whispered to her husband: 'Careful, Henryk. Be careful.' And, as she advised him, she thought: there is going to be another wedding. But her thoughts were blown apart by Jan Dombrowski.

'Very well. Oh God,' Henryk thought. 'He's swaying. He's damned well swaying.' So he stood up again.

'Pan Dombrowski has fought beside me for three years.

He has proved his courage time and time again.' Thunderous noise. 'Now he is proving it in a different way.' The noise increased as all eyes were turned on Jan and his blue-eyed widow.

'They are made for each other,' said the old men and women. 'Just look at them. Have you ever seen two people so much in love? Except of course our Henryk and Kasia?'

The blue-eyed widow had been married to a neighbour of Jan's. The man had been killed during the Confederate Wars. She was trying to maintain the small estate left to her, bordering on the Dombrowski lands. She was a fine-looking woman. They all agreed on that. No one knew much about her, but she was a woman any man would be proud of : that they all agreed.

Kasia was on her feet. 'I would like to drink a toast,' she held her glass high.

'To Jan Dombrowski and all he has done for our country.' Mugs and glasses were raised.

'And to the woman who is to become my wife.' Jan held his glass above her head.

Then he stood up, a little unsteady, and shouted something in a strangely muffled voice.

'And now, another toast.' shouted a huge voice.

Some had to hang on to the tables; some had to close their eyes and pray for strength, but they all stayed on their feet.

'God Almighty, its Nym.'

'Yes,' roared the same voice. 'It's Nym.' The only sound to break the silence was that of the wind, becoming stronger every minute, to drown the noise of the barn.

'All right,' said the huge figure, standing in the heat and smoke. 'Yes, I'm Nym. All right, I'm Nym, *Sergeant* Nym, late of Her Imperial Majesty's Bodyguard—'

'And what would you do for Her bloody Imperial Majesty?'

'You know what I would do.'

Henryk and Kasia looked at each other.

'Piotr!'

Maryshka was on her feet. His huge frame seemed to shrink. 'Yes?'

'Silence!' Her voice cut like a whip.

Henryk's voice was very hard and sharp. 'Sergeant Nym!'

'Yes, Your—'

'You have done enough for Poland. Now it is time for you to look after your wife. It is time for all of us who have been away to look after our wives and children. We've neglected them for long enough.' Henryk looked along the rows of hot, flushed faces.

'We have done all we can. Now let us start to rebuild—'

'For the day when we can throw out the Prussians, the Austrians, and the Russians!' Jan Dombrowski had stood up to join Henryk on the table.

From inside his coat of plain red velvet he produced a piece of cloth. He held it high above his head: blackened, shredded, stained with dark blood.

'The flag of Poland!'

Even those almost incapable of thought were on their feet.

'Friends,' he shouted. 'One last toast. Fill your mugs for one last toast.' Tears were pouring down his cheeks, and down those of many others as he raised his glass.

'To Poland!'

'To Poland!' The very roof shook to the answering cry. In the silence that followed the shattering of his glass on the floor was very loud and sharp.

'And now, Henryk Barinski, to you and your wife I hand over this last remnant of what we have once been.' He offered the tattered scrap of cloth to Henryk who took it wordlessly, just nodding his head, unable to speak.

'But we won't always be like this,' roared Nym. 'No, by God, we won't!' Maryshka dragged him back to his seat, angry but at the same time proud of her brave, stubborn husband who would never accept defeat, of however short duration.

'And now, more music, more dancing. Come on, Dmitri, get them going again!' Kasia clapped her hands. 'More wood on the fire. More vodka in the jugs. This is not a wake!'

They responded. The noise began again; the dancing grew wilder; more and more couples vanished into the upper recesses of the barn where the hay was soft and sweet-smelling.

'Thank you, Jan,' she said. 'It was a wonderful thing to do.' She kissed him on the cheek. 'And may you and Marya have as many happy years together as we have—but,' she smiled, 'without so many unavoidable absences.' Marya, the blue-eyed widow smiled back. 'Thank you. I hope, very slowly, to turn him into a responsible landowner.'

Henryk and Kasia went out into the deathly white silence of a windless, frozen night.

* * *

They lay together in bed.

Below, in the kitchen, Stepan and Katushka huddled close to the stove. Now and then their old eyes slowly closed.

'Ought we to go up and see?'

'See what?' Stepan asked belligerently.

'Well—if everything's all right.'

'D'you mean Master Henryk and—?'

'No, I don't, Stepan. I mean little Jacek. Is he to be forgotten completely?'

For a while Stepan stared at the stove. 'No, of course not.

'His father took on the whole damned Russian Empire on his own—'

'Yes, he did. And don't you praise him for it?'

'Of course, you silly old crone.'

For a while they listened to the rising wind. 'He'll always be Master Henryk to you, Stepan, won't he?'

'Yes.'

'Well,' said Katushka firmly. 'Put some more wood into the stove and let's try and get some sleep.'

* * *

Upstairs, in the large four-poster bed, Kasia lay awake listening to the rising sigh of the wind. Beside her Henryk slept.

From the next room she could hear the loud snores and sudden shouts of delighted laughter ringing out from her son—their son—drowning the haunting cry of a wolf, carried to her on the cold, merciless wind.

She thought of many things: many months of supreme happiness, many years of despair. The wolves called to each other across the Lipno valley but this time she was not afraid.

This time she had her husband and her son beside her—safe.

THE END

THE BANNERS OF REVOLT

(following *The Banners of Love, The Banners of War, The Banners of Power* and *The Banners of Courage*) is the fifth and last of a sequence of novels having the collective title of

DESTINY OF EAGLES

CSARDAS by DIANE PEARSON

'Only half a century separates today's totalitarian state of Hungary from the glittering world of coming-out balls and feudal estates, elegance and culture, of which the Ferenc sisters – the enchanting Ferenc sisters – are the pampered darlings in the opening chapters of Diane Pearson's dramatic epic.

Their world has now gone with the wind as surely as that of Scarlett O'Hara (which it much resembled): handsome, over-bred young men danced attendance on lovely frivolous belles, and life was one long dream of parties and picnics, until the shot that killed Franz Ferdinand in 1914 burst the beautiful bubble.

The dashing gallants galloped off to war and, as they returned, maimed and broken in spirit, the new Hungary began to emerge like an ugly grub from its chrysalis. Poverty, hardship, and growing anti-semitism threatened and scattered the half-Jewish Ferenc family as Nazi influence gripped the country from one side and Communism spread underground from the other like the tentacles of ground-elder.

Only the shattered remants of a once-powerful family lived through the 1939–45 holocaust, but with phoenix-like vitality the new generation began to adapt and bend, don camouflage and survive. . . .'
Phyllida Hart-Davis *Sunday Telegraph*

'Long, fat, romantic, historical . . . a huge canvas . . . I defy anyone to remain unaffected.' *Evening Standard*

0 552 10201 6 – £1.00

WUTHERING HEIGHTS by EMILY BRONTË

WUTHERING HEIGHTS is a classic work of artistry and genius. Today, one hundred and thirty years after it was first published, it is still a totally absorbing and utterly compelling novel of a grim passion, of a glorious love.

Catherine Earnshaw and Heathcliff must take their places amongst the great lovers of the world. Their complete obsession, and possession of each other, symbolises the oldest, the grandest, and the most romantic theme in literature . . .

0 552 10609 7 – 85p

RETURN TO WUTHERING HEIGHTS by ANNA L'ESTRANGE

In many respects Emily Brontë's great classic has always demanded a sequel. Hareton and Cathy are united, but is it possible that Cathy's daughter could be untainted by her mother's wild and tempestuous nature? Is it believable that Hareton Earnshaw, reared in the shadow of Heathcliff, could settle to the life of a country squire?

Anna L'Estrange, who grew up in the country of the Brontës, has studied the characters, the settings, the structure of Emily Brontë's great classic. And here the ghosts of Heathcliff and Cathy cast their shadow over the children they never knew. Old passions and hostilities come to life in a narrative that continues one of the world's greatest love stories . . .

0 552 10608 9 – 85p

THE WATSONS by JANE AUSTEN and ANOTHER

Emma Watson belonged to the middle order of country society and was therefore seriously disadvantaged at Dorking's first Winter Assembly. For – truly – the whole purpose of the ball was to be noticed by the Osbornes of Osborne Castle and a Watson could hardly expect to receive so signal an honour . . .

But Emma, the wittiest, the prettiest, and the most intelligent of her family, discovered she was to be singled out, patronised by no less august a person than the young Lord Osborne himself . . .

A full bibliographical record of the genesis of the present completed version of THE WATSONS is provided in an excellent Postscript to the book.

0 552 10712 3 – 80p

SANDITON by JANE AUSTEN and ANOTHER LADY

Charlotte Heywood is invited to stay with the Parker family at their home in Sanditon, a small village on the South Coat which Mr Parker is busily trying to promote as a fashionable bathing resort. Her coming arouses no little interest among the residents, and, indeed in the case of the dashing young nephew of the wealthy Lady Denham, it leads to some extraordinary and most alarming events . . .

Begun by Jane Austen in 1817, SANDITON has been completed some 160 years later, by Another Lady.

'Thanks and praise, therefore, to the Other Lady, for her tact, her taste, wit and discretion. She has provided us with a novel which like the sea which Charlotte could see from her bedroom window, dances and sparkles in sunshine and freshness.' Philippa Toomey in *The Times*

'The completed novel is entertaining and agreeable . . . There are touches of irony of which Jane herself would have been proud.' C. B. Cox in the *Sunday Telegraph*

0 552 10297 0 – 75p

MICHAEL AND ALL ANGELS by NORAH LOFTS

To the Fleece Inn, in the autumn of 1817, came the Ipswich coach, the occupants – a strange ill-assorted company – destined to change forever the lives of those who lived at the Fleece . . .

Will Oakley, landlord and host, with his two daughters, one so beautiful, and one repellently ugly, waited to receive his guests – the farmers, the merchants, the quality – and those who fitted into none of these categories – like the handsome foreigner with the scarred face – and the fat man who appeared to be gloating over some malicious secret of his own . . .

0 552 10728 X – 80p

BLOSSOM LIKE THE ROSE by NORAH LOFTS

Philip Ollenshaw was the eldest son of Sir John Ollenshaw, and heir to the Manor of Marshalsea. But there his advantages ended, for Philip was a cripple – shy, sensitive, nervous – and in his father he aroused only hatred and contempt.

But Philip physically a lesser man than his father had courage and vision. When he fell in love with Linda Seabrook he renounced his inheritance and joined a band of colonists bound for America, committing himself to a life of hardship and endeavour.

And, carving out a future from the wilderness, surviving the perils of Indian raids and the harshness of life under Puritan rule, Philip found his strength was the abiding force of the community . . .

0 552 10726 3 – 85p

I MET A GYPSY by NORAH LOFTS

It began in the old King's time – the mating of a gypsy woman with a Tudor lord – a strange union that resulted in an even stranger line of descendants.

Beatrice was the first, a novice who left the church to live in a desolate inn on the wild Norfolk coast. And after Beatrice came the others, innkeepers, harlots, adventurers – a wild strain of people whose fortunes carried them from Guinea to the Arctic, from British-India to the territories of a Chinese War Lord.

And those who came into contact with the gypsy blood – who befriended, or loved, or hated them – found that their lives were unaccountably affected . . .

0 552 10725 5 – 70p

HESTER ROON by NORAH LOFTS

The Fleece Inn stood where the three roads joined . . . the roads to London . . . to Norwich . . . and to the sea. Its trade was prosperous, its hospitality famous, and the host, fat Job, was jolly and generous – to his guests.

To his servants and grooms he was cruel, avaricious and menacing, and to Ellie Roon, the humblest and most menial servant at the Fleece, he was a figure of terror. Ellie was used to being shouted at, to being bullied and maltreated, but when her bastard daughter was born – in a rat-ridden attic of the Fleece – she decided that Hester must have a different kind of life.

And so, equipped with little but courage and a strong will Hester Roon began her eventful progress in the harsh world, of 18th century England . . .

0 552 10724 7 – 85p

HONEY-POT by MIRA STABLES

'Honey-Pot' was a nickname aptly bestowed on Russet Ingram. Lovely, well-born, well dowered, she drew all men to her. Even her rivals allowed her charms and pleasing disposition.

Yet here she was, a prisoner of the one man immune to her graces – accused of frivolously tampering with his young ward's romance! A man with manners more suited to his ancestral highland clan than London society. James Cameron – the enemy she must escape at all costs, or risk the ruin of her reputation and her beloved sister's marriage hopes . . .

0 552 10962 2 – 70p

THE SCARLET DOMINO by SYLVIA THORPE

Antonia Kelshall and Geraint St Arvan were married on a fateful night in 1791, having met for the first time only one hour earlier.

Rescued from prison by Sir Charles Kelshall in exchange for agreeing to enter into an unspecified 'contract', the rakish Geraint acquired a fortune, but with it a wife who hated him . . . an an unknown enemy who threatened his life . . .

0 552 10963 0 – 75p

THE SWYNDEN NECKLACE (A Georgian Romance) by MIRA STABLES

A diamond necklace and a season in fashionable Bath! For penniless Honor Fenton, this legacy could lead to a splendid marriage – or so Mama declared. And indeed, Honor's beauty made her the toast of Bath, but she was sadly unwordly – a defect which led her into some rather unladylike scrapes, from which she always seemed to be rescued by the handsome Mr Jocelyn, a stranger whose tender concern belied his imperious manner. Though his apparent lack of family and fortune could hardly endear him to Mama, Honor fell deeply in love, and vowed to marry no other . . . Unfortunately, Mama had already made *her* choice – the wealthy and eligible Sir Ralph Crompton . . .

0 552 10719 0 – 60p

A SPEAKING LIKENESS (A Georgian Romance) by SHEILA BISHOP

Diana Pentland, a young widow, could hardly avoid befriending the miserable, unwed girl she found on her doorstep. But when the girl refused to divulge her name, nor that of her seducer – and then disappeared, leaving behind her new-born son – Diana almost regretted her charity. An attorney persuaded her to adopt the boy, and in return an anonymous client would provide for them generously. Soon she came to love little 'Hop' as her own.

His identity and that of the mysterious benefactor remained secret, until a chance visit to Brandham Castle, when Hop's incredible likeness to the heir led Diana to believe she had solved the mystery. As she found herself drawn deeper into the family secrets, she also found protection and love from a very unexpected source.

0 552 10659 3 – 60p